TO LOVE AGAIN

By Amy Barkman

Copyright © 2016, 2017 by Amy Barkman
Published by: Voice of Joy Publications

Cover Art: Cynthia Hickey

ISBN-10: 0-9983520-5-5
Print ISBN-13: 978-0-9983520-5-3

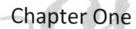

Chapter One

2007

Christy

I turned around from the computer at the sound of the door opening. The girl coming in the office was pretty, but definitely Goth, or Emo, something like that. Straight black hair, short black skirt, black sweater, black shoes, black fingernails, black purse, even black ring and earrings. The only things that weren't black were the silver ring in the side of her left nostril, her bright blue eyes, and her very pale skin.

"Hi, I'm Gina Howard. Are you the one I talk to about getting a job?"

I nodded and pointed to the empty chair at the side of my desk. "I'm one of them." When she was seated, I asked, "So what kind of work are you interested in?"

"One that will pay my rent." She screwed her face up and shrugged as she smiled.

Not professional but definitely engaging!

"Did you bring your resume with you?"

The response was another shrug. "I don't have one."

I was curious and my boss was out of the office, so why not? "Okay, let's see if we can create one for you. I'm not really busy right now." *What kind of maternal instinct is this kicking in – and*

1

for someone not much younger than I am?

"Great!" The girl reached in her purse and pulled out a pack of cigarettes. "Is it okay if I smoke?"

I pointed to the "No Smoking" sign on the wall and turned my palm up as if I was sorry for the rule, which I definitely was not.

"Shut up!" But she put the pack back in her pocketbook.

I went into Word and began a new document. Assuming that her comment was an expression of disgust instead of a command, I continued speaking. "Now give me your name again."

"Gina Howard."

"How do you spell that?"

When the answer came, I was surprised. "Oh! I'll bet people mispronounce it all the time if they just see it spelled out."

"Yep, but I just tell them that it's not like a gene you inherit – it's like gin that you drink." The appealing grin appeared again on her face.

I finally elicited the facts that Gina was nineteen years old, a high school graduate, and her only employment had been as a waitress and a babysitter.

"I'm a good babysitter," she said. "Not so good a waitress. I love to talk with the kids and they like to talk too, but customers at the restaurant didn't want to talk to me much. And all that carrying food got real boring."

Likes people interaction. That's good. Receptionist? But where would she fit in dressed the way she does? And why do I instinctively like her?

I noticed the wall clock and hastily revised my lunch plans. *Have I lost my mind?* "Tell you what. Do you have an hour or so?"

"Lady I got all the time in the world." Then she laughed, "No money but lots of time!"

I hit the intercom button. When Jan answered, I said, "I'm going to take a lunch break now. Want to come cover the front desk?"

The answer came immediately. "Sure, be right out."

Jan Conn and I were the only two employees working at Hunt Temp Service - "We HUNT the jobs for you!" - this week. By some planning mishap both the owner/manager, Elena Hunt, and Sally Keene, the secretary, were on vacation.

Jan's eyebrows raised a fraction when she saw my companion. *She probably thinks the girl's a friend of mine instead of a client. So? Don't be a snob, Christy!*

"Jan, this is Gina, a new client. We're going to discuss her skills over lunch."

When we were out on the street, I turned to Gina. "Lunch will be my treat, okay?"

Any fear that the girl would be insulted instantly fled at the joyful expression on Gina's face.

"If there is going to be any lunch, it would have to be your treat."

Certainly not embarrassed about her situation in life! I would be.

I led her to the Big Buffet a few buildings beyond my usual lunch retreat in the mall. I figured if she was that broke she needed a really good meal and the luxury of lots of choices.

I was right. She piled her plate with four fried chicken breasts, macaroni and cheese, mashed potatoes and gravy, three slices of roast beef, and three rolls. As soon as we carried our plates to the table, she went back for salad and soup. I fully expected her to deposit those and go again for dessert. But she contented herself with what she had, for the moment.

I was shocked when she picked up the chicken breasts one at a time, wrapped them each in a napkin and plopped them down in her giant black bag. I started to tell her that take out is not allowed from a buffet but then decided I'd just come back later and pay for an extra lunch and explain the situation to the manager.

She finished off the soup and started in on the roast beef with every sign of great enjoyment. *If I ate like that I'd be big as a house!*

Well, sometimes I do eat like that. It depends on how sorry for myself I'm feeling that day. And if it weren't for walking and sit-ups, I probably would be big as a house.

After Gina polished off the rest of her food including a second plate of more roast beef, potatoes and gravy, and a huge bowl of chocolate cake with chocolate syrup and gobs of whipped cream on top, I figured maybe her mouth would be empty long enough to answer a few questions.

"Gina, how long have you been without a job?"

She wiped her mouth with a napkin and said, "It depends on what you mean by a job."

"I thought you had been babysitting and waitressing."

"Yeah. Well those have been a while, like about six months or something."

"How have you made it 'til now?"

"I have an old man. Well, I HAD an old man." I guess she noticed my puzzled expression. "Like, a boyfriend. He took off with some biker chick who had her own cycle and I haven't seen him since last week. It's his apartment."

I know that I've been sheltered but I was shocked at her nonchalance. I forced my face to stay expressionless. "Maybe he'll be back soon."

She shook her head. "Na. Crater – that's one of the other bikers that hang around near where we live - I live – said that Mike and her took off for California. He'll probably never be back. He was always a biker wanna-be"

"Is the lease in his name?"

She looked at me blankly. "Huh?"

"The lease, the contract on the apartment, is it in his name."

She laughed out loud, causing people from several tables to turn and look at us.

"Lady, where I live you don't do a lease. You pay every week for the next week. He already paid for this week but I've got to come up with some money or I'm out in three days. "

I was stunned. This kind of lifestyle was so far beyond my experience I felt decades older than this street smart young woman who was only nine years younger than me.

Gina continued. "I could be doing the streets, ya know, but I just don't like the thought of that. Mike and me, well I thought it was more than a hook-up." Then she laughed again. "The hooker bit – I don't like it. So I got to do something."

I was feeling that old "I've got to do something" feeling myself, the one my psychologist found so frustrating in his attempts to get me to relax.

"How much is your rent?"

"Fifty."

"Fifty dollars?"

She nodded.

Good Lord, what kind of a place is only $50 a week paid in advance. I don't think I really want to know.

I started to ask if it would insult her if I gave her two weeks rent money and then remembered her reaction to my offer of lunch. *But is she one of those con artists who would take advantage of my generosity? Lord, what should I do?*

I knew, being me, I couldn't do anything else. I asked her to wait a minute while I went to pay and get change for the waitress who brought our drinks and cleared away the empty plates. After paying the bill, I went to the ATM machine I'd spotted in the entrance as we came in.

When I got back to the table Gina was finishing the remains of a cherry cobbler with ice cream.

I put two hundred dollar bills on the table beside her.

Her eyes widened. "I never got a tip like that when I was a waitress!"

I laughed. "That's not the tip." I put three dollar bills in the middle of the table.

Gina cocked her head to one side and her eyes met mine.

"That's two weeks rent and groceries and whatever else you might need."

"What for?' She looked at me with narrowed eyes. "I don't do women."

I felt my face heating. "I don't either."

"Then how come?"

"Let's just say I haven't done a good deed this year."

She scooped up the money and stuffed it down in the bag

with the chicken and cigarettes and whatever else she had there. *Cigarettes! How can she afford cigarettes if she can't afford food? I* had another thought. *Is my money going toward more cigarettes? Probably.* I reminded myself that we are to give as unto the Lord and not try to control how our giving is used.

We gathered our stuff and headed back to the office. "So, do you have family anywhere?"

"Yeah, my old lady. She's a hooker. Always has been. I swore when I was a kid that I wasn't going to end up like that. I could go stay with her. But then I'd have to fight off her men." She shook her head. "I'm not doing it anymore."

How did she develop that kind of determination? To have made it through high school with that kind of home life showed some guts that I obviously didn't have – me who did nothing for three years after graduating from college except daydreaming and watching television.

"I'm sure we'll find something through the agency." I spoke with more assurance than I felt.

We walked through the front door of Hunt's Temp Service. "Now let's get to that resume." *I'll add lots of descriptive words like determination and integrity...* I remembered the chicken... *well, maybe not integrity.*

I rushed to the walking track that afternoon. I couldn't wait to tell Helen about my new client. It was three years ago that I started walking at the track in the big Disciples of Christ Church near my house.

There were three of us, the purple lady, the old man, and me. One old man is very like another – baggy slacks, ugly button-front shirts, stooped shoulders, so I didn't pay much attention to him until the day he wasn't there. Of course the lady wasn't really purple but I thought of her that way because she always managed to work purple into her outfit, whether it was a whole sweat suit or just a hair band or socks.

The three of us never spoke but I knew from the sign in sheets that they were John and Helen, and I was sure they knew my name was Christy.

Finding that perfect time was a long agonizing process. I tried several time slots that didn't work out at all. During one attempt a couple who walked together always talked in loud voices to a man who walked about twenty paces behind them. That was bad enough but the woman had an unbelievably slow Southern drawl, he spoke a high-pitched raspy voice, and the content of their talk resembled the taste of tofu...by itself! I would try to remember later what they said that irritated me, but it was all so meaningless I couldn't recall a single sentence. All I knew was that it was the antithesis of peace.

Peace was my goal. The doctor said that walking would relieve stress and that was a must. For three years I did nothing except sit and zone out in front of the TV, but finally something shook me out of the complete despondency. It had to be God because nothing had changed.

I finally found this time in the late afternoon shortly before closing when the track was almost empty. There were usually only those two other people walking at that time – Helen and John. They never spoke to each other and they never spoke to me. That suited me very well.

I came to look forward to being there. It was an atmosphere of   belonging..

I supposed it was silly, but it seemed like they were my family. I looked forward to going each day and being with them, nobody saying a word, just walking. But walking together – not side by side but at the same time. Smiling hello and goodbye, knowing that we would be together again tomorrow. Strangers, but fitting together in a wonderful emotional bond, we three who walked in silence.

I didn't tell the doctor about them. I was certain he would see it as a part of my illness and say that I was replacing my parents with strangers that didn't even know each other, much less me. He wouldn't have understood. Or maybe he would have understood too well. But I didn't tell him and in a way I did find my peace there with them.

It lasted a long time, that togetherness.

I got a job after a few months of walking but whenever I could, which was most days, I hurried away from work and got there for the last part of the time period and was able to spend at least twenty minutes wrapped in the familiar cocoon of peace, walking with my fantasy parents who still never spoke to me or each another. But they both smiled as though they were very glad to see me when I arrived.

It was just a few weeks before Gina walked into Hunt's Temp Service that the old man wasn't there one day. The atmosphere was different. I didn't pay much attention to him all that time, but in his absence the general feeling of peace was shattered.

Then he wasn't there again the next day. Or the next.

Finally I couldn't stand it any longer. I broke the unspoken rule – and spoke.

I slowed down and waited for the woman and when she came along side, I spoke almost in a whisper, feeling like I was desecrating something sacred by breaking the years of silence. "I wonder where our friend is today."

I noticed that the smile and confidence were missing on Helen's face. She shook her head. "He must not be well."

"That's what I was afraid of."

"Or maybe he is on vacation."

I hoped she was right.

We began walking together then and talking. Strangely enough, although it was the old man who was the cause of the silence between us being broken, we didn't talk about him. But maybe not so strange. What did we know about him except his name, from the sign-in sheets?

The atmosphere wasn't the same after the old man quit walking but Helen and I became friends.

"I love to see the way you work purple into your outfits every day"

Helen laughed. "I love that poem, 'When I am an old lady I will wear purple.' But I draw the line at the "red hat that doesn't go".

"You don't seem like an old lady."

"I'll be sixty-five in January."

I shared about my breakdown six years earlier and how walking was a prescription for stress. "You have no idea how grateful I was to be able to walk with you and John. It was so peaceful."

Eventually I even told her how I had pretended like they were my parents. But she didn't laugh or shy away; she took my arm and linked it in her own.

I confessed to her like she was a priest. I told her everything. And it felt like somehow that she was a priest, a link to God.

One day Helen began telling me about herself. "The first time I attended the book study group at my new church, I was glad that, even though the rest of the group were all about twenty years older than I was, the teacher was just my age. I hadn't even joined that congregation yet, but a miserable marriage that shortly ended in divorce made for a lot of lonely nights and the current study looked fairly interesting. Best of all, it was somewhere safe to go and spend a few hours. And it would be that much less time alone feeling sorry for myself."

I nodded, identifying with the younger Helen.

"A few decades later I wondered if I would have done things differently if I knew how things would turn out, you know 'knowing what I know now', but the answer was 'No'. I wouldn't change a thing, I couldn't. The die, as they say, was cast. I could have no more stayed away than...than my cat could resist an open can of tuna left out on the floor." Helen laughed softly.

"I remember going home that first night thinking that it had been one of the most exciting times of my life but I didn't really understand why. Not then. It was a few weeks before I realized that Sanders, the teacher, was the age of the others, twenty years older than me and not my age at all. But he was so exuberant, so excited about life and..." She hesitated then, as if the very memory of his liveliness was more than she could verbalize.

She shook her head. "There was never anyone else like him. Never, ever. Even his name...so different." Then the smile faded,

"And I also found out that he was married, with children just a few years younger than me. At the time, it was devastating. I was very young, mid-twenties, lots of hormones." She grinned. "About your age I would say."

Too soon it was time to leave the track before they locked up for the night and I felt the way I did once while watching a movie and something broke and I was left waiting eagerly for the next scene.

The next day Helen brought a folder and left it on the chair next to her sweater and purse while we walked. "I have something for you. It's poetry I wrote to him. He never saw it and I guess..." She hesitated. "I guess I just want someone to share it with, someone I think will understand. I don't know why. I'm just a silly old woman."

"No way. You seem a lot younger than sixty four and besides, my therapy taught me that sharing feelings with others is important, not silly at all."

"Now, remember when you read the poetry, he and I met at a church book study. We were both very eager about God and truth. The poetry might be a little too...too spiritual for your taste."

"No, I need spiritual. I am a Christian and even my psychologist is a Christian. I don't believe that anything less than spiritual can help me."

She nodded. "Good. Then you may enjoy them. I hope I am doing the right thing, giving them to you, I mean."

I wondered if Helen was having second thoughts about me, speculating if I was nuts or something instead of just emotionally devastated.

I was glad to have the poetry over the weekend. I curled up on the couch that night and began reading. The poems were obviously written over a period of time.

The following Monday I reached the walking track first and when Helen arrived I walked up to her and gave her a big hug.

"Thank you."

She nodded. And sighed. "I thought so."

"Where do you go to church?"

"I go to the big Episcopal Church down town. Where do you go?"

"I go to a little Methodist Church near my house."

"Ah, one of the grandchildren."

I frowned. "What do you mean?"

Helen laughed. "I just meant that the Methodist Church came from the Anglican, or Episcopal Church. And we came from the Catholic. So that makes us the children and you the grandchildren."

Helen seemed to be able to make everything so personal and interesting. I found out that she was a librarian and since I loved to read, I've always thought that would be a wonderful job.

"The problem is," she explained, "that when you are a librarian, you don't have any time to read at work. You are always raising money and taking care of a million administrative details."

I thought it still beat the kind of job I had the past three years. My college degree was in Social Work but that proved to be too emotionally draining for me and I was working as an assistant manager at the Temp firm. Even that could sometimes get to me, worrying over the people who so desperately needed work when there often just weren't enough jobs to go around. My psychologist said there was such a thing as being too empathetic.

"Christy," Helen asked. "Have you thought about dating again?"

"Sure, I have thought about it a lot. But it seems like it would be a waste of time. I mean.... well... You understand!"

"Yes," she said sadly. "I understand."

To how many is it given to see Beauty in the face and see there, however unbelievable, knowledge of one's own beauty, though in truth it be embryonic and deeply hidden.
I would ask no greater gift than this that has humbled me to the depths of my being, but treasure it, and hold it before me always, in hope that someday I may become what Beauty has seen in me.

***

"And, believe it or not, Helen, I found her a place. She is going to start tomorrow morning at Flemings." It was almost like a miracle that when Gina and I returned to the office there was an e-mail from the factory needing a two week replacement on one of the lines. "She'll have people to talk to and the pay is pretty good. I really hope it will lead to something permanent for her."

Helen nodded. "You did good! Did you invite her to church?"

I didn't keep the horror from showing on my face. "Church?"

Helen laughed. "Never entered your mind?"

"No. Well maybe but just for a second. She wouldn't fit at church at all." Then I felt terrible at my judgmental thought. *I have a lot of room to judge!*

When I got home that evening, I thought about Helen's question. Why didn't I mention church to Gina? *Because you were embarrassed to be seen with her. It was bad enough where nobody knows you, but at church? ARGHH! I'm sorry, Lord.*

I couldn't believe that I would let my pride about what people might think stop me from inviting Gina to a place where she could learn about God's love and grace. But I'd told her to come back in when the two week were up. By then I'll work up the nerve.

When I got in bed, I couldn't seem to get comfortable. I picked up my Bible from the bedside table. I didn't read God's Word like I should, but I kept it there for times when I really needed it. I'd been reading in Matthew and the bookmark was still in the place I stopped. How long ago? Weeks? Months?

"And the King shall answer and say unto them, Verily I say unto you, Inasmuch as ye have done it unto one of the least of these, my brethren, ye have done it unto me." Matt. 25:40

I closed the book. "Lord, I gave her food and found her a job." I got the feeling that He was not very impressed. Another verse came to my mind. *"Do unto others as you would have them do unto you."*

Okay. I had her address in her file. I'd...*Surely you don't want me going to that neighborhood? Do you? Lord?*

Chapter Two

2007

Christy

Within a few weeks after we began talking, Helen and I bonded as though we really were mother and daughter. We never mentioned the old man and I almost forgot that he had been a part of our silent partnership of three years.

One day as soon as I arrived, she silently handed me a newspaper. On the front page was a picture of the old man; only he was in a suit and tie and a few years younger than when we last saw him. The headlines read "NATION MOURNS BELOVED AUTHOR".

"Oh! He was famous! Who would have ever thought it?" I looked down through the article and read aloud. "He died quietly in his home of heart failure." I turned to look at Helen. "I guess that's why he quit coming. He just didn't have the energy any more. I'm glad he wasn't sick and in the hospital."

The funeral was in two days and being held at the large downtown Methodist Church. "Are you going?" I asked.

"Are you?" Helen searched my face.

"I don't know. It isn't like we really knew him, I mean we never talked or anything. But on the other hand, I felt like I knew him. Remember, I kind of pretended that you were my parents?"

She nodded.

"I wouldn't want to go to visitation and talk to the family or anything." I looked back at the paper. Survivors were a wife and two children, several grandchildren, and one great-grandchild. "But, yes, I would like to go to the funeral." *You don't have to talk to people and explain why you are there at a funeral.* "I have some personal days due me at work. But I don't want to go alone. Will you go?"

"Yes, I will. Where should we meet, Christy?"

"There's a coffee shop near the church. Want to meet there?"

She agreed.

***

I paused at the sign-in book and looked at Helen but she shook her head. We chose seats at the back of the church and our presence was unacknowledged, just like we wanted.

The organ music was majestic and seemed a fitting tribute to someone who evidently was as famous as John had been. I whispered to Helen and asked if the library where she worked carried his books. She nodded. And I determined to read them.

Even though I was a Methodist, I belonged to a small church and was not used to the clergy robes and formality of the more "high church" service. In this church, you could really tell that the Methodist Church was the grandchild of the Catholic. The minister, looking to me like a priest, opened with a scripture and written prayer and then the choir sang.

"Love Divine, All Loves Excelling" seemed a strange choice for a funeral song but the minister introduced it by saying that John had chosen the music himself.

I couldn't help but think of David and that sometimes it's hard to let the Love of God excel the love between humans. Swallowing the lump in my throat, I turned to look at Helen and saw tears gliding down her cheeks. I suspected she too was thinking about her own love and I reached out and took her hand.

She squeezed mine tightly.

The minister talked about what a wonderful man John had

been and how he influenced so many with his books on theology for the common man. He called him "another C.S. Lewis". And then he read more from the Bible.

The choir closed with "O Love That Wilt Not Let Me Go."

I found myself crying along with Helen. It is true that God will not let us go even when we want Him to. The words to that hymn were so descriptive of my own journey for the past several years. "I rest my weary soul in thee." And "O Joy that seekest me through pain." And finally, triumphantly, "I lay in dust, life's glory dead, and from the ground there blossoms red, Life that shall endless be." That was the part I wanted to get to – the part where I didn't feel pain any more.

It made me think that possibly the old man - and that was how I thought of him instead of by his name - that the old man had a deep secret sorrow too just like Helen and me. Maybe that was why we were so peaceful in each other's company all that time. We were soul mates, each of us depending on God for our ability to get through this life.

Oh, what a drama queen I am.

John had a family. He wasn't really alone like Helen and I are. Oh well, I'd never know what caused him to choose those two hymns but he had once more touched us both, with the music he chose for his own funeral.

When it was over we slipped out the back and didn't go to the graveside service. But we had paid our respects and somehow I felt like John knew we were there and we had one last time of our threesome as we sat there with Helen and me holding hands and crying.

After that, at least once a week we began having supper together after our walk. We never got together on weekends when the track was closed; neither of us ever suggested it. But Wednesday nights were our time together and it was a good time.

She brought me one of John's books that first Wednesday night, said she checked it out in her own name and she would bring me others if I liked it and wanted to read more of his work.

The first one she brought was "The Bride Book". It was about the sanctification process of the New Creation Bride – the Church of the Lord Jesus Christ. And it was very good. It helped me see myself as part of something important, something bigger than me or my little church, bigger than denominations and movements. It helped me see myself as truly part of something eternal that God is bringing about now.

I didn't read it 'til the weekend but couldn't put it down until I finished. I was eager to see Helen on Monday.

"Wow!" I said. "That was awesome. Yes, I want to read another one. But can I keep this one until I get it from you?"

She smiled. "Yes, it's checked out for two weeks from last Wednesday. I'll bring another tomorrow."

And she did.

My relationship with my fantasy father took on a new dimension as he began teaching me across time, space, and eternity.

***

Gina

The first word out of my mouth that morning was one I tried hard not to say anymore. But to wake up with a roach exploring my nostril was enough to make a preacher cuss!

I brushed it away and watched as it scurried off the sheet and onto the floor. By the time I got my shoe on and ready to stomp it, the roach had disappeared. *Yuck!*

While I dressed, I rehearsed what I'd say to the supervisor at break time. "Is there any job here I can apply for – a permanent one, I mean." *No, that isn't right.* "I'd like to apply for a permanent job. How do I do that?" *Better, but not exactly.*
"I've really liked working here these two weeks. Is there any chance of getting on permanently?" *Yes! That's better.*

It was only a 15 minute walk to the factory and I was surprised to find out that I liked the exercise each morning. It was the perfect job for me. Some of the women were cliquish but I can live with that. And already several of them were acting more friendly. *I want to keep on working there!* If I could get on permanently I'll find a better place to live – one without roaches!

I chain smoked on the way to the factory every morning. It'd be four hours before I'd get another cigarette. I'm often the first to clock in when the doors opened. There's one woman, Clarine, who glares at me every time that happens. She's also the woman who would sabotage your work if you don't watch her. One of the friendly girls, Kim, told me that Clarine had been seen pulling items out of one basket on the conveyer belt and adding them to her own so she would get credit for another person's work.

And she was the one I overheard on my first day at lunch break. I hadn't known to bring something to eat so was getting some peanut butter crackers out of the machine in the break room when I heard a voice saying, "What can you expect from street trash?"

Just a month earlier I would have laughed but since that lady at the Temp Service had been so nice to me, I was even more determined to pull myself out of my situation and move on to better things. *I'm not street trash! And someday you will know it, lady!*

There had been opportunities to really act like street trash in the last two weeks but I'd held my temper - and my tongue. The pay was pretty good and I didn't want to spoil my chances at a full time job.

At the beginning of lunch break I asked my supervisor about openings and was told to go to the HR office. I didn't want to admit I had no idea what HR stood for, so I just nodded and headed out of the break room. When I got in the hallway I spotted a maintenance worker sweeping the floor.

"Sir, can you tell me how to get to the HR office?"

He smiled and gave me the directions. I think he liked it that I called him Sir.

The closer I got toward where I was going, the more the scenery changed. From the concrete floors and walls in the warehouse where I work, I went to tiled floors and painted walls. From there I opened a door onto carpeted flooring and walls that had pretty pictures in gold frames. I was really nervous when I knocked on the door that said Human Resources Office. *Aha! HR.* When there was no answer I opened it and stuck my head in; there was no time to waste being polite; I'd already used 10 minutes of my 30 minute break.

The woman at the large desk looked startled. "Yes? May I help you?"

"Yes, ma'am. My supervisor Terry Flynn said to come here about full time work. I've been working as a temp for the last two weeks. Tomorrow's my last day, and I wanted to apply..."

Just then an inner door opened and a man walked out. The name on the office door was Timothy Roland. He stopped when he saw me and looked me up and down. "What have we here?" I wanted to kick him.

The woman at the desk answered. "She is a temp and wants to apply for permanent work."

"Well come on into my office and we'll see what we can do." I noticed the woman giving me a strange look, lifting her eyebrows and pursing her mouth, like she was trying to warn me. I nodded to her; I knew exactly what the warning was about. But I followed the man into his office.

He pointed to a seat facing his desk and I sat down. But he didn't go behind the desk; he sat on it directly in front of me. "So, you want to work here full time?"

"Yes, uh, sir. I'm doing pretty good but my last day is tomorrow and I'd like to stay on."

He reached out and touched my cheek. "Nice pretty girl like you, I'm sure I could find something for you." His finger trailed down my neck and shoulder.

What the...? The old buzzard has to be 60 if he's a day.

His foot touched mine. "Yes, I'm sure I can find a place for you."

I pulled my foot back. "Do I fill out some papers or something?"

He chuckled. "Yes, or something."

I looked at the clock. "Sir, my lunch break is almost over and I've got to get back to the line. What do I need to do?"

The man stood up from the desk and suddenly he was all business. "You say your last day is tomorrow?"

"Yes, sir."

"Then be here in my office Monday morning. My secretary will give you an application to bring back with you. And we'll give you some tests. And get to know you better." The last remark was made in a different tone of voice.

"Thank you, sir." I got up and left the room as quickly as I could. He was right behind me and spoke to the secretary.

"Give the young lady an application. She'll be back at 8 a.m. Monday and we'll have her take the test with the others at 9."

The secretary nodded and got some papers out of a file folder. "Just fill these out and bring them with you."

I took the papers and returned to the work station. I was hungry and hadn't gotten a cigarette either. But at least I had the possibility of a job. *I wonder just how nice I have to be to...*All of a sudden I remembered a story book my first grade teacher read to the class. It was about a skunk named Timmy. *Timothy Roland? Hmm, Timmy the Skunk!!!* I didn't laugh out loud but I couldn't help smiling. Even then, Clarine glared at me.

***

I don't enjoy the afternoon walk home like I do the morning one. The guys I call "the slugs", in my mind, were hanging out in clumps all over the streets by then. The bigger gangs were mostly in the Beckley section a few blocks over but there were a lot of losers who ganged together there on Dobler Street to show off their manhood with crude remarks and obscene gestures. They always turned on the talk whenever I walked by but so far nobody tried to stop me. I have my knife if they do. When Mike gave it to me, he said to keep it out of sight all the time because it's illegal; but if I need it, it's here, and it's quick, and it's sharp.

Thinking of Mike brought tears to my eyes but I opened them wide in a defiant stare. *He's not worth crying over. Scum.*

I made it past the slugs and let myself into the building and my apartment. I relocked the door and slid the dead bolt across with a sigh. The apartment gives me a sense of safety even though

Mike isn't here anymore to protect me.

Mike Greer was the knight in shining armor I'd wanted all my childhood...the one who took me away from my mother and the screaming, and mother's men and their demands. Mike took me away from them and I became his exclusively. He wanted what the other men wanted, but he also gave me a place to live and food to eat. And he was proud of me; he liked to show me off to the other guys in the neighborhood. Everybody knew I was Mike's old lady and nobody gave me any hassle.

I fought back tears again at the thoughts of Mike. *Why fight the tears? Go ahead, get it out.*

So I did. I sat on the floor with my head on the couch cushion and sobbed until I was weak and there were no more tears. Then I got up and went to the bathroom and washed my face.

I looked in the mirror at the swollen eyes and red nose. *Aren't you pretty?*

I had to admit to myself that the visit to HR had really discouraged and frightened me. *Looks like I have to put out wherever I am. That … that Clarine is right – I am just street trash.*

Just then there was a knock on the door. Quickly I splashed cold water on my face and dried it with a towel.

"Who is it?" I yelled through the door. I didn't dare open it in case it was one of the slugs.

"Christy from Hunts...the Temp Agency."

Great! What's she doing slumming?

"Just a minute." I slid back the two locks and opened the door.

Christy stood there smiling. "May I come in?"

"Sure, come on."

When Christy was settled on the couch, I sat in the wooden chair at the table and looked at her.

"I guess you're wondering why I'm here."

"Yep."

"I got your address from the application in our file."

I nodded.

"There are two reasons, really. One is, and I should have

come last week but...well, I wondered if you'd like to go to church with me."

I didn't mean to but the laughter exploded from my chest and out my mouth before I could stop it.

Christy stared at me with her mouth dropped open.

"Sorry. It's just that...do I look like church and I would be a fit?"

"I don't know. I just thought since you were alone maybe you'd like to come."

"You're a nice lady. Too nice for people like me."

Christy began shaking her head. "No, no please don't say that. I'm not nice. I mean I try to be. But we're all alike underneath, aren't we? I mean we all have problems and need help."

Lady, you got no clue about problems! "Hey, I don't mean nothing, anything, bad but church and me just won't ever fit. I wouldn't even have anything to wear."

"You could borrow something of mine."

Gina shook her head. "What's the other thing you came about?"

"A job came in today. I know yours runs out tomorrow and this other one starts Monday. It's the same kind of work but pays a little more and I talked to the HR lady and she says this could definitely lead to a full time if you do well."

Without the help of Timmy the Skunk!

The relief that filled my heart was unexplainable. "Sounds great. I was going to apply for full time at this one on Monday but I think its going to take extra curricular activity to land it."

Christy looked puzzled. "What do you mean?"

"I mean puttin' out for the man."

"The man?"

"The boss man, the guy who hires people. He wants my body." *There, let's see how she handles that.*

Christy sat still for a few seconds before reaching in her purse. "Then this is just in time." She handed me a form.

I saw that the name of the company was a place I pass every

day on my way to work, about five minutes closer.

"Thanks. I mean I really do thank you. You're a real friend."

Color sprang up in Christy's cheeks.

"And I'm sorry about the church thing. But I don't think God likes me very much."

"Oh! But He does. He loves you, Gina."

I shook my head. "Well even if he does, church people don't." *There, let's see her deny that one!*

Christy looked me straight in the eye. "I'm a church people – church person – and I like you."

I could feel my own cheeks coloring. But I smiled and nodded. "You're different."

Christy picked up her purse and stood to her feet.

"Well, I won't bother you any more. But, you know where I am if you need anything. Do you need anything now?"

"No. Thanks to you I'm caught up, I've had plenty to eat, and didn't even have to bum cigarettes. And I've got the next two weeks rent paid. Tell you the truth I'm hoping to move from here as soon as I get a full time job."

"You will let me know, won't you? If you move?"

I agreed.

***

Christy

I missed walking that Thursday because I went to Gina's instead of to the track. So I called Helen as soon as I got home.

"Sorry I missed today. I took your advice, a week late but I went to Gina's apartment and invited her to church."

"Good for you."

"Hey, what's wrong? You got a cold or something?" Helen sounded all stopped up.

"To tell you the truth, I didn't know you weren't at the track today because I didn't go either."

"Are you okay? Can I get you some medicine?"

"No, I'll be fine. I've got aspirin and flu stuff here. Everything I need. So, tell me, is she going to church with you?"

I laughed. "No, I think she was glad I asked but she's not going. She said she and church didn't fit."

"She may change her mind later - when you get to know each other better."

Helen sounded like she knew something I didn't. On the other hand, when Gina said she wanted to move I felt a panic that I might lose track of her, before I remembered her pay would come through Hunts for a while. This could be a God thing.

"Maybe. But I think she's right. She and my church would definitely not fit. Oh! I forgot you're not feeling well. I'll let you go. Hope to see you tomorrow. Get better."

***

Helen

I replaced the phone in the cradle and turned back to the letter that lay on the table. And the opened package that lay beside it.

I didn't lie. I didn't say I had a cold. I just said I wasn't at the track today. Christy doesn't need to know I've been crying all afternoon.

***

Christy

After I left the track the next day, I went for a drive. I knew I shouldn't, and I hadn't for a long, long time – over eighteen months now. I drove through the subdivision where David lived. He would be thirty-eight now, ten years older than I am. He lived there with his wife and children.

We too had known each other from church, just like Helen and Sanders. We also felt like we had known each other all our lives. And we separated, not because of any integrity on the part of the female, but because the male was honorable.

But I didn't meet him at church. I knew who he was from church, but we didn't meet there. Our first real meeting was the stuff of which romance is made.

Chapter Three

2001

Christy

As I walked down Charing Cross Road in London, I was simultaneously startled by a heavenly sound of music and a familiar face. You don't expect to nearly run into a familiar face when you are an ocean away from everyone you know. But there it was, nameless for the moment but familiar nonetheless. And perhaps it was the very absence of a name that caused the familiar face to blend with the heavenly music and indelibly stamp an impression of destiny to the encounter.

It was my first full day in London, on the trip I had promised myself since my senior year in high school when our English teacher brought a group of students on the grandmother of all field trips. It was a wonderful five days that we spent but it was over so quickly and even when we were experiencing the wonders of England, we were at the mercy of the Tour Guide and her timing. I promised myself that when I graduated from college I would ask my parents for the gift of two weeks in England and spend as long as I wanted at the Tower of London, Westminster Abbey, Windsor Palace...and that I would go to Madame Tussaud's and Trafalgar Square and so many other places that there just had not been time for before. And my wonderful parents agreed.

And here I was, encamped in a medium priced hotel in South Kensington near the Gloucester Road Underground Station and more excited than I had ever been in my life. In fact it seemed that life, real life, was just beginning.

I was on my way that Sunday morning to Trafalgar Square and had gotten off the tube at Charing Cross so I could find the little book store at 84 Charing Cross Road made famous by Helene Hanff's book of that title. My heart dropped when I discovered a pizza place at the location but I was determined not to let the disappointment spoil my day.

I crossed the road and passed a statue, and decided not to stop and find out who it represented because I could see Trafalgar Square ahead, when the bells rang and I looked and saw the familiar face three feet from me on my left.

The familiar face looked as shocked as I felt. It wasn't exactly a déjà vu sensation but similar. Our eyes locked and there was connection between two souls. That sounds corny but that is the way it was nevertheless.

We both came to a dead stop and continued staring at each other. He got it before I did.

"1st Methodist Church back home, right?"

Light dawned. "Yes, of course. Your children come to Sunday School." We'd never met but I'd seen him drop them off.

He grinned and held out his hand, "David Bailey."

I smiled and held out my own, "Christy Simpson."   There was an awkward silence. "I just got here yesterday. It's my graduation present... from college."

"Congratulations!" He smiled. "I'm here on business but don't have to start 'til tomorrow. Are you sightseeing today?"

"Yes, and you?"

"Well, I'd like to but I don't know what I am doing, or where to go. I've never been here before. I just got in last night and will be busy all week so I thought I'd just come to Trafalgar Square and wander around from there...maybe go see the Houses of Parliament and Buckingham Palace. Where are you going?"

I was aware that there was a hint in his tone, a desire to have a tourist companion. I had been so excited about being here all alone but...

"Well, I really want to go to Trafalgar Square too. I have never been even though I spent five days here in England when I was in High School. But you've just come from there."

He quickly answered, "I'd love to go again. I wanted to feed the pigeons but felt kind of silly doing it all by myself."

"Okay then," I said. We walked down the hill to the famous site.

The pigeon food vendors were doing a healthy business that morning. Mostly it was children who would feed the flocks of birds that were obviously very tame and expectant of bounty from the humans.

David and I didn't care that there were few adults indulging the pigeon gluttony. He insisted on buying and we both scattered birdseed with great abandon. After a few minutes I knelt down and began talking to one bird that was apart from the others. There were enough seeds being thrown around that the flock ignored me. And my pigeon, the one I thought of as my very own pigeon, came over and shyly took a seed out of my hand. Then to my great surprise, he jumped up on my arm and ate from my palm. It was one of the most wonderful feelings I'd ever experienced.

David pulled a disposable camera out of his pocket and caught the moment. "Beautiful," he said.

My pigeon finished the food in my hand and then flew off to become lost in the hundreds of his fellows. We looked at the statues and then headed back toward Charing Cross. At my suggestion we stopped at St. Martin-in-the-Field Church to read the sign in front of the door. We discovered that the heavenly sound earlier was the bells of the church and also that the "Visitor Service" had just started a few minutes earlier. The attendant said we would not be interrupting if we wanted to enter. We looked at each other and nodded.

The pulpit was so very British, the preacher had to climb stairs to enter it. And it would be dangerous to the neck to sit very close up front!

We sat about halfway down on the right facing the front of the church and the charm of the place immediately made us smile at each other. The choir was awesome and we found out later that St. Martin's was famous for its music.

After the service we couldn't resist having lunch in the Crypt below the church. It truly was a crypt, with people buried below the stone floor. But it was converted into a charming little restaurant and we had the most awesome mushrooms, each bigger than my hand but they weren't portabellas, they seemed like just regular kind of mushrooms only giant sized. They were stuffed with a chicken and crème filling and topped with a filo pastry and it was one of the best things I ever tasted. David agreed. We stopped in the souvenir shop on our way out but resisted buying anything since it was the first day in London for both of us and we knew that temptations to spend would abound in the future.

After that we went across the street to the National Portrait Gallery and spent an hour or so looking at pictures of famous people. I especially love the Tudor period of English history and was in awe at seeing the originals of so many paintings I had seen on book jackets and in center sections of books I'd read.

David loved to read as much as I did so we spent the next few hours in the quaint little book shops that are peppered throughout that area of Charing Cross Road, and we didn't resist making purchases there. Then we found out that somehow we had wandered into Covent Garden. We were both amazed at how many places of interest were in such a few blocks in the great City. We laughed with the crowds at the street performers whose antics entertained us and put coins in the hats of several.

We stopped in a little Italian place for supper and talked about all we had seen and all we wanted to see. When we came out it was beginning to get dark and I realized that I would have to ride on the tube back to Gloucester Road alone at night. The thought hit me for the first time why my parents were hesitant at my coming alone. Why had I never thought of being alone at night? I couldn't just hole up at the hotel every night or I would miss much of what I wanted to do.

"Where are you staying?" David asked.

I told him and he insisted on seeing me back to South Kensington; he was staying in Knightsbridge, not far away, he said.

So we entered the tube at Charing Cross and exited at Gloucester Road. We had both bought weeklong passes and were impressed with the efficiency of the underground system.

When we reached my hotel we turned to face each other and suddenly were silent. After talking nonstop all day long, I couldn't think of what to say. Part of me knew it was because I didn't want to say good night. Strange, I had only known that face as the father of some of my Sunday School students and now he was far removed from them and from home. He, like the pigeon, was suddenly mine – cut off from the flock and uniquely attached to me.

It was obvious by the way he put off leaving that David felt the same way. Was it just because we were two people from the same hometown together in a strange country? I didn't think so. I'd never felt so comfortable with anybody in my life.

"I feel like I've known you forever," he said.

I just nodded.

***

2007

I stared down at the picture in my hand and was so glad that there was a souvenir of that day. It was the last year that seed vendors were allowed in Trafalgar Square. The pigeons were thought to be a health hazard and feeding them was discouraged. It was a time that could never be repeated.

In many ways.

***

2001

On Monday of that first week in London, I went to Hampton Court Palace and it was fun. Since I could spend the entire day I availed myself of the luxury of going on all the tours instead of just the three that my previous trip allowed.

With that wonderful sense of belonging that comes with visiting a famous site for the second time, I entered the Great Hall, and made my way around to the Haunted Gallery where it is said that the ghost of Henry VIII's fifth wife Catherine still runs screaming and crying for mercy as she did when her husband sat in chapel and ignored her. Catherine was the second wife that Henry beheaded. According to history, she was guilty of adultery, as the first had not been, but one had to pity her anyway... such a child to be married to such a gross old man.

The Chapel Royal was still breathtaking and the Tudor Kitchens as fascinating as ever, though I still could not imagine eating peacock! The rest of the Palace was new to me. I had not seen the King's Apartments or Queens Apartments or the Georgian Rooms and, honestly, did not enjoy them as much as I'd hoped to. If you don't know the history and aren't familiar with the people who lived there, the places are just not as interesting. But the Palace Gardens were awesome and I was very glad that I took the time to walk through them over to the Great Vine.

I loved it but admitted to myself that it would have been more fun if David had been there with me, making me laugh and sharing the adventure. Then, perverse creature that I was, I found myself being irritated at him because his absence was in some way spoiling the absolute joy I had been looking forward to for years in being here alone.

He'd said "I'll call you later in the week and see how you are doing." And he gave me his hotel number in case I needed anything. I didn't want to think about whether he would or would not call me. I didn't want to think about whether I would see him again. I wanted to enjoy my time alone, my freedom from having to account to anybody.

I hid my disappointment well when I checked at the desk for messages and was told that there were none. I ate in the hotel dining room that night and spent the evening reading a book I bought the afternoon before from one of the bookstores near

Trafalgar Square. The book was on Charles I, the only King ever to be executed in England. Charles was a good man, not in tune with the times in which he lived, but a good man nevertheless. I felt sad for him and determined to go to Whitehall during my stay and see the place where he was executed.

I was just turning out the light when the phone rang. It was David.

"I hope I didn't wake you up."

"No, I just finished reading. Did you have a good day?"

"Yes," he said. "But a long one." He paused. "The thing is this...I have some tickets for tomorrow night– they don't cost anything but you have to have a ticket to get in. They are to the Tower of London's Ceremony of the Keys. A guy at the office here had them, left by someone who couldn't use them because he had to fly on to Australia. They thought I might want to go experience it. And there are two of them; his wife was with him. They have the list of names for each night there at the Tower and we would have to pretend to be...uh...let's see...here it is...Bruce and Doris Sleet. What do you think?"

I laughed. "I think I could pretend to be Doris Sleet for a night!"

He laughed too. "Okay then. I'm Bruce. We don't report to the gate of the Tower until 9:30. Want to catch some supper first?"

"Yes, that would be wonderful,"

"I'll get a taxi and we'll go in style."

"Great."

"I'm not sure what time my meetings will be over so I'll call your room as soon as I get back to my hotel and we'll plan from there."

"Fine." When we hung up, I sighed deeply with contentment.

I turned out the light then. But I couldn't go to sleep. David's face was burned into my mind's eye, laughing, smiling, grinning, and just looking at me with a calm pleasure.

I got out of bed and onto my knees. "Dear Lord, help. You couldn't have planned this but it seems so right, so real. I have never felt so comfortable with anybody in my life. But he's married. I know I should have said 'No' to going with him tomorrow. He probably shouldn't have asked me to go. But here we are. Yesterday was an accident but tomorrow is a date. Lord, forgive us, please. Amen."

I got back in bed and turned the light back on and forced my mind into the 17th century and onto Oliver Cromwell and King Charles I whose problems had nothing to do with the joy of forbidden twinkling blue eyes.

The next day I slept late and luxuriated in the realization of waking up in London, England with another day of doing whatever I wanted. I could take another day trip out from the city. Or I could visit the National Gallery and see the Rosetta Stone.

After the breakfast bar at the hotel, which I made just before they closed it down for the morning, I decided on Madame Tussauds and Regents Park. I passed by the Sherlock Holmes Museum but didn't go in. I'd read all the Holmes books, including the modern ones but wasn't that enthralled by him.

Madame Tussauds was all I hoped, and more. I had no idea that we would be allowed to touch the waxworks. I loved every minute of it. And I loved Regents Park. It was beautiful and my heart ached in a strange new way when I saw the couples sitting together on blankets holding hands and laughing and feeding each other bites of picnic lunches.

I especially loved Queen Mary's Rose Garden. I had a bowl of soup in the little restaurant there in the middle of the Garden and it was the best mushroom soup I ever tasted in my life. There was a woman there with a whining child and I was glad that I was unattached and unencumbered by responsibility.

But I was also glad that I wasn't going to be alone later that evening.

2007
Christy

Helen and I finished our 20th lap around the track, marking

the end of one mile.

"Did you go anywhere other than England when you were on your graduation trip?"

"No. I intended to go to Scotland but it just didn't happen. Maybe someday. I almost went to Paris but decided against it."

Helen sighed. "I always wanted to go to Paris but that never happened either. I never got anywhere but, like you, I think England would have been my first choice."

"Maybe you will still go some day."

She looked at me with a funny look. "You know…. Maybe I will! I really hadn't thought about it. But maybe now I will."

She didn't say anything more but I thought that was strange. Why now? Could she afford it for the first time? Had I brought something into her life that would make her think that maybe now she would travel? Surely not my own travel story.

The next day Helen brought up traveling again. "Christy, if I went to England would you be interested in going too?"

I almost stopped walking. I knew I could never go back alone, but with Helen that was a possibility. It would even be fun. Money was no problem, not with the inheritance that I had barely touched.

"Yes!" I said. "That would be awesome. I'd love it."

"You could be my tour guide," she said.

I laughed. "Fun! I could show off all my knowledge."

But suddenly we were both quiet. I don't know what Helen was thinking but I was jerked out of the now into the England of 6 years earlier.

2001

David brought a taxi to my hotel and we went to Leicester Square and ate at Bella Pasta Restaurant. We saw the statue of Charlie Chaplain and a street performer that had the most awful costume imaginable. I couldn't think what he was supposed to be. His skin was painted green, and his clothes were green, and green stalks of something were sticking out of his belt and up his back and about a foot over his head. When he held out a cap for money we ignored him and walked by but then he said, "C'mon Mate, I need money for a new costume." We were a step or two away when it sank in what he said and we looked at each other and burst into laughter. David turned around and pulled a pound out of his pocket. "Yes, you do!" He laughed again and gave the man the money.

The Ceremony of the Keys was different from anything I ever experienced. It was exciting to wait there in the darkness at the iron gate to the Tower that had been closed to the public hours earlier. The guard brought flashlights to check off the names of those on the list for the night. There were many of us gathered there, waiting to be called and escorted back to the place where we would see the ceremony. The guard instructed us that no talking at all was allowed during the short ceremony or on our walk to and from the site.

As we stood by the Traitors Gate and thought of all the people who had come by boat there to the Tower, I felt as though the very stones of the place were permeated by the unknown fears that had been transported by the accused, as well as the excitement of those coming to be crowned.

We saw the Chief Yeoman Warder with his escort all in their uniforms, carrying a lantern, and we watched them walk the same paths their predecessors had walked for seven hundred years.

After the gates were locked and the Chief Warder returned, we heard the same words that were heard by both famous and nameless prisoners and members of the royal family over the years, the name of the ruling monarch being the only variation.

The challenge was issued, "Halt! Who comes there?"

"The Keys"

"Whose Keys?"

"Queen Elizabeth's Keys."

"Pass Queen Elizabeth's Keys and all is well."

The Chief Warder responded, "God bless Queen Elizabeth."

And the Guard all said, "Amen."

And then the trumpet sounded, an eerie lonely sound there

in the dark and silence, the very repetition transcending time and making those of us who heard it aware of our own finiteness.

When we were back outside the visitor's gate, it was as though the crowd who had been very noisy as we waited to be admitted somehow lost the ability to speak and even though the ban was lifted, we all dispersed without a word.

David and I didn't talk for a long time. We walked up the embankment and looked back on the Tower, which looked enchanted in the night, with only a few turrets and towers lit and shining out of the darkness. We stood there leaning on the rail and watched it in silence.

Finally he spoke. "I have to fly over to Paris tomorrow."

The violence of my reaction shocked me, it was as though someone had thrown ice water in my face, only I felt it in my stomach.

I didn't know what to say, so I didn't say anything.

"I wish you could go with me," he said, still staring at The Tower.

I just closed my eyes and bit my lower lip. What was I supposed to say to that?

"Look, Christy. You must think I am awful. I am a married man with children, a Christian, a churchgoer. I have no right to be spending time with you this way. I knew when I first saw you Sunday that I should just keep on walking. But I couldn't. I wanted to be with you. But it's selfish of me. I've interrupted your vacation."

"No." I finally spoke. "No, it's not selfish. It just seems so natural, us being together I mean."

"I know but it can never go anywhere. I am married. And I have children."

"I know." I said miserably. "And I know you love your wife...."

"No!" He shocked me with his sudden anger. "No, I don't love my wife. I have never loved her. But I had sex with her and got her pregnant and married her and then fathered another child. And that's that."

I stood there in silence for several seconds, joy that he had never loved his wife warring with sorrow that he was committed to the marriage.

"She loves you." It was part statement, part question.

"No." His voice wasn't bitter but resigned. "Judy is incapable of loving anybody."

"But then why...?" I stopped. I thought I knew why. We both believed in keeping promises; it was part of our faith.

"The children," he said. "I can't go off and leave them with her; she is not a good mother. But I can't take them away from her either."

"Oh, David, I'm so sorry." My turning to him was involuntary and by the light of the street lamp I could see that his eyes were full of longing and sorrow at the same time. And suddenly we were embracing, his arms around me, his head buried in my neck, my arms around him and my ear hearing the pounding of his heart. We didn't kiss.

I think we both knew that we dared not. But we held each other for a long time.

***

2007

Helen often mentioned 'our trip' to England as if it were inevitable. I found myself thinking of it in interesting ways. At first the feeling was one of a dread of 'getting back on the horse again' after a painful fall. Then, in moments of determined independence, I thought of the trip as a memory replacement technique. I could go back to the places I love and remember them afterwards without seeing David there. Gradually Helen's enthusiasm affected me and I began to see it as a thing unto itself and not an extension of my past.

Helen began checking into flights and dates and 'our trip' began to take on form.

We chose April because Helen had always been drawn by the line in Robert Browning's poem "O to be in England now that April's there." I began researching more periods in British History

than the Tudor and Stewart ones with which I was familiar so that I would
be better prepared to understand more of what we would see.

2001

I went to Whitehall while David was in France. I rented the earphones and listened to the history of the era, and was never able to forget the dramatic moments when I listened as Charles I was marched through the hall and out the window where he was taken to the block and beheaded.

On Thursday of that week I took the train to Windsor and toured the castle areas that are open to the public. In Saint George's chapel I childishly stomped on the place where the body of Henry VIII lay buried. Henry's treatment of his wives has always infuriated me; he personified male insensibility and feelings of superiority.

I had lunch across the street from the castle in a little crookedly shaped restaurant that has served food to hungry travelers for over three hundred years. That is one of the things that fascinates me about England – everything is so old there. If I think about it objectively I realize that there is no part of the world older than another part, but the marks that mankind has made on geographical areas most definitely cause feelings of newness or feelings of antiquity in the land itself.

On Thursday night David called from Paris. He opened the conversation with "I am sorry to bother you..." Before he could continue, I interrupted. "No, don't apologize, please. I have missed you."

"I've missed you too. Oh, Christy, what a mess! I know I should have just left it alone and taken the assignment here as a gift from God to give me strength to stay away from you. But I ..." He stopped talking and there was silence on the line for about ten seconds. Finally I said, "When do you get back?"

"Tomorrow night. Around 8."

"Shall we go to Bella Pasta again?" I asked.

"Are you sure?"
"Yes," I answered. "I am sure."

Chapter Four

2007

Christy

I confessed to Helen as we walked together. She was so easy to confess to.

"I would have moved to David's hotel for the rest of his time in London and become his lover without any hesitation. But he had more integrity than I. Or did he? It's a question I have asked myself over and over. The psychologist has no respect for his moral decisions, calls him neurotic and selfish. On one hand I can see it that way. I was so young and vulnerable and, looked at from one point of view, David played with my emotions and indulged in a fantasy affair but kept his own ideas of honor by not actually going to bed with me. But in another point of view, the view of my heart, he had no more control over his emotions than I did and could no more keep from spending time with me than I could with him. When I recognize that, I am filled with more respect than ever at his physical restraint."

***

2001

Christy

On Saturday, the two of us went to Victoria Station and took the train to Hever in Kent. I was glad of his company for more than one reason. To get to Hever Castle, home of Anne Boleyn and the place where Henry VIII courted her, it was necessary to change trains and walk over a mile from the station to the castle. I was determined to go there but experienced a little trepidation at the thought of the journey. Now, here I was, going on a trip I had dreamed of for years with the person whose company I enjoyed more than anyone I ever met.

Changing trains in a strange village in company with David was fun instead of fearful like it might have been if I were alone. And his company made the walk to the castle an adventure I would probably have never dared to experience on my own.

As we left the small station at Hever and set out down the single lane road to the castle, we hadn't walked far when on our left we spotted a stile, recognizable to me only because of pictures remembered from a childhood nursery rhyme book. Beside the stile was a hand carved sign that said 'Shortcut to the Castle'.

England's footpaths were walking trails through private property. Usage of the old paths was kept legal by being walked at least annually. This task was faithfully performed by various walking clubs.

Without a word but with grins at each other, David and I climbed the stile as our fellow travelers on the train disappeared around the curve on the pavement ahead of us.

We passed by a pond on our left that was partially hidden by the hedgerow that separated it from the path, but through the trees and bushes we could see the water and what appeared to be a floating house for the ducks that were lazing around on the porch that surrounded it. The path was narrow, and the overhanging trees gave it a secretive atmosphere until we came suddenly out into the sunlight and an open field. We stepped carefully but leisurely around the cow piles that dotted the field until David stopped abruptly.

"These might be bull piles instead of cow piles," he said. I could feel my eyes widen and he took my hand as we ran toward the metal gate on the far side of the field. Laughing, we climbed the gate and continued through more private property until the path finally joined the paved road leading to Hever.

That day was a magical day, my favorite day ever. We toured the castle, seeing all the things I had read about in novels about the beheaded Queen of England who was the second wife of Henry VIII – her bed, the Book of Hours that she carried to her execution, her portrait. We explored the maze. We strolled through all the gardens and sat on the ground by the lake under a shade tree. There was a moment there by the lake, as he helped me to my feet and looked into my eyes that we almost kissed...almost but not quite. My heart was pounding so hard from the intensity of the moment that my ears began ringing. We walked in silence back toward the castle but at some point on the way, David took my hand.

We unclasped hands when we stopped for scones and tea at the Moat restaurant. The scones were the best I ever ate and the Devonshire cream served with them was exquisite. David honestly seemed as interested as I was in the beauty of Hever as well as the history that had taken place there and we talked enthusiastically about all we experienced that day.

When we left the castle grounds, we stopped in the church where Anne's father, George Boleyn, was buried. It was deserted except for us and after we had looked at all the historical markers, David took my hand again.

I looked up at him and saw complete tenderness in his eyes. He spoke softly.

"We are alone together here in the presence of God. I wish I could make vows to you before Him that I will take care of you and protect you and spend my life with you, but I can't. I can say that, right or wrong, I love you and it would be dishonest to pretend that I don't. And I can pledge this to you right now in this place and in His presence that I will not dishonor Him or you or my love for you by allowing our relationship to become anything that we would ever be ashamed to let anyone else know about."

I swallowed against the lump in my throat. "Then I'll make a pledge too...not the one I want to make either. I promise I will never attempt to turn you from your pledge." As soon as the words were out of my mouth, I regretted them. "I love you, David. I truly love you and I will try to love you enough to respect your choice."

Once again he drew me into his arms. Once again, we didn't kiss. On the way back to Hever Station, we talked about the scenery, about how much the landscape of Kent looked like home although the architecture did not. Several of the homes had thatched roofs and were enchanting to me. We passed a driveway and a sign proclaiming that a Bed and Breakfast lay hidden through the trees at its end. I found myself sending up a silent prayer that one day David and I could honeymoon there.

The station was deserted and we waited in silence for the train. It wasn't that we were uncomfortable with each other or that there was nothing we wanted to say. It just seemed that our vows had so narrowed the relational possibilities that we were unsure as to the next step.

When we again reached Victoria Station, we crossed the street and went to a Pub for supper. It was crowded and loud and so conversation was almost impossible. After dinner, David hailed a taxi and dropped me at my hotel before continuing on to his own. I hesitated at the door of the cab and looked at him mutely.

"I'll call," he said. I nodded and closed the door.

I stared as the taxi drove away taking him from me.

2007

It was settled. The date in April was chosen, the tickets were already on our credit cards, and Helen had applied for her passport. She and I would drive to Cincinnati and leave my car in long term parking, fly to Chicago, and take the seven and a half hour flight to Heathrow.

Part of me couldn't believe I was doing this. And part of me was excited. My therapist was very pleased with the decision. I was only seeing him once a month now and he seemed genuinely happy with my newfound independence. He did ask if I was sure I was over feeling the superstitious fear that doing something that made me happy would result in tragedy. I told him I wasn't absolutely certain but I thought so.

It was the writings of the old man...John... that were helping me. I now had an assurance that God really wants me happy and also that I am a part of His life in the earth that is much bigger than just me.

Christmas would be here in just six weeks and in the meanwhile there was Thanksgiving to be gotten through.

During our walk one afternoon I asked Helen what she was doing for the holiday and she too was going to be alone. She never mentioned any family and I hesitated to ask. But today she opened up.

"I have a sister in Texas. And this year I'm flying out there for Christmas. We haven't seen each other in years."

"How nice," I said wistfully. "It's tough being an only child."

She smiled. "I used to wish that I was an only child. Beverly and I fought like cats and dogs. But at least when you get older, there is someone else who remembers the people from your childhood. We talk on the phone every few weeks and enjoy each other now much more than we did then. But since we weren't close we've never visited much."

"But you are going there this year?" I was already dreading Christmas alone...again.

"Yes." Helen smiled and picked up the walking pace. Sometimes when we were talking, we tended to slow down. And it was usually Helen who noticed and got us back in rhythm. "Beverly is now a great-grandmother and I barely know her grandchildren. I figured I need to go and get to know the only family I have."

I nodded. She was right but I felt left out. I'd started to think of Helen as my family. And it was true that she is the closest thing to a family that I have. My mother and father had relocated to Kentucky from California when I was in first grade and I barely remembered my grandparents and uncles.

She interrupted my thoughts. "Why don't we do Thanksgiving together this year? I mean really do it with turkey and dressing and the whole spread? We could both fix some things and have it at my house."

"That's great. I'd love it!" I hadn't had a real Thanksgiving dinner since my parents died.

When we parted that afternoon I resisted the urge to drive by David's house again. "Lord Jesus, help me."

He was healing me, I could tell. Because of Helen's story, I no longer felt like Christianity's only Scarlet Woman and was able to actually forgive myself for loving a married man. And for wanting him to leave his wife or commit adultery.

I was coming along about blaming myself for my parent's death. John's books were helping me understand — at least with my head. We live in a fallen world and accidents happen.

I never saw them again after they kissed me goodbye at the airport when I left on my dream trip — the day before I met David.

***

The Saturday before Thanksgiving, I headed to the grocery with the list of things needed for my contribution to the holiday meal with Helen.

CHRISTMAS GIFTS FOR NEEDY CHILDREN. The bold heading on the flier tacked up to the bulletin board just as I entered in the supermarket caught my eye. *That might be just the answer to my prayer about something to do to make Christmas special this year.* The flier announced that the Living Word Church would be meeting each Saturday morning from now 'til Christmas Eve to 1. take applications for those who needed gifts for children and 2. receive and wrap donated gifts. The Saturday meetings would be at the Conference Center in the mall beginning at 10 a.m.

I glanced at my watch. It was 10:15, so I parked the cart, went back to the car and headed to the mall.

There was a table set up in the foyer of the Center, and a pleasant looking gray haired woman directed me to the "second room on the right."

I was surprised to see that there were only three people there, two middle aged women and a younger man. They were standing behind a long table that held several sheets of paper, turned toward me. The papers were blank except for letters at the top and were obviously sign-up sheets for those who wanted toys.

A sandy haired woman smiled and said, "Would you like to sign up for Christmas gifts?"

"I'm sorry. I came to volunteer to help. But..." I looked around the empty room with my sentence unfinished but obvious.

The good looking man walked forward and held out his hand to shake mine. "I'm Kyle Martin, pastor of Living Word Church." His hair was auburn and his eyes were blue – very blue.

I introduced myself and told him where I go to church. He then introduced me to the women. The sandy haired lady who had spoken first was Jo Ann and the other lady was Selena.

"My mom is out at the greeting table." He gave a wry grin. "We thought we'd need someone to direct the crowds this way."

I laughed. "Well, you may yet. Where all have you announced this? I saw the ad at the supermarket."

Selena answered. "We put it on the Christian radio station and in supermarkets and drug stores."

"Can I make a suggestion?"

"Sure."

"If you really want a lot of people to sign up, I think you should put it on the local rock station and pass out fliers in the housing projects."

The pastor nodded solemnly. "That makes sense."

"And give a time deadline or you'll have people coming in at the last minute wanting things and you won't have them." I paused. "I hope I don't sound like a know-it-all but I helped with some things like this back in college."

He laughed, his dark eyes twinkling. "Hey, we need all the help we can get. Sound on!"

"As soon as you get some requests start posting the specific needs on the Christian radio station and on community bulletin boards. If you have a lot, you might even send requests to other churches."

"You really do know what you're doing, don't you?" He was looking at me with a grin on his lips and respect in his eyes.

I could feel myself blushing. "Well, I just watched other people put it together back then."

Around 11:30, I offered to go pick up lunch and bring it in for the volunteers. By that time one woman had come in to sign up her three children.

Two p.m. was the time announced on the flier as closing time, and after lunch only one man had come in, to request an Ipod for his son. On the spur of the moment I told him that any gifts would be delivered to his home and given to the child in person. He then said that he changed his mind. When he walked out, the four of us looked at each other and burst into laughter.

"I guess we should have just offered to buy him an Ipod." Kyle Martin shook his head.

"But heaven only knows what he would listen to on it! And I smelled alcohol on his breath."

The pastor looked at me with respect. "I'm glad you said that about delivery; I hadn't thought of people ... um..."

"Stealing?"

"Yeah. Stealing. We are to be wise as serpents as well as being gentle as doves." He sighed. "I hate that."

"Me too." I walked over and picked up my purse. "Anything I can do to help?"

Kyle followed me out into the lobby. "You've already been a big help. But please, come back next week. I'll follow your suggestions and hopefully there will be more people. Or are you going out of town for Thanksgiving?"

"No, no plans except with a friend for Thanksgiving Day."

He nodded. "You can bring him with you if you want."

Is he trying to find out if I have a boyfriend?

"It's a lady. And I'll ask her."

"And anytime you want to try out our services we'd love to have you."

"Where is your church?"

"Here."

I must have looked shocked. "Here?"

"Yep, in the conference room where we met today. We come in early Sunday morning and set up the music and all."

"Really?" I had never been to a church that didn't have its own building.

He grinned. "Really."

"What time?"

"Praise and Worship starts at 10:30." The look he was giving me with the cute little half smile was not exactly pastoral. Just then Jo Ann and Serena came out of the room. He turned to them. "Christy may come to church some Sunday."

They both smiled. Jo Ann said, "I'll save you a seat in the morning. I always sit on the left hand side."

Lord? Should I? Oh, why not!

"I'll be there," I promised.

***

The lights in the conference room were very bright and the full band seated to the right of the podium was a shock. Keyboard, drums, guitars, trumpet or coronet...I never could tell the difference...looked like a rock concert instead of a church service. All my church life had been spent in very traditional settings. *This is certainly different!*

I saw a hand waving from the rows of folding chairs on her left. Jo Anne had saved me a seat up front. Way up front. *No turning back now!*

The band began tuning up just as I reached the spot reserved for me. Jo Anne introduced me to some couples seated in front of our chairs and a lady on the other side of her. She had saved the aisle chair for me.

A group of men and women went up on the stage and a woman nodded to the band. Behind them words appeared on a giant screen.

I liked the singing but was a little embarrassed at the raised hands and movement, almost like dancing, from many of the congregation. I glanced over at Jo Anne whose hands were not in the air but busy clapping in time with the rhythm of the music.

The songs got gradually slower. At one point, I felt that I was beginning to understand the expression 'praise and worship'. The musicians had started out with fast paced music and words of praise. They transitioned into worship music that made you want to fall on your knees. Just as I was wondering if I would have the nerve to kneel down, the music came to an end.

The attractive young pastor took the platform and spoke into the microphone.

"Praise the Lord!"

The congregation echoed, "Praise the Lord!"

He looked over the audience, smiling and nodding all the while. It was not my imagination that when his eyes landed on me, his smile broadened and the nod was more pronounced.

Jo Anne leaned over and whispered. "He saw you!"

I felt my cheeks grow hot and hoped I was not visibly blushing. *He's just glad that another person has come to his church.*

"Today I want to talk to you about dating and marriage. But not the way you might think." He grinned at us. "I am hoping that when every person in this room leaves this morning, you will have decided to stop dating Jesus and be married to Him."

Whoa! I never heard that before. He definitely caught my interest. He went on to talk about how Christians are called to be the Bride of Christ but most have not accepted the proposal and others were committing adultery. I felt a prickling in my heart at his words.

That's me, one of them anyway. I've wanted David more than I've wanted Jesus.

Most of the sermon was spent illustrating how the human heart is full of idolatries. I never heard a sermon like that in my life and hung on every word. It felt like something inside had been very hungry and was finally getting food to eat. Kyle Martin closed with a call to come forward if anyone wanted to make a public declaration of commitment to be married to Jesus. I looked over at Jo Anne who was picking up her purse and Bible. Obviously she was getting ready to leave.

I don't care! I'm going up.

The smile on Kyle Martin's face was tender when he saw me walking forward. He reached out and took my hand in his before looking around to see if any others were responding to his call.

I saw that several men and women and a lot of teens were walking up to join us and realized that I had been the first one to come up front.

Kyle squeezed my hand. "I'm so glad to see you."

My heart gave a little skip. *Lord, I am coming to you to give up a desire for romance. I don't want another romantic dilemma!*

"Let's all join hands." Kyle instructed the group. Then he bowed his head. "Lord, we come with baggage, idolatries in our hearts, and idolatries in our minds. We lay them at the cross and choose to be your Bride. Take us and make us one with you. In Jesus Name, Amen.

The band and singers had come back onto the stage during their gathering and prayer and now led the worshippers in the song "Sanctuary."

When the music ended, Kyle Martin dropped my hand and took the mike to give a closing prayer and benediction.

Afterwards a middle aged man came up and engaged him in a discussion. I went back to my chair but Jo Anne had already left. I picked up my purse and sweater and began walking toward the back of the conference room. I looked back once and saw Kyle Martin watching me but he was still trapped in conversation with the same man. I thought he looked sorry that he couldn't talk to me. *Okay, Jesus, it's you and me, remember? Deliver me from temptation!*

***

Thanksgiving Day was rainy. The noises of the Rose Bowl Parade filled the living room. I don't like parades but felt like it was almost blasphemous not to tune into it.

I was to be at Helen's at 1:30 and we would eat around 3. Helen was providing the turkey, dressing, mashed potatoes, gravy, and rolls. And I was taking green beans, sweet potato casserole, corn, and pumpkin pie with whipped cream. *Cranberry sauce? We didn't even mention cranberry sauce.*

Helen answered on the first ring. "Yes. I got cranberry sauce, both kinds, jellied and whole berries. I wasn't sure which kind you would want."

"I like the berries." I was glad neither of us would have to make another trip to the store.

"Me too. Well, we've got the other in case any strangers show up."

Shortly after we hung up, my phone rang. It was Helen calling back.

"That remark I made about strangers kept echoing in my mind. And I thought about that Bible verse that says to be nice to strangers, something about some have entertained angels unaware."

I waited but already knew what was coming.

"I was just wondering. Do you think maybe we should have invited that girl? You know, the one that you found a job for?"

I didn't actually groan but I came close.

"I guess I could go by her place and ask her, on my way over."

"Okay and if she says yes, call me on your cell and I'll set an extra place at the table."

I agreed. *I don't want Gina to come with me. Lord forgive me. I am so selfish!*

I parked on the street in front of the run down apartment building in the same place I parked the time I came to bring the job information. I hadn't heard from Gina so I guessed something was working out for her. I walked up the dusty steps and knocked on the door.

Gina answered right away and her face lit up when she saw me. That made me feel even more rotten about my reluctance to invite her to Helen's.

"Wow, I don't believe it! Come in. I'm going to move and I promise I was going to come to the office and tell you."

"Is this a good thing?"

"Oh, yeah! That job you brought by worked out. I've been there a month and am now full time. I haven't found a place yet but I'm looking."

"I'm so glad, Gina."

She smiled and looked at me expectantly.

"I came to see if you would like to have Thanksgiving Dinner with me and a friend, an older lady named Helen. We're going to eat at her house."

Gina looked shocked. "Serious? You want me?"

"Of course." *And right now, I really do, Lord. So I'm not lying!*

"Awesome! I'll get my sweater."

Chapter Five

2007

Helen

I was so glad when Christy called and said Gina was coming to have Thanksgiving dinner with us. *Thank you, Lord, for urging me to invite her.*

I put the third place setting at the table and viewed the results with pleasure. The salt shakers were little chipmunks dressed like pilgrims, and silk autumn leaves were scattered all over the top of the table cloth imprinted with cornucopias. A wicker Cornucopia filled with real fruit sat in the middle of the table. I used the clear amber plates instead of my pink and blue good china so it would look more Thanksgiving-y.

This is silly to feel so excited...as if I have daughters coming home for the holiday! And I haven't even met one of them!

The doorbell sounded and I greeted the two younger women who were laden down with holiday fare. Christy laughingly introduced us as she tried to balance a pot of green beans in one hand and a pumpkin pie in the other without spilling anything.

Gina looked into the living room and spotted the television set. Her eyes widened "Oh, look! Miracle on 34th Street is on. I haven't seen that since I was a little girl."

"Why don't you and Christy go on in and watch it while I organize everything in here. I'll join you in a few minutes."

Gina looked at Christy as if for permission. Christy nodded, smiled at me, and followed Gina to the couch..

Within minutes I was beaming with satisfaction at the perfectly decorated and filled table. But when I started to call the others to come in, a thought came to my mind. *Oh, no, Lord. Surely that's not you?*

But I knew it was. I joined them in the living room and my heart stirred as I saw the look on Gina's face avidly watching the television set. Christy looked up and gave a little shrug.

When the commercial break came, I cast one last backward eye to the holiday feast spread in the dining room, took a deep breath, and cleared my throat. "I have an idea. Why don't we fill our plates at the table and bring TV trays here and eat while we watch the movie."

Gina's face lit up. "Oh, could we? That would be great."

Christy grinned. "Sounds fine to me." And she reached over to hug me on her way toward the dining room.

While Gina and Christy were filling their plates, I got out the trays and set them up in the living room. After a moment I went to the table and gathered some silk leaves to put on top of each one. The chipmunks and fruit filled cornucopia went on the coffee table. By the time the others returned with their food, the living room was looking festive too.

"Go ahead and start before things get cold. We'll say the blessing at the next commercial." I left them and went to fill my own plate.

Gina didn't exactly act uncomfortable but I saw her look over at Christy to see how to act when I began to pray. Then she bowed her head and closed her eyes in imitation.

"Thank you, Lord for this food; bless it to our body's use. And thank you for bringing us together and binding us together with your love. Amen."

"Amen." Christy echoed.

Gina opened her eyes and looked up. And nodded.

The movie came back on. I exchanged a look with Christy as we both watched Gina once more become absorbed in the story of the child who didn't believe in Santa Claus.

At the ending Gina was wiping away tears and I handed her a box of tissues from the bottom shelf under the coffee table.

"Thank you." Gina blew her nose. "I don't know what's wrong with me lately. It seems like I'm getting wimpy and crying a lot."

I leaned down and hugged her. "It's not wimpy to cry. It's healthy."

"Thank you for letting me watch it. For watching it with me. I..." Gina's face began to show signs of more tears about to arrive on the scene. "It really did seem like a miracle when I was a kid. I loved it. But my mother laughed at me and said it's stupid to believe in miracles."

"I can understand that. I've prayed for miracles that didn't happen. But you know, I'd rather be stupid than hopeless."

Gina's head jerked up and she looked me directly in the eye. "What do you mean?"

I laughed. "Well, if we just decide there is nothing beyond what we can see around us, that would bring terrible depression and hopelessness."

Gina nodded. "That's Mam – depressed and hopeless. I decided I wasn't going to be like her when I was a real little girl. But..."

I waited and Christy was silent too.

"But, sometimes I'm afraid I'm more like her than I think."

"Yes." I purposefully made my tone of voice very gentle. "Like Job said, 'that which I have greatly feared has come upon me."

"Huh? Who's Job?"

From my peripheral vision, I saw Christy give a sudden start. *She and I live in a whole different world than this child. We can't begin to understand her frame of reference.*

"A man in the Bible. He tried to do right but he was always afraid bad things were going to happen. And they finally did."

Gina nodded. "I never read the Bible. Is it good?" She laughed. "Well, I know it's called the good book, but I mean, is it interesting?"

Christy laughed out loud. "Well, it depends. Sometimes it

seems so boring I can hardly stand it and other times it's really fascinating."

"It's a big book."

I laughed. "Yes, it certainly is a big book. You know, we who are Christians believe that it is God's Word to us in this world."

"No sh...no joke?"

I heard a smothered snicker from Christy's direction. "No joke. But there are lots of different versions and some are easier to understand than others."

Christy spoke up. "One thing that's helped me is something I read in another book." She stopped and looked over at me before resuming. "Helen and I used to walk with a man at the walking track and after he died we found out he was a famous author and teacher. Helen checked his books out of the library for me. Anyway, he said that the Word of God is like water, because it says so in the Bible. But...oh, I don't know how to explain anything. Helen, you do it."

"But I don't know what you're talking about."

"You know, about Jesus changing the water into wine."

I nodded and turned back to Gina. "Did you ever hear the story of Jesus' first miracle, that He turned water into wine at a wedding?"

Gina shook her head. "All I know about Jesus is that they say when he was born there were angels and shepherds. And that when he died, he came back to life. Kind of like Frosty the Snowman."

This time Christy didn't try to disguise her laughter.

Gina turned toward her. "What?"

"Frosty the Snowman. I'm sorry." Christy didn't seem sorry since she kept laughing and was even slumped over in her chair with her face in her hands.

I said gently. "It's just that Frosty the Snowman is a fictional cartoon character. And Jesus is very real. The comparison struck Christy as funny."

Gina's eyes were still narrowed but her shoulders relaxed a little. "Anyway what were you saying about wine? I don't like wine much. I like beer better."

I told Gina the story of the wedding at Cana and the miracle of the water and wine. "It was Jesus' first miracle. A very practical, homey kind of miracle."

Christy had gained control of herself and resumed her example. "Anyway what John said was that we are like those stone pots that Jesus told the servants to fill up with water. Someplace in the Bible it calls the Word of God water. So we are to fill up with the Word, the Bible, and even though it seems boring sometimes, when we need it, it will come out as wine."

Gina stared at her blankly.

"I guess I didn't explain it very well."

Gina still stared at her.

"It made sense when I read it." Christy looked over at me and shrugged.

"I think..." I stopped and waited until Gina turned to look at me. "I think that what that means is that what we read in God's Word will come out as practical help when we need it in our daily life."

Gina nodded. But she didn't look very impressed.

"Would you like to have a Bible? I have several that I don't use." I pointed toward the bookshelf

"Yeah, sure. Why not?"

When they left, Gina had a brand new NIV translation and several containers of leftover Thanksgiving fare. After waving good-bye, I went back into the living room and sank into a chair. *Neither one of them even mentioned helping with the dishes!*

***

Christy

I dreaded seeing Kyle Martin again. I felt like I made a fool out of myself on Saturday and on Sunday both.

First I practically took over the project of that church and acted like I was some kind of an expert. Then I was completely emotional at the church service and dedicated myself to something I didn't even know how to begin doing. Marry Jesus instead of date him? What in the world did that mean?

I determined to read my Bible more but as I confessed to Gina and Helen, sometimes it was boring.

And worst of all I was feeling like a, well, like an adulteress or something. I liked the way Kyle Martin made me feel. And then that made me feel like I was being untrue to David. And that was completely silly.

David was a married man and there could never be anything at all between us. The feeling for David was adultery, not any attraction to Kyle Martin.

And besides all that, if I am going to be married to Jesus, I don't need to be thinking about any men at all. The nuns say they are married to Jesus but how does an ordinary person do that? And it wasn't just for women. Kyle said that he needed to be married to Jesus too.

There's obviously a lot I don't understand. But I'm willing, Lord. Teach me what you want of me.

***

Kyle

"Come on, Martin. Act your age." I looked at myself in the mirror. "Better still, act your calling!"

The pretty curly haired new girl at church really shook me out of my usual impersonal reactions to the congregation. There had been plenty of young women come to church over the last few years. And most of them flirted outrageously. But none of them interested me. And then Christy walked in the door that Saturday morning and suddenly I was interested.

Mother noticed and was thrilled. She often told me she was afraid I'd end up an old maid. I told her that men couldn't be old maids. And she told me that I had all the makings of an old maid no matter what sex I was.

"Too particular." She accused me of wanting the perfect woman and said there was no such creature.

But surely it wasn't wrong to want the perfect woman, want someone who loved the Lord and wanted to serve as much as I do. Someone called by God. Surely that's God's plan for my life.

Lately I realized that I'm willing to settle for someone with maybe just a few faults; loneliness is creeping into greater periods of time. When Christy answered my altar call last Sunday, the thrill I felt was more than just a pastoral joy. It seemed like it was a sign from God.

For the first time I wished my church was the kind that had people fill out cards with their address and phone number on them. But even if I knew the number, how would it look if I called her? Calling as a pastor would be okay. But it would be dishonest. Well, partially dishonest anyway.

It had been a long week. She didn't come for Sunday or Wednesday night services but she promised to be there today to help with the Christmas project. I hoped there would be a lot of families show up. All the things she suggested were carried out.

***

Christy

There was a very different atmosphere in the Convention Center when I walked in that Saturday. Mrs. Martin was pointing three families toward the sign-up room. She smiled and nodded when she saw me.

Besides the three groups in the hallway, there were five families already seated at tables filling out papers. Rev. Martin and the women helping him looked much happier than they did the previous week. There were two extra helpers besides Jo Ann and Selena. And was it my imagination or did Kyle Martin look especially joyous when he saw me walk through the door?

He laid down the papers he held and came to greet me. "Hey! How have you been? I wondered if you have been under attack since your commitment last Sunday? But I didn't know how to contact you."

"Attack?"

"Well, you know. Satan comes to take out the Word that is sown in our hearts. And that usually means we have a lot of temptation when we've made a decision to put Jesus first."

Ah! That makes sense. "Right on! But I made it."

He nodded. "Good for you!"

"Now, what can I do?"

"I thought we might put on some music for background. What do you think?"

"I think that's great. Where is a player?"

He pointed to a cd player and a stack of cd's on a table against the wall to my right. "Why don't you choose the music?"

I walked over to the table and looked through the cds but didn't recognize any of them. It was like the music at the church service on Sunday, completely new to me. I finally chose one that had a picture of a man playing the piano on it entitled Live Worship. Soon the music flowed out into the room.

Kyle Martin looked over, grinned at me, and gave a thumbs up.

Yay! I did good!

Suddenly the room was filled. Around thirty people arrived about the same time and there was no time to think about anything except taking down names and addresses and ages and sizes and requests. I certainly hoped someone was there to offer help and gifts but all the people I spoke with were signing up to receive.

It was after one o'clock when the crowd thinned out and we all looked at each other with widened eyes.

"Quite a difference from last Saturday, huh?" Jo Anne laughed and shook her head. "Christy, you really know how to do this."

"What's bothering me is where are we going to get the gifts and finances to meet all these needs?"

"Oh, the idea you had about the Christian radio station paid off too. We've had a lot of calls pledging donations of money and gifts." Kyle Martin looked very happy.

I breathed a sigh of relief. "Great!"

"What are we going to do about lunch today?" Joanne put her hand on her stomach. "I'm starving."

"I was thinking we'd wait 'til we close at two and then go get something."

I offered to bring something in like I did last week but Kyle didn't seem to like that idea.

He looked at Joanne. "There's nobody here and I doubt there will be many more in the next forty minutes. You can go on if you want."

The other three ladies asked if the offer applied to them too and he assured them it did. "Christy and I can manage and pack up at two."

Evidently the offer to leave early didn't apply to me. I had to suppress a smile.

When the others had gathered their purses we walked them out. Mrs. Martin smiled as we approached. "Are we calling it a day?"

"Christy and I are going to hang around 'til two but everyone else is going on. I think the rush is over and we can handle it."

"It looks like we were a success today."

He nodded and leaned over to hug his mom. "Yep. Thanks."

"Anytime." She pushed the folding chair back under the desk and picked up her own purse.

As she went through the door she called back over her shoulder. "Don't do anything I wouldn't do." And laughed.

I looked over at the pastor and his face was red; he was definitely blushing.

***

Christy

"Are you sure this is okay?" He pulled in the parking lot of Jumbo Buffet, a Chinese restaurant in the other shopping center.

"Yes, I love Chinese. And they have my favorite stuffed mushrooms here."

"Great! I love the grill best. I always get a piece of steak and a pork chop."

"A meat man!"

He grinned at me as he put the car in park. "Definitely. Meat of the world and meat of the Word."

The pretty Chinese girl showed us to a booth, took our drink order, and pointed us to the food laden steam tables.

"Okay, we're on our own!" Kyle took off for the grill and I headed toward shrimp and mushrooms.

I got back to the booth first and waited for him before I began eating. I figured he would want to say the blessing, even though I never did out in public.

Sure enough, when he was seated, he reached across and took my hand and bowed his head. "Thank you Lord for this food. Bless it to our body's use. And thank you for this time of fellowship. Guide our conversation. In Jesus name, Amen."

I began the conversation. "So what did you do for Thanksgiving?"

"Mom had the usual family extravaganza. My sister and her husband and kids came in. Dad's brother and his family came too - lots of cousins and their kids. In other words, the typical American chaotic holiday."

"It sounds great."

He looked at me quizzically. "What did you do?"

I explained that I was an only child and orphaned, and that my only family was on the other side of the USA. He looked horrified.

"I'm sorry. I remember now that you said you were having Thanksgiving with a friend...a female friend."

I smiled. "But I had a wonderful Thanksgiving. I've become close with a really nice lady." I told him about meeting Helen at the walking track and about John and that we didn't find out who he was until he was gone.

Kyle nodded. "Yes, I've read one book of his. About the Bride of Christ."

"Yes! Wasn't it great?" I rushed on without waiting for an answer. "It's so strange that we never suspected he was somebody famous. His name was on the sign-in sheet but I didn't recognize it. And I guess Helen didn't either, or she would have said something. She saw about his death on the front page of the paper."

"So, you're reading his books now?"

"Yes, and I love them." I hesitated before confessing. "Sometimes I have a hard time reading the Bible but I love to read explanations about it."

When he didn't say anything, I started suspecting that he was not in agreement with John's writings. And I felt defensive toward my departed friend.

"So, I get the impression you don't like his explanations?"

Kyle grimaced. "I'm just not sure about a few things."

"What things?" I could hear that my tone of voice sounded belligerent.

"Oh, things about the role of the Holy Spirit in God's people in the end times.

"How do you differ from what he believes?"

"I don't know. It wasn't anything he said. It was just that he didn't say a lot of things I was looking for."

Curiosity replaced my defensiveness. "Like what?"

"Well, he doesn't really mention the gifts of the Spirit at all. There's a lot about the fruit of the Spirit and the transforming power of the Holy Spirit but he never mentions the gifts."

"So, what did you think he should have said?"

"I just would have liked him to mention that God still moves supernaturally and that prophecy and words of wisdom and healing and all the gifts are part of what God uses to get the Body of Christ ready for Himself."

I nodded, even though I really wasn't sure of what he meant. I really didn't know much and was realizing more and more of how little I do know about God or beliefs.

"But that's enough serious talk." Kyle Martin grinned at her. "What are you doing tonight?"

Hmm. What do you have in mind? "I'll go on back to my house and watch TV for a while. I'll probably just fix a salad for supper since we're pigging out here. Take a shower go to bed. Exciting, huh?"

"Would you like to go somewhere with me?"

"Where?"

"I'm going to check out a street preacher. I heard about him the other day. He preaches every Saturday night outside some of the joints down in the Beckley area."

NOT my idea of an exciting date!

But on the other hand, maybe the street preacher would be someone Gina could relate to and I could tell her about him.

"Okay."

Kyle grinned from ear-to-ear. "Great!"

It was 3:30 when we left the restaurant and Kyle took me back to the mall and my car. I gave him my address and cell phone number; he said he'd come by in about three hours.

I went home and crashed. I wasn't sure what to think about our "date." It was mostly just about God but I could tell the way Kyle looks at me that he is interested in more than my eternal soul.

I slept about an hour. When I woke up I took a shower and picked up the front room and dusted the furniture. I couldn't figure out what my emotions were about Kyle Martin. When I thought about him, I got excited at the idea of his obvious interest in me. But still, I couldn't feel the way I felt about David, no matter how hard I tried.

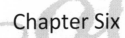

Chapter Six

2007

Christy

At 6:30 promptly my doorbell rang and there he stood. He had on jeans and a t-shirt that read "I work for a Jewish Carpenter" on the front. The black shirt was fairly tight and showed his muscular chest. Maybe not what they call a six pack but definitely very masculine.

"Come on in. I'm going to change clothes if that's okay. I didn't know what to wear to check out a street preacher. But I'd like to put on jeans too." I had on dress slacks and a nice baby doll top. I decided to keep the top and just change to jeans and substitute the sandals with sneakers. I also grabbed a jacket. The temperature was still in the high sixties even in late November, but it might cool off later.

When I came out, Kyle had picked up one of the books on my coffee table. They were all written by John but this one was not the one we had discussed. It was one on spiritual warfare.

He looked up when I came in. "Nice!" His eyes swept me from head to foot and back up. "Perfect checking-out-street-preacher attire." He sounded so serious that it took a minute to realize he was teasing me.

When he grinned, I laughed out loud. He laid the book back on the table and we left without discussing it, or John.

He opened the door of the car for me, as he had earlier. I wondered if David was the kind of man who opened car doors for females. I thought he probably was. He was so polite everywhere we went but I never rode in a car with him. Oh, yes, there was the taxi. *Stop it! You are with a very handsome man who is obviously attracted to you. Forget David!*

Kyle slowed the car as we drove through a part of town I'd never been in, though I thought it was just a few blocks from where Gina lived. The sidewalks had paper lying around and there was grass growing in the cracks between the squares. He pulled up to a curb beside a garbage can without a lid. As soon as I got out of the car, I could see and hear the flies hovering and buzzing over it. And I could smell rotting garbage. *Yuck!!!* I controlled my facial expression and smiled up at Kyle.

Rap music drifted out of a bar across the street and all I wanted to do was to run. A couple of tough looking guys approached us.

"You lost?"

Kyle didn't look at all intimidated. "Nope."

"Whatcher doin here?"

"Came to see somebody."

"Who?"

Just then several people walked around the corner and Kyle pointed at the tallest man. "Him."

The one who had been doing the talking just nodded. And they walked away.

Kyle and I stood watching as the preacher unfolded a small table. A young woman with him took some papers out of a sack and began to arrange them on the table. The second man pulled a guitar out of the case he carried. As they worked, the preacher pulled a Bible out of his pocket and walked over toward us.

"Hello! You're new to the neighborhood!"

Kyle laughed and stuck out his hand. He introduced himself and me.

I noticed that the street sign on the corner read "Beckley Street" and vaguely remembered an article a few years ago that talked about the police having a lot of problems in that area. While the two preachers were talking, I walked over to the table where the woman was laying out folders.

"Hi, I'm Christy. I came with Reverend Martin."

From a distance she looked to be about my age but when she turned to look at me, I was surprised. Her face was lined and strained. Her eyes narrowed. "Why are you here?"

I sensed heat spreading on my own face. "I don't know. Reverend Martin wanted to meet ... what's his name? The street preacher?"

"Jim Sutton. He read about 'im in the paper?"

I shrugged. "I guess so. I don't know. He just asked if I'd like to come with him to see a street preacher."

She turned back to the table. "We don't need no other preachers. Jim does just fine."

I realized the woman was being protective of "her" preacher.

"Kyle Martin just wanted to meet him, not take his place." *Well! Sounds like I'm being protective of "my" preacher too.*

I smiled at her and looked over at the man who was tuning his guitar. "Do you sing along with him playing the guitar?"

"Na, I can't sing. He and Jim sing. I just come along for ...well, just to be here."

Jim and Kyle walked over to where we stood and the street preacher introduced the woman as Cherrie Pitts.

I had to really control my face and the desire to burst out in laughter. It just sounded too much like cherry pits and made me think of the name of a stripper or something similar.

Kyle solemnly shook her hand and said he was glad to meet her.

Lord, this sure couldn't be you putting me with this man. I could never be a preacher's wife and act dignified no matter what comes along.

The guitarist began playing a praise song and all the men sang. I'd never heard it but it was a catchy tune. Suddenly people began to gather. They came from the apartment buildings up and down the street. Mostly children, some women. The only two men that showed up looked like street people and as if they had been drinking alcohol. As soon as that thought came to my mind I noticed that one of the men held a paper sack in his hand. He put it to his mouth and took a drink.

There were twelve or fifteen people standing around but no one sang except Kyle and Jim and the guitarist. When the song was over, Jim began to pray in a loud voice for God to join the group there on the sidewalk and rescue His people from sin and poverty.

When he finished praying, he started his sermon. At least I guessed it was a sermon. He yelled a lot and didn't seem to have any particular message to teach, just talked – loudly - about what sinners we all are and how we need Jesus.

It's not that I disagree with what he said. But I sure didn't like the way he said it.

I didn't look at Kyle during the message...just stared at Jim Sutton. He preached for about ten minutes and then the guitarist started singing "Just As I Am" and Jim yelled for people to come and repent. A lot of them did. They went toward him, some with tears streaming down their faces. *How different we all are. That is not the kind of thing that gets me to repent!* But it was obvious from the response that the street preacher was just what these people needed.

The man who drank from whatever bottle the paper sack covered was hugging the preacher and sobbing all over his shoulder. My heart went all melty. *I really hope he gets his life straightened out.*

Some new faces showed up in the crowd and some of the familiar ones disappeared. Soon, Jim began his message all over again. And again it was followed by an invitation to repent. Different people responded than the first time. Finally Kyle looked down at me.

"Ready to go?"

"Sure." I was more than ready, though I didn't want him to know it.

When we were back in the car and safely off of Beckley

Street, Kyle sighed.

"What'd you think?"

I gave him a weak smile. "Not exactly my style."

"No." He agreed. "Mine either. But he sure gets results."

"How'd you find out about him?"

"Newspaper. The article said that several of the street people have quit drinking and a few guys turned themselves into the police for previous crimes."

"Really? That's impressive."

"Yes, real impressive. I get so…" He sighed. "I shouldn't complain but it's hard to preach and never see any real change in people."

I protested. "But last week I came forward and so did a lot of others."

He turned and looked at me before putting his eyes back on the road. "Yes, and how has your life changed since you answered the call to be married to Jesus?"

I thought about my attempts to enjoy Bible reading and that hadn't changed. I thought about how I did go by and invite Gina to Thanksgiving dinner, but that was really because of Helen, not me. Had that commitment not meant anything to me? It seemed like it did at the time.

I couldn't think of anything to say.

"I thought so. I tell you Christy I really wonder sometimes if God called me or if I just called myself."

That subject was completely out of any area of expertise on my part. So again I didn't say anything.

"I'm sorry. That is completely unprofessional of me. Saying that to someone who is not in ministry."

"It's okay." Then a thought struck me. "But Kyle, I think you are a really good preacher. I've never gone up at an altar call in any other church."

"You haven't?" He turned to look at me again.

"No. Never. So there's nothing wrong with you. It's me that isn't letting God do what He wants to do to make me one with Him." I thought back on Thanksgiving Day.

"Or maybe I am. I thought it was just Helen, not God." And I told him about Gina.

Kyle Martin was fascinated with the story of Gina Howard. He looked at me with renewed respect.

"That's a neat story. What did you say when you went back to the restaurant to tell the manager about the chicken?"

My mouth dropped open. "I didn't! I completely forgot."

He laughed. "But that's the kind of thing, taking her to lunch, that happens when you are one with the Lord. And only He prompted you to do that, nobody else."

"You know, I didn't really realize it was God at the time. I thought it was just me. I've had a problem..." I did *not* want to tell the preacher about my therapy so I wanted to word this right. "...a problem with wanting to help people too much, I think. To tell you the truth, I'm not sure what's God or me."

"If it's a good deed, it's God."

That sounded very simple but my psychologist is a Christian and he didn't think that was true. "But what about people pleasing? I've always had a problem being a people pleaser."

His eyes searched mine before returning to the road ahead. "I'm afraid I don't know about all that. I'm a real simple guy. Good things are from God, bad things are from the devil. So what is a people pleaser?"

"Well, I think it's someone who gets their self-image from pleasing people. They don't make boundaries for themselves." I hastened to correct any wrong impression that might make. "Don't get me wrong. I've made lots of boundaries by being a loner. I don't go around people much but when I do, I tend to do whatever they want."

"Is that all?"

"No, it's hard for me to know what I truly want. I think..." I searched for the right words. "I think I censure myself on a really deep level. You know?"

He shook his head. "No, I don't know. Sorry."

"I don't want to want wrong things so I don't let myself..." I gave up trying to explain that one. "And I never get angry. It's easier to be nice."

He nodded as if I'd finally said something he understood. "Well, the Bible says to be angry and sin not."

He is clueless. The night started out so promising but now I was just frustrated. "Anyway, I wasn't sure if taking Gina to lunch that day was me wanting to fix things for her or if it really was a good deed."

"Turns out that it was a good deed, didn't it?"

"Yeah, I guess it was."

"Wanna stop by for a burger or something?" He grinned engagingly.

"Okay." *Just relax, Christy. Have fun. Don't be so serious.*

The rest of the evening, Kyle made me laugh with stories about funny things that happened to him during his time in seminary. One day he and two fellow students went to Walmart and when it was their turn at the checkout, one of the guys turned around and started frisking him. The other one turned to the clerk and said. "Our friend is a kleptomaniac and we have to check him out whenever we leave a store."

"I laughed and told her they were just kidding. But they just smirked and winked at her. I think she really believed that I was a thief."

I loved the story but couldn't help thinking how humiliated I would have been if it were me.

When we returned to my neighborhood, he walked me to the door. "I won't kiss you goodnight because it's a first date." He grinned boyishly. "So when can we have our second date?"

I laughed.

***

Gina

On Sunday afternoon I made the rounds of apartments for rent in the area near my new job. I'd spent Saturday doing the same thing. So far I couldn't find anything as good as my current place, much less something better.

Then I walked into the yard of the tiny house at 93 Southern Street. This was different! Everything in my price range so far had been in buildings that held at least four apartments and this was a one family dwelling with a tiny fenced in yard.

Just as I went through the gate, the front door opened and two men walked out. The one who had a key in his hand looked at her quizzically. "Can I help you?"

I nodded and held up the real estate magazine I picked at Burger King. "I saw this ad and came to see the house."

He turned to look at the other man. "You're sure?"

The second man nodded. "I'm sure. I need a garage with enough room for a small shop. I should have asked about a garage before I wasted your time."

The realtor smiled and shook his hand. "No problem." He nodded toward me. "Looks like I was here at the right time to help this young lady."

The other man left through the front gate and I joined the real estate agent on the tiny porch.

"This looks kind of like a doll house." As soon as the words were out of her mouth, I wished I could take them back. When I was a little girl, a doll house was my greatest dream but Santa Claus never brought it. A few years later I heard a girl in school talk about the playhouse in her backyard. It was like a large dollhouse, with rooms for children to play in. The girl had a table and chairs and a tea set as well as a pretend stove and sink. I couldn't imagine the luxury behind ownership of such a thing. And now I wished I hadn't voiced my excitement. *But there's no way he could know how I much I want a doll house.*

The realtor's face lit up. "I always thought so too. And I figure a woman would like it more than a man. That guy..." And he jerked his head toward the direction the man had taken when he left. "He was trying to be polite but I knew that even if it had a garage, he and this house would never be a match."

"You can tell who matches with houses?"

He shrugged. "Sometimes." Then he stuck out his hand.

"Sorry. My name is Keith Sullivan."

I shook his hand. "Gina Howard."

"Well, Ms. Howard, are you ready for the grand tour?"

"Yes, and please call me Gina. I don't think I'm old enough to be Ms. Howard."

He laughed but then the smile left his face. "Are you eighteen or over?"

"Oh yes. I'm nineteen."

"Then we have no problem." He opened the door and motioned for her to enter.

"If you were under eighteen, you wouldn't be able to legally sign a lease and the owner wouldn't want to rent to you."

I nodded. So glad Christy clued me in on leases so I didn't show my ignorance.

When I looked away from him and around at the room we stood in I almost gasped. The doll house impression not only remained but deepened. Chair railing topped white paneling on the bottom three feet of the walls and a pattern of roses sprinkled on white background wallpapered the rest of the way to the ceiling. The room was empty and it hit me that I would have to buy a lot of things if I didn't get a furnished place.

Keith Sullivan was standing in a doorway to my left. "This is the kitchen." He stepped aside and I went in. The room was painted a bright sunshiny yellow and at the back a sliding glass door showed a tiny fenced in yard beyond.

"It's small," the realtor was saying. "But you can see there's room for a dinette set there in front of the door. He began opening cabinets. "Plenty of room for storage of dishes and canned goods. And the refrigerator and stove go with it. The only problem is no dishwasher."

Dishwasher? I've always been the dishwasher. I wanted to say "Who cares? This place is wonderful." But if I showed how much I liked it, they might raise the price.

He opened a door that I assumed was a closet. "The washer/drier unit is in here by the water heater. You can see that it's tiny, but for one person..." His voice trailed off with a slight question mark at the end.

"It will just be me. Tiny is fine." *No more trips to the Laundromat? Yes!.*

I followed him back to the main room. At the back there was another door leading into a small hallway. He opened a door to the right and showed me a closet. Past the closet was a bathroom. The floor was tiled in white and cobalt blue and the appliances were white porcelain.

One last door in the hallway was straight ahead and opened onto a bedroom. White translucent lacy curtains had been left at the window and there was a soft apple green carpet on the floor. The living room floor had been just wood so the luxury of the carpet surprised me. The bedroom was larger than I had have guessed. When I walked over to the window and looked out, I could see the kitchen doors to my left. The tiny yard contained an empty garden edged with bricks that gave evidence someone had cared about in the past. *To be able to live in a place like this!*

"How much is it, Mr. Sullivan? Is this right?" I pointed to the magazine in my hand.

He glanced at the ad and nodded.

"I want it."

"Great. How soon?"

"Now." *Next week's rent is due tomorrow.*

"Now? Don't you have to give notice somewhere else?"

She shook her head. *How do I explain about places that don't ask for leases?*

"I was living with someone. I can move in today."

Keith Sullivan glanced at his watch. Then he got his cell phone from a clip on his belt.

"Mrs. Baxter? This is Keith Sullivan. I have a young lady who wants to rent your house today."

He listened for a minute. "No, not yet." He held his hand over the phone. "She wanted to know if we discussed the deposit. Was that in the ad?"

"No." I could feel my stomach tighten. *I thought it was too good to be true.* "I have the first month's rent. How much is the deposit?"

"The same as a month's rent. That way if you leave before the lease is up it gives her a month to rent it again. Or if there is some damage left, she has the money for repairs."

I shook my head. "I don't have that much. I guess I can't rent it." I was determined not to show how disappointed I felt, but the words weren't sounding right coming out of my throat.

"Excuse me. I'll be right back." The realtor left the bedroom.

God, if you really love me the way Christy said you do, please, please help me.

I started to walk back to the living room but didn't want to intrude on the phone call. I went in the bathroom and saw a little plaque on the wall that I didn't notice the first time. "With God all things are possible." Matthew 19:26.

I stared and tried hard to believe what was written there, and then I heard Keith Sullivan's voice behind me.

"I told the owner that this is your first rental and you didn't realize about deposits. She said that if you want it, you can pay the deposit over four months. Think you can manage that?"

"I'll manage it if I have to starve for four months." The words flew out my mouth before I thought. *So much for not showing how much I want it.*

He laughed. "It just so happens that the owner is my future mother-in-law. I don't have that much persuasive power with every homeowner."

"Thank you so much." I pulled my checkbook out of the pocket of my jeans. "How do I make the check out?"

"I'll have to run back to the office and get the lease agreement." He hesitated a minute. "Want to come with me or stay here?"

"Stay here, please."

He grinned. "First homes are a real joy, aren't they?"

I just smiled and nodded.

"Make the check out to Beulah Baxter." He waved as he walked out the door. "Be back shortly."

When he was gone, I leaned against the wall and looked

around the living room. *A dolls house. Thank you God. I guess you really do love me.*

But what about furniture? I hoped Keith Sullivan didn't offer to help me move my stuff in so he wouldn't see that I have no stuff to move except clothes. *Wait. Everything in the apartment wasn't furnished. Mike's Mom gave him some things from her house. Think, Gina think. Which things?*

The table and chairs, just a small set with two chairs, but it would look great sitting there in front of the glass doors in the kitchen. The formica top was gray but that would go okay with yellow. No bed, but the pillows and sheets were Mike's. And the bedroom floor was carpeted so that would be no problem. There was even a comforter and I can sleep on that if the floor is too hard.

Mike's mom also gave him the dishes and pots and pans so I'll have those too. No chairs but who cared. A whole little house all to myself. *My doll house.*

But how would I get the table and chairs there? I really didn't want the realtor to see my old place. He might have Mrs. Baxter change her mind. The term *street trash* still haunted me.

Christy! I'd call Christy and ask her if she could help me move. Even if we had to make two trips, we could do it. And surely she wouldn't mind. Not after inviting her for Thanksgiving.

***

Christy

It took two trips in my car but we got Gina's table and chairs, dishes, and clothes moved to the little house in under an hour. I've never known anybody who owned so few things.

Her eyes were sparkling as she looked at the table and chairs sitting in front of the glass leading to the back yard. The chairs were placed so that there was no problem opening or going through the sliding doors.

I know no one was squeezing my heart but when I watched her childlike enthusiasm, there was definitely a reaction.

I was trying to decide how to offer her some furniture without insulting her when I remembered back on our first meeting and her eagerness to be taken to lunch.

"Gina, I don't know if you'd be interested but..." I paused and scratched my ear. "I never told you but my parents died about six years ago and I've never done anything with the stuff that I don't really want. There's a bedroom set in the spare room that I don't need or want. I hate to offer you something used but if you're interested..."

Before I could even finish the sentence, Gina let out a whoop!

"Yes!" She made a ball with her fist and jerked her bent elbow downward in a gesture of victory. "That would be awesome. I planned to sleep on the floor."

I walked into the living room. "There may be some stuff for in here too. If you want it."

"Are you kidding? Of course I want it. Anything. Oh Christy, the best thing I ever did was choose the agency where you work."

I reached over and hugged her. "It was a wonderful thing for me too. I never had a sister before."

When I released her shoulder and could see her face, I saw the tears sparkling in her eyes.

"Me neither. Okay, I'll confess. I didn't have enough money to get this place. They wanted a deposit and I didn't know about that. But while the real estate guy was talking to the owner on his cell phone, I prayed. I told God if he really loves me like you said, that he would help me get this place." She beamed. "And he did. They're letting me pay the deposit a little at a time."

"That's great, Gina."

I was very happy for her and for me too. This relationship was surely a God thing.

Chapter Seven

2007

Helen

pulled out the poems and read them all again in order from the time they were written. With each poem his face and the surroundings that prompted the writing leaped into my mind. *Why do I torture myself? It does no good to remember.* And yet, to forget would be to kill something that was essential to my very existence. What would I be without the love Sanders and I shared? At least in remembering there was some joy, even in the last one.

To run from pain by running from this love I have for you is sin.
I who mentally reject philosophies that call for sacrifice
 beyond His own for us at Calvary,
I live with daily bleeding.
Or else I live in half-life shadows
of escape and lies and plastic dreams that negate who I am.
So once again it's Life I choose
and you, and love, and pain
and Him who bleeds with us
and makes our sacrifice a holy thing.

Then I pulled out my old journal.

***

Helen's Journal
1973

I went back to talk to Pastor Tom once again about my relationship with Sanders. I married Ken four years ago and it became obvious very soon that he was not about to give up other women. I made an appointment and was seated on that same couch where I had first confessed my feelings for Sanders, who was Tom's best friend.

He was not as warm or relaxed as when he entered the room on that earlier occasion. But he was polite.

I looked at him without disguising my anguish, and saw him take a deep breath as though the pastoral office must break through to assuage such pain, even when that pain was in me. I told him about Ken's other women, the venereal disease and its permanent effects - no children ever.

"I am so unhappy. And it's all my own fault."

"What do you mean? You can't blame yourself for his selfishness or his promiscuity." This time his reaction was protectiveness toward me.

I nodded, swallowing and wiping away tears as quickly as they spilled out onto my cheeks. "I know that. But I can blame myself for getting involved with him in the first place. Do you know why I married him?"

Tom shook his head. He was the one who performed the marriage but asked no questions about the haste of the wedding. I believed that he was just relieved to have the situation resolved for his friend.

"I married him because I had gone to bed with him. And do you know why I went to bed with him?" I didn't wait for a response. "I went to bed with him because I admitted to myself that I would always love Sanders and, contrary to what you thought, he had too much integrity to either get a divorce – or have an affair. " I looked up at my pastor defiantly. "I offered, you know. I loved him so much I would have done anything to be with him, be anything he wanted me to be. But he turned me down. You didn't know him as well as you thought you did. He really is the best man I ever knew."

Tom said nothing and we sat in silence for several minutes before I continued.

"I didn't want to live a holy life of celibacy!" I made a noise somewhere between a laugh and a cry, maybe a combination of both. "Dear God, what a mistake! You have no idea..." I shook my head. "But that's not what I am here to talk about. What I want to say is this...it hasn't gotten any better. If anything, it's worse. The love I mean. Not worse - stronger. The love just gets stronger. And you know as well as I do that it is not one sided. It can't go anywhere, I know that. But what can I do about feeling this way? God is merciful. How do I receive His mercy for me and stop feeling this constant loneliness except when I am with Sanders?"

Tom give a start and I quickly added, "We are not together often, don't worry. And we never talk about our relationship any more. Sometimes though he comes to the library and we spend a few minutes there, in public. Nothing has changed."

"For either one of us." I added firmly.

Tom didn't say anything at first. And then after a minute he just sighed. "You know, there are some things that only geography will solve." There was kindness in his voice.

"What do you mean?"

"If you were to move away then you wouldn't see him every Sunday or be anticipating the possibility of running into him on the street or having him come in the library. He wouldn't be so present in your life."

"Oh, my God!" I stared at him and his eyes looked down at the desktop.

After a moment of silence, I spoke again. "I've been offered a job at a library in a town about two hours from here. It would mean moving. You know, don't you, that it would be like killing a part of myself?"

He looked up at me and I could tell by his eyes that he hadn't known.

"I convinced myself it was just a rebound crush after your first divorce," he said. "I thought it ended with your second marriage. I see I was wrong."

"I prayed before I came that the Lord would give you wisdom to help me know what to do. Now I wonder if I really wanted that prayer answered."

"I'm sorry." The pastor's words came out in a hoarse whisper.

And I could tell that, finally, he meant it and felt the empathy that I sought from him years earlier.

"I imagine that I'll be going through another divorce soon. But I'm going to give Ken one more chance. He can move with me if he wants and if he can stay away from women I'll stay with him." I sighed, "And maybe if I am away from Sanders I can concentrate more on saving the marriage."

"I am so sorry." Tom repeated.

"Thank you. But as you often say 'We live in a fallen world.' What can we expect from fallen people in a fallen world?"

The week before I moved I called Sanders at his office and told him. He was very quiet and I wondered if Tom had already told him I was considering the move. I wondered if they ever talked about me at all.

Finally Sanders said, "I hope you will be happy."

I said, "You too."

That Sunday was my last at church and when I left, just as I reached the end of the sidewalk, I turned and saw him standing there on the step watching me walk away. Our eyes met and the connection was so complete that it was as if there was no building, or people around us. There was only love and pain that crossed the space between us like lightning, revealing the truth that no distance, no time, no space, could ever really separate us.

I wasn't sure that my legs would take me to the car but they did. When I was safely in the driver's seat, I put my head on my arms over the steering wheel.

"My God!" I whispered. "I can't do this without You."

Helen's Journal

1990

We moved. I started my new job and eventually Ken and I divorced. At that point I was glad I had no children; the split could be final without future obligations on either of our parts.

I settled in to the new town better than I thought I would. I found a church whose size suited me, large enough to allow anonymity and small enough to be friendly. I didn't make friends that first few years but preferred being alone with my heartache and secrets. There were the study groups at the library and acquaintances made there, even coffee or a quick supper with them, but no one that I felt a connection with enough that I would even consider inviting to my home.

I enjoyed decorating the apartment and eventually bought a small place within walking distance of the library. It was an older house, built in the first decade of the 20th century but remodeled in the sixties with the plumbing and heating systems updated. It had a little room off to the side of the main entrance with a fireplace surrounded by pretty tiles and a decorative mantle. I had fun fixing it up with Victorian furnishings, some inherited and some purchased one at a time as I wandered through antique shops on days off work. I called it my parlor.

Sometimes I didn't go to church on Sundays even though breaking that lifelong habit felt strange at first. But before too many weeks elapsed, I found that my new habit of sleeping late on most Sundays and lounging around in pajamas and house slippers really suited me. I made myself go to a service once a month.

I began to realize that I've never really relaxed much but had always been on the go. I even began watching television, a first, since I'd been primarily a reader, reserving TV for news and weather information alone.

I thought that I really should find some volunteer work to do but it was just too much trouble. After a day at work, I deserved to come home and crash. And after five and a half workdays, I deserved Sundays free.

Soon the once a month Sunday morning church attendance disappeared and four times a year at services served to prove that I really wasn't missing anything. The preachers on television were more interesting and I could enjoy their messages in the comfort of my own home.

Since I never joined the church or attended a Sunday School class or made any friends there, there was no one to notice when the weeks turned into months and the months into years and I was not among the worshippers on Sunday morning.

It was in the fall, seven years after I moved to my new job that the world tilted into a new perspective for me.

His name was Steve and he was very distinguished looking, a decade or so older than I. He came in the library one morning with a request for help with a research project. I happened to be at the front desk when he approached.

He was apologetic. "Usually my secretary does this kind of thing but there are a lot of purely clerical things that have to be completed right now so I said I'd handle this myself. Only I don't know what I am doing." He paused and chuckled. "I hated to admit that to her."

I laughed and offered to help him. We went to the newspaper archives, where I did the research as he looked on. When the information was gathered and the data documented, Steve breathed a sigh of relief.

"What can I do to thank you?"

I laughed. "That is our job."

"Well, then... How about doing another favor for me?" Steve smiled, with dancing eyes.

"What?" I grinned back, very aware that I was being flirted with...and liking it.

"Go to lunch with me?"

I looked at the clock. It was 11:40. "I can't leave 'til after 1 p.m. A lot of people come in on their lunch hour and none of us take lunch between twelve and one."

He grimaced. "And I have an appointment at 1:30. How about tomorrow?"

I hesitated, looking toward a wall.

He moved into my line of vision. "Please?"

I couldn't help but laugh. "Okay."

"I'll be here at 1 tomorrow. Is Ryan's okay?"

"Lovely."

And so it began. We had lunch several times the first two weeks and then attended a play performed by the local college theatre department.

Steve's divorce was finalized a few months before his first trip to the library and he was delighted to find someone companionable. When he took me home after the play, as we stood in front of my front door saying goodnight, he leaned down to kiss me.

I turned my head away.

"I'm sorry," he said. "I didn't mean to move too quickly. I don't know what the rules are...haven't dated since college."

"No," I said, the sadness I felt filling my words. "Don't apologize. You didn't do anything wrong. It's me." I hesitated only a minute and then said, "Would you like to come in for coffee?"

He looked surprised that an invitation followed the rebuff, but quickly agreed.

Over coffee I told Steve my story.

"And you are still not over him?"

I shook my head. "I don't believe I ever will be. So, you see...it's not fair for me to date."

He started to say something but I stopped him.

"No, listen. I married once thinking that would distract me from loving Sanders and it was a nightmare. Now, I know we are not talking about marriage, we barely know each other, but at our age people do date with the future in mind. And I am just not...well, it is just not fair to you or any man to waste time on me."

The tone of Steve's voice became even more kind. "Why don't you let me be the judge of whether spending time with you is a waste or not?"

At that her eyes filled with tears. "Truly, Steve, it's not just marriage. I can't...I mean I don't want any romantic involvement."

"You've taken vows of chastity?" His tone was light but the question was serious.

"Yes."

"Well, that's honest."

"So you see, I really don't think we should see each other any more. There is no future in it."

There was silence for a moment. And then he said, "You don't think that I could make you change your mind? Sweep you off your feet?"

I had to laugh. "You really are fun to be with, Steve. And I've enjoyed our times together a lot. It's been a refreshing change in my old maid existence. But, no. I won't change my mind. And I like you too much not to be honest. You deserve to find a woman who will not only appreciate you but will enter wholeheartedly into a meaningful relationship with you."

I stood up then, indicating that it was time for him to leave.

At the front door, he turned. "If you change your mind..."

"I won't." I smiled and watched him walk down the path before I closed the door.

The next day, I did something I'd never done before - called work and said that I didn't feel like coming in, giving the impression that I was sick. I wasn't physically ill, but felt like I'd been sick for a long time.

I put on my coat and went out the back door before returning for a scarf and gloves. It was a bitterly cold day.

Hands thrust into pockets and with the wind stinging my face, I walked. And walked.

I came to a park, deserted now by school children and toddlers alike. A swing swayed gently in the wind and I sat on it, placing gloved hands on the metal chains. In front of me was a tree. Brittle leaves lay in a heap at the tree's base and all the limbs were bare. Except one.

There on one limb, on a small branch at the middle of the tree, was one last leaf.

Why is the tree clinging on to that one last leaf? Then I

realized that if I'd thought it through I would have surmised that a leaf would cling to a tree, not the other way around. But my impression was strongly that the tree was clinging to the leaf.

It's me, that tree is like me. I am clinging to that one last dead leaf of the love between Sanders and me. And it is useless. It's dead. I need to let it go.

I sat there and watched as the wind blew the leaf. Surely it would fall to the ground like its mates. But though I sat there until I feared for my nose and toes and fingers, the leaf remained, clutched by the tree that had more strength than the wind which sought to tear the leaf from its branch.

I took a walk today, this bitter, cold, December day.
Somehow the day and I agree.
I saw a tree
clinging to one last leaf; I don't know why.
The leaf was colorless and dry.

I never remembered making a choice or a decision but after that day things were different. I never called Steve. It would have been fun, filling hours with someone intelligent who made me laugh. But it wouldn't have been fair to him. And sure enough a few years later, Steve brought his new wife by the library to meet me. They had just returned from their honeymoon.

He and his bride were obviously very much in love and she smiled warmly at me. "Steve says you are a very wise lady and were a good friend to him at a time when he needed one." I smiled back and was glad for them.

No, I didn't call Steve and I didn't try dating any more.

But I did begin volunteering, at an orphanage.

I did go back to Church and move my membership there, and got involved in Sunday School and visiting shut-ins. I did take over as Vacation Bible School Director.

And I did find a measure of peace.

***

2007
Helen

The weather was finally turning cold after an unseasonably warm fall. I looked at the clothes spread out on the bed and wondered what to pack away and what to keep out. I'd need some light clothing for Texas but definitely switch to winter wear for home in Kentucky.

It was two weeks before my scheduled flight. *My scheduled flight. Good for me. Flying to Texas in December and England in April. It's about time.*

I opened the drawer to my bedside table and removed the address book.

"Beverly? Hi, it's Helen. What's the weather supposed to be out there Christmas week?"

I was surprised it would be in the 50's. I always thought of Texas as having a hot southern climate. After talking with my sister for a few minutes, I hung up the phone and packed away all the clothes I'd been considering for the trip.

When I replaced the address book, I picked up the bound booklet that held the hand written poems. I kept that beside my bed always in easy access. Sometimes when I was horribly lonely they brought comfort. The copies I gave to Christy were typewritten but these seemed more personal somehow.

I caressed the book for a moment and then threw it back and slammed the door shut.

Lord, I'm sixty-five years old. I've wasted my life wanting something I can never have. It's too late for me but please help Christy not make the same mistake. And use me to help her if you can.

I picked up the phone again and called Christy's cell phone. She sounded genuinely glad to hear from me.

"Helen! I was just thinking about calling you. What's going on?"

"Not a thing. I was just feeling a little lonely."

"I'm so glad you called. Guess where I've been today?"

Christy sounded excited.

"Back to church with the good looking preacher?"

Christy laughed. "No, but we had a date yesterday."

"Really? Good for you."

"I'll tell you about it at the track tomorrow but right now I want to tell you about Gina."

"What's going on?"

"She called my cell phone today. I gave her the number on the way from your house Thursday. I almost didn't answer it 'cause it was a strange man's name on the caller id. But it turns out the phone belonged to a realtor and she has rented a house. She needed some help to move."

"Is it a nicer place than the one you told me about?"

"Like a hundred times nicer...a thousand. It's a doll house. That's what we call it – The Doll House. Anyway, you wouldn't believe it, Helen. The girl has no furniture. I mean none, zero, nada. She has a little chrome and formica kitchen table and two chairs but that's it, and those belonged to the man she was living with. She was planning on sleeping on the floor of the bedroom. And the living room is bare too."

"Oh, poor child."

"She doesn't seem to mind at all. She is too entranced by the house to care about anything else. And it really is cute. Tiny but cute. I'm going to give her the bedroom suite in my spare room. I never liked it that much and don't need it at all. To tell you the truth I want an excuse to turn the room into a library but hated to just throw the furniture out."

"Good for you, Christy."

"I'm going to see if Kyle Martin, the preacher, will help me move it to her place. And I wondered if you have anything you would like to contribute."

"Hmm. Let me think. I know there's a chair in the basement I saved in case I have a yard sale some day. Which I probably never will. It's a recliner. And there are a couple of end tables too."

"That's wonderful. At least she will have someplace to sleep and something to sit in."

"I'm not through thinking what stuff I've got. When are you going to be moving the bedroom suite over there? You think your preacher will take my things too?"

"I haven't called him yet. Oh, I just looked at the time. Church starts in twenty-five minutes. I'll go and then ask him afterwards. What time do you go to bed?"

"Around ten thirty or eleven."

"Okay, I'll call you."

I laid the phone down, and smiled. *Lord, it seems like you are doing a good job setting Christy free without my help.*

I picked up my Bible and went to the kitchen. After brewing a cup of mint tea, I sat at the table and opened the book. I glanced down and read aloud the first verse I saw.

"He maketh the barren woman to keep house and to be a joyful mother of children. Psalm 113:9." Tears leaped to my eyes.

Are you giving me two daughters now in my loneliness, Lord? Thank you.

Chapter Eight

2007

Christy

Several people were up by the stage area talking to Kyle Martin after the church service but he looked over and grinned when he saw me waiting for him.

I hope he isn't disappointed when he finds out I'm waiting because I have a favor to ask.

Mrs. Martin stopped to say hello on her way out. "I'm so glad to see you back again. I understand you and my son went to see a street preacher last night."

"Yes, Ma'am." I didn't want to tell her how much I did not enjoy that event.

"I fussed at Kyle. Told him that's no place to take a young lady. I don't know what's wrong with his head."

I couldn't keep from laughing out loud. "It wasn't my favorite church service by far. But it was educational."

Mrs. Martin patted my shoulder. "He means well. And he's a good boy...I mean man."

"I know he is, Mrs. Martin. Probably because he has a good mother."

Just then I felt a hand on the back of my neck. "Hey! I'm glad you're still here." It was the preacher and goose bumps rippled over my body.

"I've got to get on home. You two be good." Mrs. Martin hurried out into the hallway without a backward glance.

"She's a nice lady, your Mom."

He nodded. "What are you doing now? Want to go get an ice cream?"

I looked at my watch. "I guess but not for very long."

As soon as the hall was cleared, Kyle locked the doors and we walked to the ice cream parlor that was just two doors away from the Convention Center.

When we were seated at the cute little coca cola tables with our ice cream, I brought up the subject of moving.

"I confess that I have a favor to ask and that's why I hung around after church."

"Ask away." Kyle was devouring his ice cream sundae like a kid who was starving. And it occurred to me that maybe he didn't eat before services.

"Have you eaten supper?"

"What's the favor in that question?"

I shook my head. "Silly. No, that's not the favor. I'm just curious. You look hungry."

He grinned. "I ate a late lunch. You're right. I'm hungry. But I was really in the mood for ice cream for some reason. I'll pick up a sandwich on my way home. So...what's the favor?"

"You remember me telling you about Gina, the girl who came in the Agency and I was able to help her?"

"Yes, I said that was a 'one with Jesus' thing to do."

I told him about the little house and the need to move furniture.

He grimaced. "I'd love to do that but it will have to be during the day if it's this week. I've committed to a local pastor's conference that's meeting Monday through Thursday in the evenings. I know you both work. So...what do you think?"

"Hmm. I guess I'll go by Gina's tonight and then call and let you know."

"That's fine. Want me to go with you?"

I shook my head. "No, I need to get on home as soon as I

leave her place. I'll just call."

Kyle looked disappointed but he agreed.

I left The Doll House thirty minutes later and called Kyle on my way home. "Okay, I have the spare key. Which day would be best for you?"

"Tomorrow's alright if everything's ready."

"I'll need to check with Helen about picking her stuff up. What about Tuesday?"

"Tuesday is fine. What time can you get away from work?"

"I'll take a long lunch break, so around 11?"

"Do I meet you at your house with the truck?"

"It's a date."

"Ah, our second date?"

Remembering what he said about the kiss, I blushed - and was glad he couldn't see me over the phone. "I don't think so! This is work, Pastor Martin."

"I stand corrected."

"Okay, I'm home now. See you Tuesday at 11."

Next I called Helen and told her about the moving time. She was excited about her list to donate to Gina.

"I've got the recliner and end tables and I found another chair too, a wingback, not as nice as the recliner but comfortable."

"That's great, Helen."

"And...does she have a television set?"

"No, she doesn't. There was one at the apartment but she left it behind so I guess it came with the place."

"She does now. I have a small one in my bedroom that I've never used, not even once."

"I'm glad. She'll be so happy."

"I also have some silk flower arrangements to go on the tables if you think she'd be interested."

"Helen, she has nothing. I saw everything she owns. Two pots and a skillet, two wooden spoons, a spatula, a paring knife, four plates, four bowls, three glasses, four each of knives, forks, and spoons. That and the kitchen table and two chairs are it. You can't imagine."

"What about towels and sheets?"

"I'm giving her two sets of sheets and pillowcases with the bed. And I can't recall seeing any towels. Surely she has at least one."

"I've got plenty that I never use since I changed color schemes in my bathrooms. What color is her bathroom?"

I thought back over the rooms in the Doll House. "Blue and white."

Helen laughed. "Guess what color my old towels are? Wait, don't tell me, it's dark blue, right?"

"Yes, how did you know?"

"Because it's just like God to plan that I have lots of bathroom towels and washcloths and a mat and decorations in dark blue sitting waiting for Gina."

Just like God. I like that.

***

Kyle

I backed the truck up into Christy's driveway, really looking forward to the hours we would spend together moving furniture. Not that I like physical labor. But I really like Christy for some reason. Sure she's pretty but there've been plenty of pretty girls in my life. This had to be either chemistry with a capital C or God. I wondered if she felt the same attraction. She didn't act all silly like some girls I've taken out in the past, but she laughs a lot when she's with me. And she actually called me to help her. That's a good sign. I wished I hadn't made that comment about the second date and kissing. Now I'm afraid she'll think to accept another date would give me permission to kiss her.

Christy came out the front door of the house before I could get out of the truck. She was wearing jeans again with a sweatshirt that said she was a bookaholic.

"Hi! Let's go through here. It'll be less distance to carry the stuff." She led me through the garage, past a laundry room and into a bedroom which had already been denuded of bedclothing or accessories.

It took us thirty minutes to dismantle the bed and get all the furniture stacked in the back of my pick up, and another fifteen minutes to drive to Helen's house.

I felt a little nervous about meeting the older lady, like I was going to meet Christy's mother or something. I hoped she approved of me.

The friendliness with which I was greeted ended any discomfort. Helen made me feel like family too. No wonder Christy cared so much about her.

Helen had collected a lot of things to send for the new home. Boxes full of artificial flower arrangements and dishes and framed prints sat in the foyer.

"But before you take those out, you'd better pack the furniture." She led us down some steps into the basement where a grouping of chairs and tables and lamps stood waiting to be transported to their new home.

When all was neatly packed in the truck bed and tied down with bungee cords, Christy turned to Helen. "Do you want to come with us?"

She shook her head. "No, I better get back to work." After a moment's hesitation, she asked. "Are you going to pray over Gina's house?"

I grinned. "I'd love to do that." I turned to Christy. "Is that okay with you?"

"Sure." Christy shrugged her shoulders.

When we arrived at "The Doll House", as Christy insisted on calling the place, I had to admit it was appropriately named. And even though I'd been warned of the scarcity of the girl's belongings, the emptiness of the house shocked me.

I shook my head and looked at Christy. "We don't have a clue, do we? How a lot of people live?"

"No, we don't. I feel ashamed at how much I've taken for granted."

"Well, let's get busy. This place won't be the same when we leave." I grinned. "And it should always be that way when

Christians come and go, shouldn't it?"

Christy smiled and nodded her head.

It took another hour to move everything in and set the bed up. Christy tilted her head when she looked at me. "Are you in a hurry?"

I looked at my watch. "I need to be home in two and a half hours to get ready to leave for the meetings. But I'm free 'til then."

The next thing I knew I was helping her put sheets on the bed and hanging towels on rods in the bathroom as well as stacking the rest of the linens on shelves in the closet.

She placed flower arrangements on tables and counters but left the boxes filled with house-wares on the floor in the kitchen. I plugged in the TV, turned it on, and was relieved when the local station came into focus.

"It's not cable but it's something."

Christy was viewing the living room with a contented smile on her face.

"Oh." I remembered Helen's question. "Let's do the house blessing."

I took Christy's hand. It felt very small and warm in mine. I swallowed a lump that sprang up in my throat before I began the prayer. When I had asked the Lord to guard the house from all evil and make His presence known there, I closed by saying Amen. But I didn't turn loose of Christy's hand and she didn't pull it away either.

She looked up at me with shining brown eyes that held a plea in them. "Please keep praying for Gina."

"I will. I promise."

***

Gina

I unlocked the door of The Doll House Tuesday afternoon after work and picked up the envelope that lay on the floor just inside. I could feel the spare key but opened it to see if there was a note from Christy. There was!

"Hope everything is where you want it. If not, we'll come back and move it. The living room and bathroom things and house-wares are from Helen. I'll stop by later. Love, Christy."

When I looked up, I could hardly believe it. There were two chairs in the living room, each with a table beside it. One of the tables held a lamp and both had flower arrangements on them. A foot stool sat in front of one of the chairs and the other was obviously a recliner.

I walked through the living area and into the bedroom. There was the promised bedroom suite. I put my hand out and touched the pretty pink spread and pink and white pillows. When I looked over at the dresser I saw my own image staring like a child in awe. A pink silk flower arrangement sitting in front of the mirror was also reflected there.

After a minute of filling my eyes with the sight of the prettiest bedroom I ever saw, I left the room and opened the bathroom door. The first thing I spotted was another flower arrangement sitting on the counter by the sink. A navy blue shower curtain was in place and dark blue towels and washcloths hung from the rods. There was even a dark blue cover for the toilet lid and a bath mat on the floor.

I felt the tears fill my eyes as I once again spotted the plaque on the wall. "With God all things are possible." Matthew 19:26

God, you really have helped me. Thank you.

When I went back into the living room I saw something to the left of the front door that I missed when I came in. There on a cabinet was a small television set. *Awesome.*

When I finally made it to the kitchen to fix my sandwich for supper, I stopped in surprise again. A cheerful yellow and green plaid cloth was on the table and in the middle was another silk flower arrangement, this one of yellow tulips and daffodils.

I also saw two large boxes with no lids. Brightly colored bowls and plates sat in one of them and the other was filled with cookware and cooking utensils.

A ringing noise broke the silence and it took me a few

seconds to realize it was the front doorbell. I'd never had a doorbell before. I hurried to open it and Christy stood there with a sack announcing that Kentucky Fried Chicken was inside. The fragrance announced it to my stomach as well, and was answered with a rumble.

"I hope you like KFC?" Christy thrust the sack into her hands.

"I don't know. I never had it."

Christy's mouth dropped open like she was surprised. But she quickly closed it and didn't say anything.

I hugged her with her free arm. "Girl, you rock. I couldn't believe all this stuff. This is the best place ever."

Christy smiled and looked around. "It really is a Doll House, isn't it? And looking better all the time. Most of this is from Helen."

"She's a nice lady, isn't she?"

Christy nodded. "The best. It's hard to believe I've only known her for a few months."

"Shut up! I thought you'd been friends forever."

"No. Well, we walked at the track for years at the same time but we never talked until recently." Christy smiled at me. "But God can make close friends real quick."

"Yeah, I guess He can."

"I'm hungry. I didn't get any lunch today."

"Because you were moving my stuff?"

"I could have worked it in or taken something back to the office but I wasn't that hungry and didn't want to spoil supper."

After we devoured the extra crispy chicken and rest of the meal, we emptied the boxes that Helen sent and put their contents in cabinets and drawers.

"She washed them all before we picked them up so they are already clean."

I hadn't thought about washing them first but didn't say so. I was learning a lot from Christy about how nice people live.

When everything was neat and clean, Christy picked up her purse and pulled out the keys. "I better get on home. If you need anything at all, call me."

"I will. And thank you. Oh, thank Helen for me too. I wish I could do something for her."

Christy laughed. "She's great, isn't she? We'll think of something to do for her for Christmas." Then she frowned. "But she'll be gone at Christmas. What are you doing?"

"Me? Nothing. I never do anything for Christmas."

Christy pursed her lips. "Then we'll have to think of something for us for Christmas too, right?"

"Right." *Yay. Christy's going to include me in Christmas.* "Oh, and thank your preacher for me too."

Suddenly Christy looked embarrassed. "I hope you don't mind. I asked him to bless your house while we were here. And he said he would pray for you every day."

I didn't know what it meant to bless a house, but figured prayer couldn't hurt anybody. "Thanks."

I stood at the door watching until the tail lights of Christy's car disappeared around the corner.

Then I turned back in to the house and closed the door. As I slid the dead bolt into place, it occurred to me that maybe a house that was blessed was a safe house.

Chapter Nine

2007

Christy

"**H**unt Temp Service." I answered the phone since Sally was at the filing cabinet. "We Hunt the jobs for you! How may I help you?"

"By having dinner with me tonight?"

I recognized Kyle Martin's voice and disguised mine, affecting a nasal tone. "I'm sorry sir, we don't take this kind of phone call."

"Oh, I uh. I thought... I must have the wrong number."

I laughed out loud before he could hang up. "Wait, Kyle. I was just teasing. It's me."

"Christy! You skunk. I was mortified."

"Yes."

"Huh?"

"Yes, I'll have dinner with you."

"Well, I don't know. After scaring me and making me feel like a fool, maybe I won't take you to dinner after all."

"Suit yourself." I winked at Sally who had stopped filing and was staring at me.

"What time do you get off work?"

"Around five. But I want to go home and change first. Is six thirty too late?"

"No, that's great."

"What should I wear? Street preacher clothes or something else?"

"You don't stop giving a guy a hard time, do you?"

"Only when he doesn't deserve it anymore."

"Where would you like to go? I'm rich this week."

"Reverend Martin, you never ask a girl where she wants to go. You choose and take her there. Just tell her what kind of clothes to wear."

"Okay. But can I give her several choices, since I don't know what kind of food she likes?"

"I guess that would be allowed."

"Is it okay to drive to Lexington?"

"That's fine with me."

"Then...P.F. Changs, Red Lobster, Olive Garden, or Outback."

"Red Lobster or Outback. Now you have to make the final choice."

"Determined, aren't you?"

I laughed at his feigned irritation. "But whichever you choose I know what to wear now. Unless you plan to go all dressed up in a suit or tux or something?"

"No tuxes, I promise."

"See you at 6:30."

Sally grinned at me. "I'm glad for you, Christy. You seem a lot happier since you met that preacher."

She was right. Life was definitely more exciting since Kyle Martin came into my life. He was good looking and funny. I hadn't felt so feminine since...since England and David.

I liked the idea that Kyle was helping me get over David. But I didn't want him to just be a distraction. He was a nice man and I wanted him to be special to me for his own sake.

"This is your second date, isn't it?" Sally went on filing papers, unaware that she had dropped a bomb.

"Yeah, it is." *Second date – the kissing date. Oh Lord, am I ready for this?*

When Kyle arrived at the house I had changed clothes three times.

"Wow, you look great." He made a gesture like he was taking a photo. "Picture perfect."

"So do you." And he did. His sports coat was blue and made the color of his eyes look more ocean-like than ever. Kyle was a slightly built man but very masculine.

While we drove toward the city, he made light conversation but I couldn't help but wonder if the term "second date" was looming as big in his mind as it was mine.

"Do you play tennis?"

I admitted that I was not much into sports of any kind.

"What do you do for fun?" He seemed truly interested.

"I'm pretty boring. I like to watch movies and read novels."

There was silence for a few minutes. I wondered if he was wishing he hadn't asked me out.

I decided to ask some questions of my own. "Do you play tennis?"

He smiled. "Yes. I love it. I took lessons when I was a kid. And it's the greatest relaxation to me."

"Really? It would be stress to me. I was never good at any sports. And I was terrified of a ball coming at my face. Nobody wanted me on their volleyball team in gym."

"It's funny, isn't it, how different people are?" He didn't seem to be completely disgusted with me. So that was good. But what now?

"So how did you end up as a pastor?"

He shook his head. "Long story. I don't want to bore you with it."

"I wouldn't be bored. I love stories."

"It started when I was a kid...a little kid, like around five. I wanted to be a preacher when I grew up, like my Dad. But then one day when we had planned for weeks to go to see some movie as soon as it came out, a Disney thing I think, he couldn't go because somebody died and he had to preach a funeral that Saturday afternoon." Kyle gave a soft chuckle. "I was disappointed

and even though we went to see the movie later, I made up my mind right then that I'd never be a pastor."

I laughed. "Because you didn't want to have to do a funeral?"

"I don't know whether it was that, or that I realized a pastor's time is not his own."

"So what changed your mind?"

"God." He laughed. "I had my wild times in high school – a typical PK, preacher's kid. Proving to the world that I wasn't weird just because my parents were religious. Then I went off to college. And it was strange. Everybody, or most everybody, was being wild. It was almost expected. And after a few weeks it all just looked stupid. I saw people making themselves sick drinking and partying all the time. They were wasting money on that, and on tuition because they weren't studying. It was just crazy. I guess I had already gone through my rebellion against my parents lifestyle and I started rebelling against my peers lifestyle."

That struck me as funny. "So what did you do? Get all religious?"

"No, not at all. I got all intellectual. But it just didn't fill whatever it was I was hungry for. I got into scifi – movies, books, even joined a Treky group. Had a uniform and everything."

"I want to see it."

He grinned. "I don't tell many people this but I still have it. Spock Jr. – that's me. Someday I'll show it to you."

"So how did God rope you in?"

He did a double take. "That's good. That's exactly how it felt. He roped me in. Actually, it was through a girl, another Treky. She was quite a babe and I was attracted. But she wouldn't go out with me after I turned down an invitation to attend church with her. I thought who cares about a religious nut? But she haunted me. She had convictions but she was just as nice to me as ever when the Star Trek group met. I dropped out after a while. Then one day I was driving along and suddenly felt like somebody was in the car with me. And I remembered the story of Saul on the road to Damascus and how Jesus said "Why are you persecuting me?" It was so strong I said out loud, "I'm not persecuting anybody." And then... I know this sounds nuts, but it was like I heard a voice in my head say "No, but you're ignoring me." I heard it really clear. I knew I didn't make it up. And I knew who it was."

I was impressed. "Wow. How neat. I wish I could hear God like that."

"You can. I didn't want to at the time. But it was kind of funny. I hadn't been boozing and stuff like the other guys but when I got back to the dorm, I got in my mates drawer and took out his bottle of gin, poured about a third of a glass and drank it straight down."

"You didn't?" I was completely shocked!

"Sure did. I was really shook up by hearing God talk to me. I needed something to settle my nerves."

I laughed out loud. "I would never have guessed that reaction. So what happened next?"

"I went for a walk around campus and talked to God man to man. Well, you know what I mean. I just told him that I wasn't the churchy kind and I needed him to tell me straight up what he wanted from me."

"And did he?

"Yeah. He said he wanted me to be a pastor but he didn't want me to lead a normal church. He wanted something different, something anybody would feel comfortable coming to. So I said okay and after college I went to a divinity school and here I am."

"And here you are." I liked Kyle Martin, a lot.

He ordered us a Bloomin' Onion as an appetizer before the steak dinner and as always the food at the Outback was great. We talked about Star Trek over dinner and he obviously enjoyed sharing his expertise on the subject.

On the way home we both seemed to run out of things to say. He switched on the radio to an oldies station and they were playing real old oldies, like Stardust and Slow Boat To China, and some I'd never heard. But he sang along with those two. The words were so romantic that I didn't know whether to be embarrassed or not. Maybe he just liked to sing. But "I'd love to get you on a slow boat to China, all to myself alone" certainly was in harmony with the thoughts of the 'second date kiss' that was moving with great acceleration to the forefront of my mind.

When we pulled into my driveway, he stopped the car and turned it off. But he didn't get out. Instead, he turned to face me. My heart was pounding and I wasn't sure what to expect. *He is a preacher!*

He reached toward me and his fingers caressed my cheek. "So beautiful."

My throat was suddenly dry and it was hard to swallow.

"Christy, I don't want to push you. And maybe I shouldn't ask, but can I kiss you?"

The mind is so insane at such times. I had an overwhelming urge to remind him that the correct grammar would be to ask *may I kiss you* instead of *can I kiss you?*

His fingers had moved to my ear and he traced the contours. My stomach was fluttery. *Come on, Christy, say something.*

"I'm sorry, that was stupid of me." He leaned over and pulled me into his arms. I didn't resist. I couldn't. I had wanted to be held and kissed for so long. And he was very good at it.

***

It was silly to wait in the cold and watch as the plane taxied the runway and took off into the sky. But because of the horrible accident the previous year at Bluegrass Field, where nearly everyone was killed on departure, I wanted to make sure that Helen got in the air safely. *Please bring her back Lord, healthy and happy. And give her a good Christmas.*

I looked at my watch and hurried toward the parking garage. There was just enough time to get back, pick up Gina, and make it to the Christmas party. Snowflakes began to fill the air and I hoped it wouldn't slow me down. I was already fighting guilt that I couldn't help with the decorating. And it would have been a good time to bond with Kyle's mother. I felt my cheeks warm as I remembered the time alone in the car with Kyle last week.

Nothing wrong had happened but...

While I drove home I weakly tried, as I had all week, to resist the temptation to wonder if kissing David would be as exciting. But even as I cast down mental images, something in my heart told me it would have. "Stop it, stop it, stop it!" I turned on the radio and let Christmas music fill the car. Worshiping the babe of Bethlehem helped drive other loves from my mind.

I hate driving in snowy weather and would rather have gone home to curl up with a mystery. But I couldn't miss the Christmas party, not after all the work everyone put into it, buying and wrapping presents. And besides that, Gina was going with me. It wasn't exactly getting her to church but close. I just hoped the snow wouldn't turn to ice before we got safely in for the night.

An hour later, I pulled up to the curb in front of The Doll House and blew the horn. When Gina came through the door and turned to lock it, I saw that she had on only a windbreaker, and quickly took a mental inventory of the coats in my own closet.

Gina opened the car door and a blast of wind entered with her. "Brr, it's cold! I'm glad I don't have far to walk to work."

I never thought of that. She has to walk to work in every kind of weather.

"The next thing we need to pray for is a car for you." I put the car in drive and looked back to make sure there was no traffic.

"I can't drive."

I put the car back in park and turned to look at her. "What?"

"I can't drive. Never had a need to learn. No car. Mam didn't have one either. So why bother?"

"Well then, we'll have to start with the driving and then work toward a car."

Gina laughed. "You are something else, girl."

We pulled into the parking lot for the convention center and found a slot not too far from the front door. I glanced at the car clock. "Hmm, we made good time. We're fifteen minutes early."

When we entered the lobby, Mrs. Martin greeted us with a smile. "Hi, Christy. And you must be Gina?" The lady turned a warm smile on her, and I was grateful.

"Mrs. Martin, I want you to meet my friend, Gina. Gina, this is Mrs. Martin, the pastor's mother."

Gina looked a little shy but smiled back at Mrs. Martin.

There were a group of about twenty people lining the walls, adults and children. I spoke in a low voice so they wouldn't hear me. "Are they here for the party?"

"Yes, I told them they couldn't go in until one, because things aren't ready yet. But you two go on back."

There were a few frowns as we passed by the waiting crowd but mostly people just stared. When we entered the conference room, Gina gasped.

I was surprised too even though I knew what the decorations were going to be, and even helped paint some of them. I just hadn't expected it to be so beautiful when it was all put together. Everything was ice blue and white and silver. Puffy cotton clouds dotted with silver sprinkles hung from the ceiling, and the fronts of winter cottages and shops were stationed around the walls. Even the Christmas tree on the stage was white with blue and silver ornaments. The food tables were covered with blue cloths and held white plates and cups.

The quaint little shops and cottages all had blue mailboxes with letters of the alphabet painted on them in silver. After the luncheon and program, the families would go to the mailbox corresponding to their last name and the gifts hidden behind the facades would be passed out to them.

We stood mesmerized by the scene until Kyle Martin came over to join us. He put his arm around my shoulders and I could feel myself blush again at the possessive gesture.

"You must be Gina."

I shook myself loose from his grip. "Gina, this is Kyle Martin, the pastor here, the one who helped move your furniture."

"I'm glad to meet you, Sir. And thank you for helping me."

Kyle held out his hand and she extended her own. Then he turned back to me. "Tell her I'm not a Sir. She makes me feel old."

Gina pulled her hand away and lowered her head. I quickly

explained. "He's just kidding, Gina. He *is* old, older than me, even."

Gina raised her head and, with a slight smile, looked uncertainly from my face to his. I wanted to kick him for making her feel awkward.

***

Gina

I fought a feeling of déjà vu that came over me when the preacher shook my hand. I'd never seen him in my whole life but I felt like it had happened before. It made me a little dizzy. And it made me uncomfortable.

This was Christy's new boyfriend. I didn't want to go having some kind of freaky karmic vibes about him.

He had the bluest eyes I ever saw. Okay, if I was honest with myself, he had the bluest eyes I ever saw besides my own. Maybe he was my brother or something. His hair was even the same color as mine without the black dye. Maybe Mam gave him up for adoption and the lady in the hall was his adopted mother. Or maybe his father was one of Mam's clients and I was the result of their transaction. Mam never told me about my father but I always figured it was because she didn't know who he was.

The preacher and Christy were both looking at me and I knew I ought to say something. But what? I couldn't say what I was thinking and couldn't think of anything else to say.

The preacher broke the awkward silence. "Let me take your coats." He reached over and took hold of the shoulders of my jacket and I shrugged my way free of it. When he had helped Christy with hers too, he walked off toward the back of the room and waved us to a table covered with cans of pop and bottles of water. "Help yourselves before the crowd hits."

Christy went over and picked up a bottle of water and I got a can of Mountain Dew.

"Well, what'd you think?" Christy gestured toward Pastor Martin who stood across the room hanging the coats on a rack.

"He seems nice."

"He really is." She sighed kind of deeply and I wondered if that meant she was falling in love.

"What can I do to help?" I agreed to come because Christy said they needed lots of help.

"Let's find out." Christy walked across the room toward the preacher, and I followed.

"What's our assignment, boss?"

His grin and wink included me and I felt my stomach do a flip.

"Boss. I like that. But actually Jo Ann is in charge. She's got it all lined out."

Just then a lady holding a clipboard joined us. "Hi, Christy. And you must be Gina?" Her smile was welcoming.

I nodded that I was who the lady thought, and she took me to the little storefront where I would be passing out gifts. I was glad that my place was named "Miracle Manor." Maybe that was silly but I was still glad. The mailbox had the initials G,H, and I. Behind the façade, gifts were all wrapped with the children's names on them, and all the gifts for each individual family were in a box together. Jo Ann showed me a checklist with a pen attached, hanging on a nail at the back of the wooden decoration. "You just check them off when they pick their presents up."

She led me toward the food tables and waved for Christy to join us. "If you two would just stand here, that might make sure that people don't take too much. Some of them may want to take food home with them and that's fine - after every one is fed. I'm going to have Kyle say the blessing and he'll explain that we'll bag up the leftovers for later. But if someone's standing here, I think it will help."

I thought back on the first day I met Christy. I took food home for later. But that was different. It was a restaurant. No one would go hungry because I took extra.

When the minute hand moved to one p.m. Jo Ann nodded to a woman standing by the closed doors, the woman opened them, and the party was on. Within minutes the large room was filled with people, mostly children, but a lot of women and a few men.

They rushed in but stopped, like Christy and I did earlier, to look at the decorations.

Pastor Martin was on stage beside the Christmas tree with a mike in his hand. His voice boomed out over the loud speaker system.

"Welcome. We at Living Word Church welcome you to our first annual Christmas party. We're going to say the blessing, and then everyone can go through the lines and fill their plates. After lunch, there will be a short program and then we'll distribute the gifts for you to take home. We'll give you instructions on that later. We'll also package leftovers and you can pick them up on your way out."

After that he said a prayer over the food like Helen did on Thanksgiving day.

The crowd rushed to the food tables like fans pouring down the bleachers and on to the floor toward a winning basketball team. Christy and I watched as they filled their plates with fried chicken from the grocery deli along with home cooked vegetables and salads donated by the church members. There were three other food tables, one for drinks and two for desserts.

When all the guests were seated, the volunteers filled plates and joined them wherever there were empty seats. Jo Ann suggested they scatter themselves so they could sit with as many guests as possible. Christy sat at one table and I found a spot at the next one. I settled in beside a tiny little girl whose mother was helping her eat.

I smiled at the mother and then looked at the child. She had auburn curls and blue eyes. *See! There are a lot of people with curly auburn hair and blue eyes. Kyle Martin is NOT your brother!*

"What's your name?" The girl looked away from me and at her mother.

"It's okay, Shelby, you can tell her. She's one of the nice church ladies." She turned to me. "I've been trying to teach her not to talk to strangers."

The girl smiled shyly. "My name Shebby."

"My name Gina." I grinned at the little girl. "What do you

want for Christmas?"

But she just looked at her Mom again.

"Shelby really hasn't asked for anything. I just put down her age and size and trust that they'll pick out some good things."

There was something about the child that tugged at my heart. *One of the nice church ladies.* I wish I were. *No, I don't. What's wrong with me?* Well, maybe not a church lady, but it sure did feel good to be one of the helpers here.

Just then I was aware of someone pulling out the chair on the other side of me. When I turned I recognized Mrs. Martin.

"Hi, Gina," the lady said. "Who's your friend?"

"This is Shelby. And her mother." I shook my head. "I don't know your name, Shelby's mom."

The woman laughed and nodded at Mrs. Martin and me. "I'm Kelly Denton."

"How old is Shelby, Ms. Denton?" Pastor Martin's mother smiled at the lady.

"She's three."

I watched as Mrs. Martin began talking across the table to some of the others. By the time the meal ended, she managed to call everyone by name.

A lady got up on the stage and sat at a keyboard like I'd seen some rock bands use. There was also a guy with a guitar. Surely they wouldn't have a rock concert for the church Christmas party.

"We're going to sing some Christmas carols. We chose the ones we thought everyone would know. But just in case, the words will be on the screen." And sure enough there were the words to "Joy to the World" on a large screen to the right of the lady.

I leaned over and whispered to Mrs. Martin. "Do you have one of the places where we give them the presents?"

The older lady nodded.

"Which one?"

"D, E, and F."

"Would you trade with me? I'd love to give Shelby her present."

"Of course. I don't mind at all."

When we finished singing some Christmas carols, Pastor Martin got back up on stage and announced a Christmas Nativity play. All children were invited to come on stage and join the ladies who were bringing piles of material up with them. Again, there was a mass rush and the pastor talked about Jesus while in the background children were being draped with cloths and robes transforming them into angels and shepherds and wise men. Two special ones were dressed as Mary and Joseph.

I'd never paid much attention to the Christmas story. It was something that happened a long time ago and since Mam said there were no real miracles, I put that in the category with Santa Claus and Frosty. But I could tell that the Pastor believed God really was Jesus' Daddy. That meant Joseph was his stepfather.

I loved watching the children parade on and off as the pastor read the story from the Bible. I especially enjoyed watching Shelby as one of the littlest angels. Her Mom had to stand at the edge of the stage, but the child joined in. And when they returned to the table, Shelby grinned at me.

"Did you see me be on TV?"

I didn't want to disappoint her. She obviously thought the video cameras were television. "Yes, you were the prettiest angel on TV."

When it was time for gifts, I really liked being the one to hand out gifts not only to Shelby but to a lot of other children. When Shelby left clutching one of the three gifts with her name on it, she turned around to smile at me one last time.

"Bye, nice lady."

"Bye, Shelby." I felt tears spring to my eyes and a lump form in my throat. *What is wrong with me lately? Gettin' soft.*

Christy and I stayed and helped clean up. Some of the kids had ripped their gifts open as soon as they got them and there was brightly colored wrapping paper all over the floor across the conference room. We offered to pick up the paper and each took a large garbage bag. When that was done, the others had finished the rest of the cleanup.

Pastor Martin hurried up to us as we were leaving. "You're not going without saying goodbye?"

Christy answered. "I've had a long day, taking Helen to the airport and all. I just want to get home, take a hot bath, and curl up with a book."

"Not in the mood for preachers, street or otherwise?"

I watched as their eyes flashed amusement at one another. But Christy stood her ground.

"Nope, just hot water and a cozy mystery."

He leaned over and hugged her. "Will you be at church tomorrow morning?"

"No, I'm going to my own in the morning but I may make it tomorrow night."

"Great. And what are you doing for Christmas?"

"I told you that Gina and I have plans."

I felt sorry for the preacher. Christy didn't seem nearly as interested in him as he did in her. I didn't see why not. He was a real hottie. *Uh oh. Is it a sin to call a preacher a hottie.*

It was snowing harder and getting colder when Christy dropped me off at The Doll House.

"Would you like to go to church with me anytime tomorrow? I'll go to my own church in the morning." She glanced through the window at the sky. "Well if it's not too icy in the morning. And I'll go to Living Word tomorrow night if the weather is okay."

"I don't think so. But thanks anyway. And thank you for taking me today. That was really fun."

Christy smiled from ear to ear. "I'm so glad you liked it. So, we never decided where we're having Christmas. My place or yours?"

"I don't care." I really wanted to see where Christy lived but hated to invite myself.

"Okay, let's say mine. I'll come and pick you up – what? About eleven that morning?"

"Perfect. And I'm bringing dessert, right?"

"Right."

When Christy drove off, I felt a warm glow for several

seconds before it was replaced with a twisting in my stomach. I needed to check on my mother. I hadn't seen Mam since I went off with Mike last March.

This was no kind of weather to walk all that distance, especially without a warm coat. But maybe it wouldn't be so cold in the next two days. I sure wasn't going to ask Christy to take me to the neighborhood where Mam lived, on Beckley.

Chapter Ten

2007

Gina

When I looked out the window that morning, all the tree branches were coated with ice. I was really glad I didn't have to go to work. The weekend combined with Christmas Eve and Christmas Day gave me four days in a row, two days of it with pay - a big treat. When I turned on the TV, a close up of a preacher's face and the blast of his voice shocked me.

"If you died tonight, do you know where you would spend eternity?"

I had no idea. Mam didn't believe in church. I went to a kids group of some kind once with a girl from school but another girl made fun of my shoes and the girl who took me went off with the other girl and I hated it and swore I'd never go back again.

But the Christmas party was fun. And Christy and Helen and Pastor Kyle Martin believed that the whole God thing was true. They were the nicest people I ever met. So maybe there was something to it all. And then there was my plaque in the bathroom.

I went to the bedroom and got the Bible Helen gave me out of the drawer. I took it back in the living room, settled in the recliner, opened to the first chapter. "In the beginning..."

After a few minutes, I laid the Bible down. *Sorry, God. This is really boring. I made it through to the talking serpent but come on...*

I got up from the chair and went to the bathroom. "With God, nothing is impossible." I stared at the plaque.

"Okay, God. If it's really you that got this house and all the stuff for me and not just nice people, I want you to show me something that nobody else can do for me. I want you to make me quit smoking and make me like the Bible." I caught a glimpse of myself in the bathroom mirror and was surprised at the defiant look on my face. "Sorry, God. But I mean it. I want to see something that only you can do."

With that I turned and settled myself back in the armchair to watch TV for the rest of the day and evening, even if there was a lot of preaching at first.

On Monday morning I woke up realizing that I had enough money to get a cab if I really wanted to visit my mother. I looked at the clock. Too early for Mam. Maybe this afternoon. But how to get a cab to come here? At my old place there was a pay phone on the corner but I hadn't seen one around here.

I got up and looked out the window. The ice had melted from the trees and even the snow was patchy on the yard. I could do this. I could walk to Mams; it wouldn't be much farther than to find a pay phone.

I scrambled eggs and made toast for breakfast and just as I was washing the dishes, the door bell rang.

It was Christy with her arms full of sacks.

"Hey, hope you don't mind. I remembered you said you were off today."

"No! Come on in."

"I brought some things I don't use and wondered if you wanted them." Christy made her way into the living room and put the sacks on the floor next to the recliner. Then she took off her coat and sat in the other chair. "Go ahead. Go through them."

"Shut up!" I pulled out a heavy winter coat with a hood from the first sack. "Boy, do I want that! That will be great for walking to work." I remembered my decision to visit Mam. "Or anywhere else." I started through the other bags.

A pair of bright red gloves and matching hat were the next things that came out. Three sweaters - two pull over and one button up joined the pile mounting on the floor.

Last there was a flannel nightgown, soft fluffy robe, and a pair of slippers that looked like two pink pigs.

Christy explained. "We do gag gifts at work and last year the secretary gave me those. I'm ashamed to say I never wore them. But if you want them, they're yours."

"Yes!" I clutched them to my chest. "They are wonderful. I love 'em."

Christy turned to pick up her purse. "I'll be going. I didn't want to ruin your day at home but wanted to get that coat to you especially."

"You aren't ruining my day. Want some coffee? I have instant."

"No thanks. I can't drink it. Or eat chocolate. Can't take caffeine."

"No chocolate? That... that's awful."

"Yeah, but I make up for it with caramel." Christy laughed and patted her stomach.

"Hey, you're not fat." Christy wasn't skinny like me, but she wasn't fat either.

"You should have seen me three years ago. After my parents died, I put on about thirty pounds. But most of it's gone now."

"I didn't know your parents died." I thought back on our conversations - they'd always been about me. I didn't know anything about Christy.

"Yeah, over six years ago. I'll tell you about it some time. By the way, that's why I have such a nice house. I didn't want you to think when you come tomorrow that I was so successful I could buy a place like that. I inherited it. And they left enough money to keep it up. I couldn't do it on my salary."

I'd heard of people with parents like that but couldn't imagine it. I stood at the door and waved until Christy drove away, then turned back into The Doll House and began getting ready to visit my own parent.

My stomach heaved at the familiar smell of rotting mice and baby diapers that filled the hall and stairway. But I gulped down the acid that filled my mouth, and kept climbing the steps.

I knocked on the door of the third floor apartment to my right. Home. Not anymore and I was so glad. "Mam? Are you there?" This was not a usual time for business but my mother might be sleeping. "Mam?" I knocked louder and waited.

When the door opened I was shocked. "Mam? Are you okay?"

Mam looked at me with no emotion on her face or in her eyes. "What are you doing here?"

"I'm your daughter. That's what I'm doing here. Now, what's wrong? You look sick. You must've lost 20 pounds." I pushed my way past her and looked around the small apartment, relieved to see no signs of a visitor.

"I'm okay. Just a cough." She followed with a spasm of coughing that sent alcohol permeated breath right into my face.

"Oh, Mam. You've been drinking again." I remembered times when Mam didn't drink gin and they were the good times. I also remembered when I was told about my name. "You were named Gina because gin is my bestest friend." Her mother had giggled when she said it. "Remember that. Gin helps you forget or at least not care what you remember." And Mam had exploded with that loud raucous laughter that invariably ended in a cough.

Now she just shrugged. "So I been drinking. So what? I guess you're still Miss Goody Two Shoes, huh?"

"Not hardly."

"Still with that guy Mike?'

"No, he left." I swallowed the lump that came in my throat every time I thought about Mike. He wasn't the smartest guy in the world or even the handsomest. But he rescued me from this place. And I'd always be grateful. "I got a job."

"Where?"

"Factory. And it's not bad."

Mam stretched out on the couch and reached over to the coffee table to pick up a cigarette and lighter. Watching Mam smoke made me want to kick the habit even more.

"So who's your man now?" Mam blew smoke rings into the air and I remembered being a little girl and thinking my mother was magic to be able to do that.

"No man. Just me." I sat on the wooden chair at the table that used to be my place at mealtime, whenever that happened to come.

"You make enough money?"

"Yep. Sure do." All of a sudden I didn't want to tell my mother about The Doll House. It seemed like to tell her would be to pollute something sacred. "No extra but enough."

"Good. I'm glad. I wondered about you. But figured you'd come back when you wanted to."

"Mam? I want to know something."

"What's that?"

"My father. Who was my father?"

A fit of coughing delayed the response.

Finally Mam gasped out. "Who knows?"

"You don't have any idea?"

"We've gone through this before, Gina. I don't know." Mam's words slurred together and a gesture of dismissal caused the burning tip of her cigarette to fall on the carpet between the couch and table.

I leaped out of the chair and picked it up between her thumb and finger. "Ouch." I dumped it into the ashtray. "Mam, you can't smoke while you're drinking. You..." A snore drew my attention away from the ashtray back to the couch. I removed the rest of the cigarette from Mam's hand and used it to put out the burning ash.

No sense in trying to talk to her now. I looked at the small space that served as living room, kitchen, and dining room. Then with a sigh, I started collecting trash and dirty glassware. An hour later the dishes were washed and put away, the garbage was bagged and ready to take downstairs when I left, and everything was dusted and cleaned.

I opened the door to the bathroom and the smell of vomit hit me in the face. I closed it again and turned to the room that had been mine. Everything was just like I left it last March. I went to the shelf and saw my high school textbooks from previous years. The last semester books were in a drawer at The Doll House. That was another wonderful thing Mike had done for me. He insisted I finish senior year and get my diploma.

There on top of the books was Raggedy Ann. I picked up the doll and held it tightly to my chest. Raggedy Ann was my friend when I didn't have any other friends. I'd been embarrassed to take the doll when I left with Mike but now I didn't care what anybody thought.

With Raggedy Ann tucked under one arm and the garbage bag in the other hand, I left the apartment, giving one last look at my sleeping mother. I'd done what I could. But it wasn't enough. It never had been enough.

I'd come back though. Tomorrow, on Christmas Day.

***

Christy

I pulled up in front of The Doll House right at eleven a.m. Before I could honk, Gina opened the door and waved. I settled back to wait on her, singing along with "We wish you a Merry Christmas" on the radio. She opened the door and slid into the passenger seat just as the song was ending and I greeted her with a musical "Merry Christmas and a Happy New Year!"

Gina laughed. "And Merry Christmas to you too. But you don't want me to sing it."

"You don't like to sing?"

"Oh yeah, I love to sing but nobody else loves it when I sing."

I pulled away from the curb but not before I noticed a wrapped gift in the plastic sack at her feet. I was glad because I bought something for her and was afraid she'd feel bad if she didn't have a gift for me.

When we got to my house, I pulled into the garage and then let the door down behind us. Gina was wide eyed.

"I never saw that before."

"An automatic garage door opener?"

"No. I mean yes, I never saw one of those before. Can I try it."

I handed her the control. "Here, play with it, Eeyore."

"Eeyore?"

"From Winnie the Pooh. Did you ever read it?"

"Nuh uh." She pushed the opener several times and the garage door went up and down and up and down. "That's great."

I laughed. "Eeyore is the donkey in the 100 acre woods where Pooh Bear lives. He gets a broken balloon and an empty honey pot for his birthday but has lots of fun putting the balloon piece in and out of the pot."

She nodded with a half smile. "Oh, I get it."

But I wasn't sure she did. She really got to my heart. No belongings, never read Winnie the Pooh, and never ate Kentucky Fried Chicken. We lived in two different worlds here in the same town.

When we walked into the living room, Gina's eyes widened at the sight of the Christmas tree. It was a seven foot artificial tree my parents bought years ago, a nice one that looked real, only shaped more perfectly than a real one. This was the first year I'd put it up since they died but now I had Gina to share it with. The tiny lights were not spaced as perfectly as when Dad put them on but they looked okay. And the ornaments were as awesome as ever. Mom had chosen each one. There were some round balls in varying shiny colors – green, gold, red, silver, purple, pink, and blue. But mostly the ornaments were miniature toys or cups or old fashioned shoes or trees or nativity scenes or bells. And every inch of the tree was filled. We always put icicles on our tree. The shiny strands shimmered in the tiniest breeze reflecting colors and making the tree look alive with light.

"Whoa." Gina grinned from ear to ear. "Now that's a Christmas tree."

I laughed out loud. I just knew she'd love it.

I took her coat and hung it in the hall closet where it used to live. "So what first? Presents or start cooking?"

She handed me the sack. "Here's your present."

I shook my head. "No, we have to do this right." I went to the stereo cabinet and pushed play. Bing Crosby's voice filled the room with "God Rest Ye Merry Gentlemen." Not one of my favorites but it was the first on the cd. "My parents always had Bing Crosby singing when we opened gifts. Okay?"

"Okay." Gina pulled the gift out of the sack and held it toward me. It was obviously gift wrapped in a store and I was very curious as to what she would have chosen for me.

I placed it under the tree next to the one waiting there for her. "First we have to get hot chocolate. I only drink it on Christmas Day." I led the way into the kitchen. "I hope you don't mind. I haven't done all this traditional stuff since my parents died."

"I don't mind. I like it. We never had any traditions."

"I just couldn't face doing it all alone but with someone to share, I've been looking forward to today." I didn't tell her how different it was with just two gifts under the tree, mine to her and hers to me. The whole floor used to be filled with gifts to me from my parents and theirs to each other and mine to them. But I did have the stockings that she hadn't spotted yet.

When we each had a Christmas mug filled with hot chocolate and marshmallows we went back into the living room. When she was settled on the couch and our mugs were on coasters on the coffee table, I went to the fireplace and turned on a switch. The fake logs blazed with golden color, making the room look warmer.

"Wow. I never saw those either. Oh, yes I did, on TV. But they seem different here in a real house." She looked around the room. "And you grew up here?"

"Yes." I blinked back tears and grabbed the stockings hanging from the mantle. "Look what Santa brought us."

Her face lit up. "Shut up! A stocking?"

I handed her the one filled with things for her. It was brand new but just as big as the ones our family used; I couldn't make myself use Mom's for somebody else.

Gina reminded me of the children at the Christmas party who were all excited about the stockings we passed out after the program and before they got their wrapped gifts to take home. I wondered at the time if she was envious but her face filled with pleasure watching their joy assured me how much she loved being a part of the giving.

Now she didn't seem to mind a bit being a receiver.

The first thing she pulled out was the teddy bear that stuck out the top. It was a girl bear with skates on and she hugged it to her chest. "Now I've got two."

"Two?" I didn't remember seeing that bear in her stuff, or any bear for that matter.

"Two toys. I got my old Raggedy Ann doll from Mam's yesterday."

I was surprised at the reference to her mother. She'd never mentioned her since that first day when she told me her mom was a, how did she put it, a street person or something like that? But I figured she meant a prostitute.

"Mam. That's different. Have you always called her Mam?"

"Long as I can remember. But I have a flash memory of her pointing her finger at me and saying 'You will say mam to me – yes mam and no mam' so ever since, I guess I've called her Mam – don't know what I called her before that." She shrugged and turned back to the stocking.

Next came a candle with a hazelnut fragrance. "Mmm. That smells good. Makes me hungry." She pulled out several plastic eggs with pantyhose in them, a brush and comb combination, and a little angel holding the letters that spelled JOY. Mixed throughout were Hershey's Kisses in red, green, and gold wrappers along with Reese's peanut butter cups also dressed up for the holidays.

Then from the toe of the stocking came the jewelers box. The small earrings were gold set with tiny pink sapphires, and I hurried to explain.

"I know you just wear one but I thought some day you might want to pierce your other ear and so I...I mean Santa...got a set."

She laughed. "I've been thinking about that. And some other stuff I want to ask you about sometime." She looked intently at the jewelry in her hand and then said in a voice full of wonder, "These are beautiful. I've never owned anything so beautiful in my life."

Gina was always making me have to swallow lumps in my throat and hold back tears. I quickly dumped out my stocking. Santa left me the same candy and stockings and brush and comb set. But my bear was dressed in ballet slippers and my angel said PEACE. My earrings were tiny crosses with no stones inset.

"That's no fair. Next year you don't do your own stocking, okay?"

The lump came back. Next year. *Thank you, Lord.* "Okay."

She got up and retrieved the present to me from under the tree. She thrust it toward me, suddenly looking shy. "I hope you like it. It's not nearly as nice as the earrings."

I tore off the paper and opened the box with mounting interest; it was heavier than I imagined. When the top layer of tissue paper was removed I drew a deep breath. There nestled in the box was a silver and white egg on a pedestal. Tiny faux diamonds were imbedded in the design and around the middle were flowers of deep pink and white with green leaves and each centered with more sparkling gems.

"Open it," she said.

I pulled it out of the box and saw that where the flowers were, the egg split. When I opened it, a familiar plaintive tune poured out into the room.

"A music box! How perfectly beautiful."

"I don't know what the song says or if it has words. But it was so pretty and the name on the tag said it's called "To Love Again.""

This time I didn't stop the tears from coursing down my cheeks. I put the music box down and turned to hug her. "Oh, Gina. There couldn't be a more perfect gift. You just don't know."

I think my tears surprised her but she acted happy that I liked the gift so much.

"And now for yours." I wiped away my tears and got her gift from under the tree.

"Whoa!" She pulled the cell phone out of the box. "For me? Is it a trac phone, where I can buy minutes? I've heard some of the women at the factory have these."

"No. It's not a trac phone. It's part of my plan. And we can talk to each other free anytime."

"Shut up!" Gina stared at the phone. "A real cell phone?"

"Yes. And it's as much a gift to me as to you. I won't have to go out in the snow every time I want to ask you something."

She laughed.

We had fun in the kitchen cooking while Christmas music played in the background. I didn't fix the whole menu my mother used to provide but we did a lot of it.

I put the rump roast on before I went to pick Gina up and by the time we finished with our gifts the delicious aroma filled the house making my stomach growl. We peeled the potatoes and got them on to boil and I put together Mom's special broccoli casserole. It went in the oven with the roast.

"We've got an hour til it's all done, over a half hour before time to mash the potatoes and make gravy. Want to play a game?"

"What? I don't like poker."

"I was thinking about Sequence or something like that." Poker. Again what different worlds we came from.

"What's that?"

I pulled the board game from the cabinet where it had been sitting, neglected, for over six years. Gina was a quick learner and beat me the first two games.

"I'm glad we're not playing for money." I drained the potatoes and put them in the mixer. "Would you get the butter dish out of the fridge?"

Gina opened the refrigerator and stood silently for a minute. "I've never seen a refrigerator so full."

"It's in the door, second shelf." Then it hit me that she wasn't looking for butter; she was amazed at the bounty. "It's Christmas. Extra food." I had a moment of gluttony guilt. Mom used to talk about starving Armenians but there were lots of hungry people right here.

While I was making gravy, Gina put the rolls in the oven and set the table. We were using Mom's Christmas china with matching glasses.

"Special plates just for Christmas." Gina shook her head.

After our dinner we cleaned up and played several more games of Sequence. I finally won a few but she was the winner of the day.

"The game fairy likes you," I said.

"Huh?"

"Just a joke." I packed the cards and markers back in their storage packages. "Mom and I used to play games a lot and we'd make jokes about the game fairy being mad at the one who lost, stuff like that."

"It must have been wonderful to have a mother like that."

"Yes, it was." I grabbed a Kleenex from the box on the counter. "I still miss her so much. My Dad too, but mostly Mom. We spent a lot of time together."

"How did she die?"

"In a car wreck. Coming to the airport to get me. I've felt like it was all my fault." I didn't want to go into all the reasons and was casting around in my mind how to change the subject when Gina did it herself.

"Airport? You've flown on a plane?"

I always saw my life as kind of average and mediocre but from Gina's viewpoint I guess it was pretty magic.

"Yeah, I went to England after I graduated from college."

"Shut up!"

I laughed. "That's me, the world traveler." I kind of hated to tell her but decided it wouldn't be fair not to. She was firmly entrenched in my life, and Helen's. "I'm going back in April. And Helen's going too."

Her eyes opened wider. "Both of you? What are you going to

do?"

"Just tour. See stuff. You know, stuff we've read about." She couldn't have gotten through school without knowing a lot of things we were interested in. "We're going to Stratford-upon-Avon where Shakespeare was born. I've never been there before. And we're going to Bath, where Jane Austin lived. You read Pride and Prejudice, didn't you?"

Now the blue eyes were sparkling. "Now that's really interesting. Yeah, I love to read. I didn't like Shakespeare so much but I liked Jane Austin. Her people were funny."

We talked about books for a while and then it seemed that we ran out of things to do or say. But I hated to take her to an empty house on Christmas Day. "Oh, I just remembered. I've got an old video tape player in the basement that I don't need. Would you want it?"

"Sure."

"And we've got lots of videos too if you want to borrow some." I pointed her to some shelves near the TV.

She picked out four tapes and gathered her gifts together. I had to give her an extra plastic bag to carry her stocking stuff. And I also loaded her up with enough leftovers for several days' suppers.

"Do you have to go back to work tomorrow?" I know some factories close down for a week at a time over holidays.

She nodded. "Yes, and I'm glad. When they close we don't get paid."

I drove Gina to The Doll House and saw her light a cigarette as soon as she got out of the car. I didn't even think to tell her to go out on my porch if she wanted to smoke. She was probably having a nicotine fit or whatever.

I was back home by 3:30 and feeling very blessed. I didn't have to go back to work 'til the day after New Year.

When I let myself back in the house it seemed empty. But I was glad for the silence. I'd lived alone so long that I was used to it. I picked up a book in Jan Karon's Mitford series. I'd discovered them through Helen and loved to escape into the mountain town with its quirky inhabitants. Just as I was snuggled into the couch, the phone rang. With a sigh I put the book down. I knew it couldn't be Gina because she had my cell phone number programmed in and that's how she would contact me, not by the house phone.

"Merry Christmas!" It was Kyle.

"Merry Christmas back. I didn't expect to hear from you today. I thought you were out of town."

"I am but I couldn't let the day go by without talking to my girl."

His girl? I didn't say anything.

"We'll be back in town around eight tonight and I wondered if maybe I could come by for a little while?"

I hesitated and then thought about Gina's gift to me. *To Love Again.* "Okay. But I didn't get you a Christmas present."

"I didn't get you one either so we're even."

I laughed. "See you around... when?"

"Eight fifteen."

I laughed again.

When we hung up I found myself still smiling. Kyle Martin always made me smile.

I went to the hall closet and got down a stack of old records that belonged to my Mom that she got from her parents. But I couldn't find the one with the song I was looking for. I loved it when I was a little girl. Mom thought it was a strange song for a little girl to like so much. I knew it must be here somewhere but finally gave up and put the records back on the shelf.

I opened the music box again and the haunting melody filled the air. I remembered the words.

No heart should refuse love.

How lucky are the ones who choose love

But if we should lose love.

We have the right to love again.

I do have the right to love again, David.

In a world full of faces few hearts ever find their places.

In many cases hearts have lost their way.

Did we lose our way? No, we did the right thing. I know that but it still hurts. I thought you were my place but I was wrong. And because of it my parents died.

Don't live in the past, dear.

For you and me the dye is cast, dear.

But if love won't last, dear,

We have the right to love again.

No, the dye is not cast for you and me, David. And I won't live in the past. I choose the right to love again.

I closed the music box and headed to the shower to get ready for my Christmas date.

Chapter Eleven

2007

Gina

I let myself in the front door of The Doll House the day after Christmas just as the cell phone started ringing. My coat fell onto the floor as I picked the phone up from the table and punched the green button.

"Hello?"

"Hi, it's me." Christy's voice came through loud and clear.

"Hey! I just walked in the door."

"You didn't have the phone with you?"

"No." It never occurred to me to take it with me. And why not? I saw people talking on cell phones everywhere, in the grocery, driving along in their cars, walking down the street.

"Doesn't matter. Anyway I wanted to talk to you about Saturday. I pick up Helen from the airport at 4:45 and wondered if you'd like to ride to Lexington with me and then the three of us could go out to dinner – my treat."

"Yeah. I'd like that."

"We said we were going to do something for Helen for Christmas but never talked about it anymore and I can't think of anything except to go to dinner, can you?"

I looked around in my mind for an idea but spotted nothing. "No. But I think she'd like that, and she can tell us all about her trip."

"That's what I thought. Well..." Christy paused as if she wanted to say something else. I just waited.

"I had an interesting night after you left."

"What happened?"

"You remember Kyle Martin, the preacher?"

"Yeah, your boyfriend."

Christy giggled. "Well, I guess he is turning into my boyfriend. He came over last night."

"You go, girl! He's a hottie."

Christy laughed out loud. "I never thought I'd hear a pastor called a hottie. But he is cute, isn't he?"

"You gotta ask?"

"I think he's really interested in me. And I like him a lot. He makes me laugh. But..."

"But?"

"Well, I think I'm getting more and more attracted to him."

"So?"

"Well, you know. Sex and all that. It's weird, feeling that way about a preacher. I can't believe I'm talking to you about all this. But, well you lived with a guy."

"Yeah?"

"Gina, I'm a virgin."

"Get outta here!"

"Sure am. And I know that he is committed to purity."

"Committed to purity?" The term meant nothing to Gina.

"Staying a virgin 'til you're married."

"Shut up!"

Christy laughed. "Well, it's what the Bible says we're supposed to do."

"It does?" I hated to admit that I'd only opened the Bible that Helen gave me on Thanksgiving Day one time. But it was so big that maybe Christy would think that I just hadn't gotten to that part.

"But here's the deal. Since we both believe that way, it makes it difficult to date. I mean, kissing and all. It leads to wanting more. And Kyle loves to kiss."

I didn't know what to say. I was trying to picture the preacher and Christy kissing and then walking away from each other. It wasn't working.

Christy went on. "And I really, really like to kiss him too."

"So, are you going to get married?"

"That's what's scary. I don't believe in getting married to somebody until you know them really well. I mean, it's not that I haven't wanted to be with people I hadn't known very long. But, oh, I don't know. I mean, he didn't ask me to marry him or anything but I think he's, well I guess it's what they used to call courting me. I think he is dating with the idea that we'll end up getting married."

"So, do you want to marry him?"

"I don't know." There was a long silence. "If it weren't for the sex thing I wouldn't even be thinking about such a thing after three dates."

Why was Christy telling me all her personal stuff? I don't know anything about it. Everybody I knew just had sex with whoever they wanted to. I probably would have had sex before Mike if it hadn't been for my mother's men. I fought off so many of them for so many years that I wasn't about to be with anybody that didn't fit my picture of a knight in shining armor.

Christy sighed. "I'm sorry to bother you with this. I know you don't have the answer. I just don't have anybody else to talk to about Kyle."

"Hey, you can talk to me about anything. But I sure can't help you with the purity stuff. I never knew a virgin before, I mean one that was a virgin on purpose."

"Gina, don't think I'm good or anything. There was a man once that I would have gone to bed with. But he wouldn't because…well it just wasn't good timing. Anyway, I guess I needed to think out loud. I was glad I was off work this week and now I'm wishing I had something to keep me busy."

"Hey, I'll trade with you. I'll stay home and you can go do my job."

"I think I'll pass but thanks anyway." Christy chuckled.

"Hey, what if we go early Saturday and look for something for Helen. They have sales after Christmas and I could put in…" I thought about my budget. With the leftovers Christy gave me packaged and in the freezer, I wouldn't have to buy many groceries for a while. "I could put in $20."

"That's a good idea, Gina. How about if I pick you up after lunch, around one thirty? That'll give us a couple of hours at the mall before time to go to the airport."

"Great!"

When I punched the red button, I thought about the question I asked myself earlier. Why didn't I take the cell phone with me? *Probably because my life with Christy seems way far separate from the factory. Which is silly since she got me the job.*

Clovers was a much better place to work than the first factory and on a cold morning like this I was glad it was only ten minutes from The Doll House. I crushed the last of the cigarette under my heel right before I walked through the door to clock in on Thursday morning. I was second in line which was unusual. I prided herself on being the first every morning. It was a man in line in front of me and when he turned, I got a surprise.

His eyebrows went up. "Gina Howard? What are you doing here?"

"I work here. But I haven't seen you before." It was Billy Benson from school. He was a big football star and I thought he went off to college on a scholarship.

He shook his head. "First day. I hurt my back and can't play ball anymore. Had to get a job. And I better get to it. See you later."

I was sorry for him. I was always glad to see anybody get to go to college, especially kids like Billy from my own neighborhood whose families couldn't send them and who weren't smart enough to get a scholarship on their grades.

I found myself daydreaming as I stamped the leather pieces going by on the conveyer belt. Why hadn't I applied for a scholarship myself? Life could have been so different. I'd thought about it. Several teachers tried to get me to apply, but Mike said it was stupid, that it wasn't what we wanted out of life. And I thought Mike was my life, the only good thing that ever happened to me. Now I wished I had sent in that application I filled out. But it was too late now. I'd missed my chance.

I jerked my attention back to the conveyer belt. Daydreaming was dangerous. If I didn't stamp in the right place and make spec and if I didn't get at least 750 per hour, I'd be in trouble. And I couldn't afford to lose this job.

At break when I went out to smoke, Billy was there lighting a cigarette too. He jerked his head for me to join him and walked away from the other smokers.

"So how long have you been here?"

"Just a couple of months."

"How's Mike?"

"Don't know. He left for California."

"Stupid."

"Stupid?"

"To leave something as gorgeous as you behind? Stupid."

I laughed. "Yeah, I thought so too. But who needs him?"

"I always thought you could do better."

I felt a twinge inside. Better than Mike? Nobody could have convinced me of that three years ago. Or three months ago. But maybe.

He put out his cigarette in the ash tray provided for the workers. As I leaned down to do the same, he put his hand on mine. "So what are you doing Friday after work?"

"N..nothing." I'd never gone out with a guy besides Mike. But Billy was really cute. And let's face it, I was a little jealous when Christy talked about the preacher last night.

"Wanna go get somethin' to eat? I got enough to get us a burger. I sold my books and have more than enough to get me through 'til payday."

We walked back in the main door before separating to our stations. "Okay, I guess."

He grinned and slapped me on the behind. "That's hot! See ya."

When I got home that afternoon, I called Christy. "Guess what?"

"What?"

"I've got a date tomorrow night."

"Awesome. Who with?"

"A guy I went to school with. He just started working at Clovers, had to quit college. Anyway, he's not as hot as your preacher but pretty warm."

"Gina! You're bad."

I laughed. "I wouldn't mind being just a little bad."

Christy's voice changed. "Oh, I forgot. You won't...? Oh, Gina, be careful."

"Don't worry. I'll be okay."

I went to the freezer and pulled out one of the neatly wrapped packages of roast beef and gravy. While it was warming on the stove I thought about what Christy said. "Oh, I forgot. You won't..." *She forgot that I wasn't a virgin like her. She's afraid I'm going to do it with Billy.*

When I finished cleaning up after supper, I went to the bedroom and got the Bible out of the dresser. When I was settled in the recliner, I opened it. The contents page showed lots of different names on it. I decided to start on page one again. But I'd do it right this time.

1:1"In the beginning (a) God created the heavens and the earth. (b)." At the side, note (a) said Jn. 1:1,2. I turned back to Contents. The first thing that looked like it might be that reference was Jonah 1:1 I turned to the page and read, "The word of the Lord came to Jonah (a) son of Amittai (b). Go to the great city of Nineveh (c) and preach against it, because its wickedness has come up before me."

That didn't seem like it had anything to do with in the beginning but maybe if I looked up that note in Jonah (a) Mt. 12:39-41. Back to the contents page. Mt. must be Matthew. Okay Matthew 12:39 – 41. Most of the words were in red. "He answered." Who's he? Looking back at the previous columns I figured it out. Jesus. Every time Jesus said something the words turned red. Okay, Jesus is talking about Jonah. Good. That reference made sense. I read on. "Jonah was three days and three nights in the belly of a huge fish..." *No way. But that's kind of interesting. Wonder if it's a fairy tale?*

Okay so Jesus was talking about Jonah but what did that have to do with in the beginning? I turned back to Jonah 1:1.Maybe it would explain it better in the next reference "son of Amittai (b) 2Ki 14:25. Back to Contents. Ah, that one's easy. 2 Kings. I read it silently and then read it out loud, hoping it would make more sense. "He was the one who restored the boundaries of Israel from Lebo (e) Hamath (a) to the Sea of the Arabah, (f,b) in accordance with the word of the Lord, the God of Israel, spoken through his servant Jonah (c) son of Amittai, the prophet from Gath Hepher."

I decided to give it one last chance. (a) referenced Nu. 13:21. From the Contents page, that would be Numbers. Closer to the front of the book. Maybe I was getting somewhere. "So they went up and explored the land from the Desert of Zin (d) as far as Rehob,(e) toward Lebo(b) Hamath.(f)."

I closed the Bible and looked at the clock. After thirty minutes I had gotten three words into the Bible, well ten if you counted the ones before the next reference (b) which I hadn't looked up. And the only thing I knew was that in the beginning when God created heaven and earth, it had something to do with somebody being in a fish's stomach. And that person had a daddy that came from somewhere with a lot of weird names.

The Bible gave me a headache.

I lit a cigarette and turned on the TV.

***

Christy

I pulled up in front of The Doll House and honked at exactly one thirty on Saturday afternoon. Gina came out with a cigarette in one hand and a purse in the other.

She didn't look happy. When I called earlier and asked about her date she said "not so hot", so between that and the look on her face I figured it must have been a fiasco.

She dropped the cigarette on the sidewalk before opening the car door.

"Hey." I smiled, hoping to get a smile out of her.

"Hey." She didn't smile back.

I waited while she buckled her seat belt. "I've been meaning to apologize. I didn't even think about you smoking all day on Christmas. You could have gone out on the porch or something."

She shrugged. "It's okay. I go a long time at work without a cigarette. If I couldn't stand it, I'd have said something."

We drove in silence for what seemed like a long time.

"Christy? I want to ask you something."

"What?"

"What do you do when guys try to put the make on you?"

I thought for a minute how to answer her. But the truth was the only response I could give her. "They don't."

"What do you mean they don't?"

"I mean that I've never had a guy try to do something other than kiss me."

I could see her shocked look out of the corner of my eye.

"Get outta here!"

"But it's true."

She slumped down. "Then it's probably me. Street trash. They just expect street trash to put out."

I wished I wasn't driving so I could put my arms around her. "Gina, you are not street trash. That guy give you a bad time last night?"

"Yeah. I mean he didn't try to rape me or anything but he was surprised that I didn't want to. And he kept trying to get me to 'admit it' as he said. But I didn't want to."

"Scum."

"Maybe. But he knew about me and Mike and I guess he just figured that I put out for anybody. I been thinkin' about it ever since you said that about we're not supposed to do it 'til we're married. I guess I'm just messed up now for good."

"No. God can change things. He'll give you a new beginning."

She shook her head. "Christy, I tried to read the Bible and I just can't do it. My mind can't seem to make sense of any of it."

"I know what you mean, Gina. I can't keep my mind on it sometimes either."

"No. I could keep my mind on it. It just didn't fit together."

"What do you mean?"

When she told me about trying to read every reference, and especially about reading Jonah instead of John, I couldn't help it. I had to pull off on the side of the road until I quit laughing.

She glared at me. "What's so funny?"

I snorted one last time. "Oh, Gina. You are something else. I don't know anybody that would go to all the trouble to look up all those references. Most of the time I don't even notice them."

"Shut up! I thought you had to for it to make sense."

I pulled back on the highway. And explained about John 1:1 "In the beginning was the word, and the word was with God and the word was God."

She nodded. "Okay. I see. It makes sense that way."

"But we should have told you to start in the New Testament. Genesis is okay but after that you get into a lot of stuff that doesn't make sense unless you know about Jesus."

"New Testament?"

I laughed. "The part where you start getting words that turn red. The first part's the Old Testament and that means old covenant. God made a deal with a guy called Abraham and that's the old covenant. And the New Testament is about Jesus and the new covenant."

"A new deal?"

"Yeah, I guess it is. A new deal." Gina was a sharp cookie. "Anyway, my favorite book of the Bible is the gospel of John. Why don't you start there."

"Gospel?"

"Gospel means good news. The stories about Jesus, the books

by Matthew, Mark, Luke, and John are called the Gospels."

She perked up. "I read some in the Matthew one. About the guy in the fish's stomach."

By the time we got to the mall, my Sunday School teacher time paid off and Gina knew a little more about the Bible.

There were a lot of sales but after an hour we still found nothing that seemed right for Helen. We picked up a really neat musical Christmas card on sale at 2/3 off the original price. But that was it. Until Gina had an idea.

"When I was in fourth grade the teacher was out sick for a long time." She laughed. "Who knows, in fourth grade it could have been three days or three months. Anyway, when she came back we had a lot of signs and some balloons telling her welcome back and stuff. She really liked it."

"And so would Helen. Great idea." We left the mall and went to the WalMart just a few blocks away.

Armed with heavy poster boards and markers, we marched into McDonalds and took up two tables for our project. Gina got everything out while I picked up coffee for both of us – decaf for me, regular for her. Then we started coloring. On one sign, "Merry Christmas" in large letters was surrounded by our artwork of Santas and snowmen. On the other "Welcome Home" and "We Missed You" nestled appropriately in smiley faces and frowny faces with teardrops.

By the time we finished the posters and the coffee, it was time to head out to the airport. We attached the balloons to the back of the signs with white duct tape.

"I hope she doesn't have a lot of stuff." Gina looked at the back seat full of posters and balloons.

I gasped. "I didn't think of that. But it's a big trunk. I'm sure it'll be okay." But I made a face and she laughed and crossed her fingers.

We pulled up right outside of the baggage claim area.

"Do you want to go in while I wait with the car?"

"But what about the signs?"

Gina was right. I circled the lot again and parked in short term parking. We each took a sign and walked into the terminal.

We didn't have long to wait until a crowd of people descended on the escalator.

"There she is!" Gina held up the "Merry Christmas" sign and I lifted the "Welcome Home" one.

Helen's face morphed into a huge smile and soon she was hugging us both.

"What a wonderful welcome. Aren't you two something?"

While we waited for her luggage, I asked about the rest of the evening. "If it's okay, we thought we might take you to dinner before we head home. Or are you too tired?"

"No. I'd love it. Where are we going?"

"Your choice, our treat."

***

Helen

I was afraid it would be a downer for the two younger women but I chose Red Lobster anyway. I just wasn't up to some yuppy place with loud music. But I had a surprise in store.

"Oh, Helen. I'm so glad," Christy said. "That was my Mom's favorite restaurant and the last time I was there was for lunch the day I left for England almost seven years ago."

I frowned. "I don't want to make you feel sad. We can go somewhere else."

Christy hugged me. "No, it doesn't make me sad. It will be good." She winked at me. "To go there with my new Mom."

I could feel the muscles in her shoulders relax. "Okay. But what about you, Gina?"

The younger girl looked startled for a second before she laughed. "I never went out to dinner anywhere with my mother so it won't make me feel sad."

"Then it will be fun to go to Red Lobster with my two girls." I wanted to make sure Gina felt included in the family allusions. And the glow on the girl's face made me glad that I did.

Gina said she'd only eaten shrimp once before but followed

Christy's example and got a mixture of scampi and fried shrimp. I got an order of scallops and a tossed salad. Gina went wild over the garlic cheese biscuits and I determined to ask for some in a take-away box to give her.

When we were all complaining over being too full, Christy pulled out a card from her purse and handed it to me.

"The Christmas Fairy Loves You" announced the fairy on the front of the card. When I turned the page, the notes of "When You Wish Upon A Star" began playing and I saw the message "May all your Christmas wishes come true" in sparkly letters. Christy and Gina had each signed it.

"How beautiful. You girls are too much. I don't have a thing for you."

"We didn't have anything for you either. We just did this today because we are so glad you are back." Christy smiled at me.

"I'm glad to be back." I looked around at the couples and families seated at the tables near us. Now I had a family too.

"Tell us about your trip." Gina acted really curious.

"Not much to tell. Nothing's really changed. I was glad to see my sister but we still got on each other's nerves. It's better over the phone. It was good that I went and saw her children and grandchildren. But to tell you the truth, they were all so busy with parties and their friends, they didn't have much time for an old-maid aunt."

"Their loss." Gina's narrowed eyes showed her indignation.

I laughed. "I didn't mind, really. I enjoyed just lying around in the guest room reading. And I took a walk every day." I looked over at Christy. "Did you walk?"

Chagrin showed on Christy's face. "No, and I'm afraid the scales will show it next week."

I remembered to ask for the biscuits and Gina was thrilled as she tucked them under her arm.

***

Gina

When I crawled into bed that night, I remembered the

thought that came to me when Christy mentioned going to Red Lobster with her mother. *I didn't go see Mam on Christmas Day.*

Chapter Twelve

2007

Gina

I went an hour without smoking on Sunday morning. It didn't make sense. If I could go for three hours at a time at work without a cigarette, and over four hours at Christy's on Christmas, why not more than an hour in my own home where there was no stress at all?

Then I remembered that with sleeping that made over eight hours without a cigarette. Yay, Me!

Maybe if I got some cigarettes with less nicotine and started timing myself and not letting myself smoke over one an hour, someday I could quit. But already I was thinking how I was going to time smoking on the walk to work and breaks. The rough one would be in the mornings. I usually had at least four cigarettes before clocking in.

Clocking in...that brought up the memory of Billy Benson and Friday night. I didn't tell Christy how he grabbed at me or how he sneered when I slapped his hand away. It wasn't going to be fun facing him in the morning.

But today I needed to decide whether to visit Mam or not. Maybe my mother wouldn't be drinking if I got there early enough. Sunday mornings weren't a busy time for her profession. I put down my coffee cup and went to get my coat. *Just do it. As they say.*

This time I put the cell phone in my pocket with the key to The Doll House and two of the five twenties that Helen slipped into my hand when she left us the night before. I put a pack of cigarettes and a lighter in the other pocket.

The smell on the steps wasn't so bad this morning. The mice must have rotted away. And the diaper smell was faint. When I knocked on the door, Mam responded immediately.

"Who's there?"

"It's me, Gina."

The unlocking sounds came and Mam pulled the door back. "What's going on with you? You disappear almost a year and then come twice in a week?"

I shrugged. "Christmas."

"Well come on in." Mam moved back and let me enter.

I could see the gin bottle on the counter next to the sink but hopefully that was from last night and Mam wasn't already into it today.

"You're up early."

"Yeah, and you're out early."

"Mam, I was worried about you the other day. You don't look well."

"I'm fine." But the words were followed by a cough. "Sassie got me some new cough medicine she says helped her and I think it's made me better."

I walked over to the counter and picked up the medicine beside the gin bottle. "It's just like all the other over-the-counter medicine, Mam. Why don't you go to a doctor?"

"And why don't you go to Hawaii?" It was as close as they ever came to joking. The Hawaii thing was her mother's response to any question that involved spending money.

"But Mam, if you get really sick you won't be able to earn any money. And then what will you do?"

"Die, I reckon. Who cares?"

"I do, Mam." And suddenly I realized I did care. Now that I was away from the day to day embarrassment of being Hazel

Howard's daughter, my mother seemed vulnerable and in need of protection.

I walked over to the kitchen area and began filling the sink with hot water.

"You took your doll." Mam followed me and sat down at the table.

"Yeah, that was okay, wasn't it?" I couldn't believe Mam noticed.

"Sure. Is that what you came back for?"

"No, I came to see you. And I wanted to ask you some things."

"Yeah about who your father is."

"Mam, this is important. I met a guy who looks a lot like me and I need to know if he's my brother. Did you have any kids before me and, like, give 'em up for adoption or something?"

"No, you're the only one."

"But his father could have been one of your clients."

"I guess so." She lit a cigarette and inhaled deeply. And coughed.

"Mam, are you sure you don't know?"

"Who is this guy?"

My heart beat faster. Mam hadn't answered. Maybe she really did know but didn't want to tell.

"He's a preacher."

Mam started laughing and ended up in spasms of coughing. I put the dish cloth down. "Mam, you've got to do something about that cough. Why don't you quit smoking?"

"Why don't pigs fly?"

I pulled out a chair and sat across the table from her.

"Tell me what you know about my father. I know there's something because of what you said on my birthday when I was five."

A look of alarm came on her face. "What?"

"You said I had my daddy's hair and when I asked who my Daddy was, you said you meant your daddy, my granddaddy. But I knew you were lying."

"Gina, there's a lot of stuff you don't need to know. Tell me what this preacher's name is."

"Kyle Martin. And I don't know anything about his daddy."

"Martin isn't it. Don't worry. But what are you doing with a preacher?"

"I'm not with him. He's dating my best friend."

"Best friend? When did you get a best friend?"

"When I had to get a job. She worked at the temp agency. She's nice, Mam. She's older than me. Her parents are dead and she lives in a real nice house. And she's been to England. And she has a friend, an older lady who invited us for Thanksgiving... Hey, that reminds me. How come I never met my grandparents? Are they still alive?"

Her mother sighed deeply. And coughed again. "Gina, why? Why now after all these years?"

"Because before I was a kid. Things just were what they were. But after I left I got to wondering about stuff like relatives. I mean I wondered when I was little but it seemed like there was never a right time to ask. And lately I just thought I'll make a time, whether it's right or not."

"You want to know about my family?"

I nodded.

"Okay, they kicked me out. They didn't want to have anything to do with me. Or you."

"They knew about me?"

"That's why they kicked me out."

Ouch. "Because you were pregnant?"

"Yep."

"I'm sorry."

"Wasn't your fault."

"I know. I just meant I'm sorry that happened to you. So that's why you ..."

"Became a hooker? No. That was later. Okay, you asked for it. I got pregnant and my parents wanted me to have an abortion. I said no. Now don't get me wrong. I've had abortions since but that was different. I thought that your daddy would marry me because of you. But he didn't. He dumped me. And told me if I tried to tell the welfare people he was the father, he'd get a bunch of his buddies to say they'd had me too. But it wasn't true."

"You mean he was the only one before me?"

She nodded. "Well, before I was pregnant with you. There'd been lots of others by the time you were born. They kept a roof over our heads and food on the table."

"Why didn't you get a welfare check and food stamps?"

"I just told you. You had to tell 'em who the father was and he said I better not say it was him. So I didn't apply."

"Oh, Mam. How awful. I'm so sorry."

"That's life."

"Who are your parents? Are they still alive? Do they live here?"

Mam shook her head. "Doesn't matter. They didn't need us and we don't need them."

I thought Mam needed somebody. Maybe I could find out some way.

"Did you ever go back? Did they know I was born?"

"No. Never went back. I haven't seen 'em for nearly 20 years."

"Maybe they changed their mind and tried to find you."

"Dream on."

"Did you have any brothers or sisters?"

"Hey, that's enough, okay?"

"Okay about your family but what about my father. I need to know who he was."

"He was scum. That's all you need to know."

"I want to know if he was related to my preacher."

"Your preacher? You going to church now?"

One Christmas party didn't make me a church goer but... "Yeah, I'm going with my friend, Christy."

Mam nodded. "That's good, Gina."

Shock! "I thought you didn't like church, Mam. You said they were all just a bunch of somethings, I forget."

"Hypocrites. A bunch of hypocrites. My parents were good

church people. Ha! They would have thrown the first stone for sure."

"Huh?"

"Never mind. I've just seen the bad ones, probably. There are some good church people."

"Yeah, Christy's one and Helen. And I think Kyle Martin and the people that go to his church. They had this Christmas party for poor kids. I helped."

Mam nodded again. "Good, Gina. I'm glad."

"But like I said, Mam, he's got my hair and eyes. Exactly."

"Your father was not named Martin. I promise." She lit another cigarette, the fifth since I walked in the door.

I got up and put the now dry dishes away. "You got anything for lunch?"

"Tomato soup in the cabinet."

"Mam, you can't live on gin and tomato soup."

"Peanut butter and crackers in there too."

"Mam, you ever eat Kentucky Fried Chicken?"

"Yeah, years ago. Why?"

"Christy brought some by my place once. She seemed surprised that I'd never eaten it."

"Too far away to walk and too expensive. Good, isn't it?"

"Yes, tell you what. Why don't you get dressed and I'll call us a cab and we'll go there for lunch. My treat." That felt good to say 'my treat' to my mother like Christy always did to me. It felt good to be able to do it.

"A cab? When did you get rich?"

"I got some money for Christmas, enough for a cab and lunch for both of us."

"Okay, you go on to the corner and I'll change clothes."

"Don't have to go to the corner. I got a cell phone for Christmas too." I pulled the phone out of my purse. "Oh, I guess I will have to go to the corner and use the phone book. I don't know the taxi number."

"Okay, be down in a minute."

When Mam went to the bedroom, I left the apartment and

walked to the phone booth. They said a cab would be there in minutes.

While I waited for the cab and my mother, I looked at the familiar surroundings, debris in the gutters, metal garbage cans overflowing with trash, cigarette butts smashed on the sidewalk. *Thank you, God that I'm out of here.* I wanted to call Christy and ask her to pray for the visit with my mother but it was church time. *Okay, God. I know you're there. You've proved it. Please let me help Mam.*

The taxi pulled up at the same time that Mam walked out the front door. We climbed in the back seat and I told the driver to take us to the nearest KFC.

My mother added in a tone I knew well, "And it better be the closest one too! I may not know the street address but I know where it is."

It was good to be driven through the streets. I thought this must be the way rich people feel when they have a chauffeur. When we pulled up in the parking lot, I looked at Mam and saw her nod. I paid the driver and gave him an extra dollar.

It seemed to me that my mother's head was held a little higher when she walked through the door of the restaurant.

"Hey look, a buffet." I was glad that Mam would be able to eat all the chicken she wanted.

"Can you afford it? We've got to take a taxi back too."

"I can afford it. It's our Christmas present, remember?"

Mam smiled. I paid for the buffet for both of us and we took our plates and headed for the steam tables. There was a sign at the end "No carry-outs from buffet." I thought back to the day I met Christy and the chicken breasts I put in my purse. I wondered if there was a sign there too and I just didn't notice.

When we got our drinks and settled in a booth, I smiled. "This is nice, Mam. I'm glad to be with you."

"Me too, Gina. I've missed you."

"You have?" I was surprised. My mother never seemed to enjoy my company back when I lived with her.

"Yeah, it gets awful quiet when you live alone."

I thought guiltily of The Doll House. I loved every minute of the quiet. "So how are Reva and the kids?" The downstairs neighbor was the one that I babysat for during the sophomore and junior years of school. I worked as a waitress during my senior year, until Mike took me in with him and said he "didn't want his woman to have to work."

"They're fine. I've kept the kids for her a few times."

"Really? I didn't think you like kids, Mam."

My mother gave a little snort. "It's not that I don't like 'em. I just never knew how to talk to 'em." When she finished her third chicken leg, she tilted her head and looked at me. "Do you remember why you call me Mam?"

"You told me to. You said I always had to call you Mam."

She snorted again and shook her head. "You used to call me Mama and then one day I asked you something and you said 'Yeah' and I told you to always say 'yes Ma'am'."

"I remember. It's the first memory I have. You said to call you Mam."

"That's what I mean about not knowing how to talk to kids. I was trying to teach you to say 'yes, ma'am' and 'no ma'am' to be polite but you thought I wanted you to call me Mam instead of Mama."

I stared at her. "Shut up! You mean you didn't want me to call you Mam?"

Mam shook her head. "No, I liked Mama but I guess I said it mean or something and scared you because you've called me Mam ever since."

I tried it out in my head. *Mama.* Then looked at my mother and shook my head. "I don't think I could go back to Mama. It doesn't feel right."

"No, I wouldn't expect you to now. So tell me about your job." Mam lit a cigarette and I got out my own. That was the nice thing about a buffet; you could smoke a cigarette and then go back for more food.

"It's factory work. You know I been thinking lately and wanted to tell you. You were right about Mike and right about I

148

should have applied to go to college when the teachers tried to get me to. I really messed up. I should've listened."

"Baby, I wouldn't have listened to me either if I was you. Big success I've made out of life."

I felt a lump in my throat. Was this the same woman I lived with for nearly eighteen years? The one who yelled and complained all the time? I wanted to reach across the table and hug her but it would be awkward.

Mam stubbed out the cigarette and got up. "I'm going to get some of that bread pudding."

I wanted to ask Mam more about her family but this visit was going well and I decided not to spoil it.

When Mam came back to the table, she was carrying two bowls of bread pudding. "I didn't know if you wanted any but here's a bowl." She placed the dessert in front of me.

"I remember this!" I smiled at the memory. "You used to make it sometimes when I was little. Only you put raisins in it."

Mam nodded. "Yeah. But the best part is the caramel and cinnamon with the bread. And this has the best part." She took a bite and smiled. "I love this stuff."

"Mam?" I hoped she wouldn't mind the question. "How old are you?"

Mam finished chewing and swallowed before she answered. "Thirty-six."

I couldn't make myself speak for a few seconds. *Only eight years older than Christy.* I did some rapid calculations. "I was two years old when you were my age?"

"Um hmm." She was scraping the last of the caramel sauce from the bowl.

I tried to imagine having a two year old child to take care of every second of every day all by myself. Without any financial help. Something inside twisted into a knot. "Oh, Mam. How awful."

She looked up from the bowl. "I made my bed, as my parents said, and I had to lie in it."

A fury at my unknown grandparents melted the knot of pity

for my mother. "I hate them for what they did to you."

Mam shrugged. "I used to hate 'em too. Stupid. Wastes energy."

"Mam, what's happened to you? You seem different from when I left last March."

"I don't know. I got real sad after you left. I mean I was glad you got out but I wished it had been to go to college, not off with that Mike guy. I always hated it that you had to stay locked in your room when the customers were there." She gave a short mirthless laugh. "I hated it even more when they saw you." She looked up with a pleading in her eyes. "Oh baby, I'm sorry for the life I made you live. I really hope you get a good one now."

Tears welled up. "Mam." I swallowed. "Thank you for giving me life. It sounds like you're the only person who wanted me to exist."

She nodded. "I'm getting some more pudding. Want some?"

I almost laughed. We were not used to deep discussions, or discussions of any kind for that matter. I guessed too much emotion made Mam want to eat. "No thanks. But I think I'll have another chicken breast."

When the taxi pulled into the street where Mam lived, I decided to splurge further. "You go on in, Mam. I'm going to have him take me home."

Mam got out onto the sidewalk. "Thanks, Baby. Merry Christmas."

"Merry Christmas, Mam."

I looked out the back window as the cab pulled away. Mam was coughing as she pulled a cigarette out of the box in her hand.

Chapter Thirteen

2008

Christy

I lifted the music box from my dresser and let it play it's reminder of hope again. Tonight I would see Kyle Martin. I decided to keep going to my own church on Sunday mornings and go to Living Word on Sunday nights every week. It made me feel not quite so...so smothered to not go to Kyle's church every service. My cell phone rang and I ran to the living room to get it. It was Gina.

"Hey, are you going to that convention center church tonight?"

"Living Word Church? Yes, do you want to go?"

"Yes."

"Great! They meet at six so I'll pick you up around fifteen 'til. Okay?"

"Okay. What should I wear?"

"At this church you can wear whatever — jeans, sweats, whatever you want."

"I don't need to borrow something from you?"

"Nope. Just come as you are." I heard Gina sigh. She was probably relieved about clothes.

"Thanks. I'll be ready."

When I hung up, I felt an excitement stirring in me. *Lord, you are working in Gina. Thank you!*

I pulled up outside The Doll House at exactly fifteen 'til six and Gina opened the door right away. She was more silent than usual on the drive.

"Are you okay, Gina?"

"Yeah." Her voice was more subdued than usual. "I went to see my mother twice this week. Monday and then again today. Hadn't seen her since I moved out last March. She seems different. I was mad at her all the time when I lived there. But this week I just...well, I just feel sorry for her."

I waited for her to continue.

"I know God helped me because you asked him to, you and Helen. And I want to ask him to help Mam. She needs it worse than me."

I just nodded. We pulled into the parking lot just as snow started falling. "I hate snow."

Gina' eyebrows raised. "I love it. It seems so clean and soft. I loved it when I was a kid. Everything was always so dirty when I looked out my window – until it snowed. And then it was all white and beautiful." She looked out the car window at the falling flakes with a sparkle in her eyes. "I always wanted to go downstairs and out the door to dance in the snow."

I opened the door and stepped out into the falling whiteness. "You make me feel ashamed, Gina. I've always seen it as wet and cold. I never even liked to make snowmen or go sledding or anything."

She lit a cigarette as we walked through the parking lot. "One last smoke." She grinned at me. "I wish I could quit but I'm trying to cut down."

She put it out before we walked through the doors. Mrs. Martin was there greeting people as they entered. Her face lit up when she saw us.

"Christy. Gina. I'm so glad to see you. Did you get wet from the snow?"

I laughed. "Not too wet. Gina loves snow."

"Kyle always did too. When he was just a little boy, around

three and four, I had to watch or he'd run outside to play in it without getting a jacket or anything." She chuckled. "Once I remember I looked out the window while I was washing dishes and there he was, dancing in the snow."

I looked over at Gina to laugh with her, but her face was pale and she had a strange look in her eyes. I thought I'd better not comment on the similarity.

The congregation was larger than the first time I attended just a month ago. That would make Kyle happy. We found a seat near the back because I thought Gina might be more comfortable there. It occurred to me that this might be the first time she'd ever attended a church. I leaned over and whispered to her. "Have you ever gone to a church before?"

She shook her head and then whispered back. "Just seen 'em on TV."

The praise team got up on the stage and the projector illuminated the large screen. Out of the corner of my eye I could see Gina watching intently. I wondered what she would think about the raised hands and exuberant worship. It didn't seem to surprise her but if all she'd seen of church was on TV she was probably used to that. I was the one who didn't really fit here.

When the music was over, Kyle got up on the stage and looked around at the congregation. His eyes lit up when he saw me and he grinned and winked. Right there in front of the whole congregation, he winked! I could feel my cheeks growing warm. Then he smiled at Gina and nodded before he bowed his head and led us in prayer.

"Tonight we're going to talk about the prodigal son and his older brother."

It was a good message. All about the Father's love for both sons and how he ran out to meet the returning sinner but also went out in the field to the pouting one who was always obedient. I think it was primarily geared toward those of us who had been Christians most of our lives. Feeling proud of myself was not my problem but I guess it was for a lot of others. I glanced over at Gina to see if she was bored but she was staring at Kyle Martin and appeared to be fascinated with every word.

When Kyle gave the invitation he said it was a twofold one. If there was anyone there who needed to repent and come home to the Father and receive a new life, they should come. But also if there was anyone who thought they were better than anyone else, they should come too, to repent and begin again a life of humility.

The musicians began playing and singing Just As I Am and Gina looked at me with widened eyes? "Can I go?"

"Of course you can go." I moved back a step and watched as she walked in front of me and down toward the front. Kyle spotted her right away and his smile made me think of the expression 'grinned from ear to ear'.

He reached out and took her hand and leaned down to say something. I saw her nod and whisper something back. He asked her something else and she answered. Finally he looked back out at the congregation.

"Gina Howard has come to ask Jesus into her heart. She did it once when she was a little girl watching a program on TV but she wants to do it again." He turned to Gina. "Gina, I believe with all my heart that it is because you asked Jesus into your life all those years ago that you are here tonight. He heard you then and has guided you to this moment when life will begin again. Do you believe that Jesus is the son of God?"

Gina nodded.

"Do you believe that He died for your sins?"

She nodded.

"Do you believe that God raised Him from the dead?"

She nodded again.

"Then repeat after me. I believe that Jesus is the Christ, the Son of the Living God, who took my sins on the cross, who died in my place so that I can have everlasting life. I receive Him now as my Savior and I make Him my Lord."

When Gina had repeated it all after him, he continued. "Do you believe that God sent His Holy Spirit to live in you?"

Gina tilted her head to one side. "I don't know what that

means."

He smiled. "Jesus said He would send the Holy Spirit to live with us and in us to guide us and give us power."

"That's good."

"Do you want to ask Him to come into your life too?"

"Well, if Jesus sent him to me, sure."

There was a low sound of amusement across the congregation and Kyle continued. "Repeat after me. Holy Spirit, I receive you in my life and give you permission to change me and make me like Jesus and guide me in all that I do. Amen."

When Gina had repeated it all, a smile, as big as Kyle's was earlier, spread across her face. He reached down and hugged her and Mrs. Martin went up and joined them and hugged her too. Kyle turned away and began speaking silently with a man who had gone forward.

Mrs. Martin brought Gina back toward where I was and I met them on the way. I hugged Gina. "I'm so glad. Now we are really sisters."

Gina was still grinning. "Sisters?"

I nodded. "Sisters in Christ. Forever."

***

Kyle

I was so frustrated. My relationship with Christy was not going like I wanted. Now that I'd found her, I wanted to marry her asap. When I thought about the planned trip to England in April, I groaned out loud. That meant a wedding would have to be put off until summer. It was February and I was ready to be married NOW! I was twenty nine years old and needed a wife.

Christy was going to make the perfect pastor's wife. She had great administrative skills, a heart of compassion for those less fortunate, and was obviously from a good background. And she was a virgin. But I shouldn't even think about that. It made the waiting worse.

I opened the door of the convention center and walked

through the hallway to the small office I lease. The guard nodded. I wished we had our own church building and believed that would happen within a year, two max. But in the meanwhile the convention center had worked out well for the two years I'd been here. I had the office whenever I wanted and the conference room on Sunday mornings and nights.

The familiar strains of Forgiven Again signaled that he had an incoming call on his cell phone.

"Hi, Pastor Kyle. It's Gina. I've been praying about what you asked me."

"About teaching the kid's class on Sunday mornings?"

"Yes, and I still think somebody else ought to do it. I don't know enough."

"But Gina, the kids love you and you can learn along with them."

"Christy would be so much better at it."

"But Christy isn't here on Sunday morning." I hoped I didn't sound as irritated as I felt about that subject. Christy still refused to leave her church. Once we were married that would change.

"And there's nobody else?"

"No. All the new kids who are coming because of the Christmas party need somebody who cares about them and understands them. You're perfect."

"Yeah, I guess because I grew up poor."

Uh-oh, I hadn't put that right. "That isn't what I meant." *But wasn't it?* "I meant that you have a real rapport with children. They love you." *That was true.*

"Well, okay then. If you're sure that's what God wants."

"I'm sure, Gina." I purposely made my tone gentle. Gina Howard seemed so fragile.

"Okay. But I'll miss being in your Sunday School class. I've really learned a lot."

"Tell you what. I'll go over the lessons with you in the car or by phone or something." Mom or I always picked Gina up on Sunday mornings before Sunday School. Christy brought her to the night service.

"I wouldn't want to be a bother."

"No bother." And it was true that Gina was an eager student and any teacher would welcome the opportunity to help her. "Aren't you working today?"

"I'm on my break. I just wanted to let you know I trust you and if you think I'm supposed to do this, I will."

When we hung up, I opened the ledger and looked once again at the figures set aside for building. But I couldn't seem to concentrate. Finally I closed the book and picked the phone back up. My mother answered on the first ring.

"Mom, I know I'm a grown man but I need help."

I could almost hear a smile in her voice. "All grown men need help. What kind of help do you need?"

"I want a romantic way to propose to Christy. Something different and that she won't be able to resist." I had to wait while Mom laughed for several seconds.

"Sorry, son." She cleared her throat. "Let's see. I need to think about that for a while. A unique and irresistible proposal? Hmm. I'll call you back when brilliance strikes."

I hoped she called back soon. I had less than six weeks before Christy left for London.

***

Gina

I put the phone back in my pocket and looked at the cigarette in my hand. *Okay, God. I'm still waiting for you to take this smoking thing away. I can't teach kids if I smoke. So it's time. Please?*

I took one last drag and put the cigarette out in the ashtray. As I leaned over I felt someone bump up against me.

"Well, if it isn't the Ice Princess." Billy Benson's voice was taunting as usual. He'd been calling me that since our date back in December, but I always just ignored him. It seemed lately though that a Christian shouldn't act like that.

I turned around and smiled. "Hi, Billy." The shocked look on his face almost made me laugh. "Everything going okay?"

He ground out his cigarette. "Yeah. You?"

I nodded. "Everything's great. See you later." As I walked through the door, I could feel his stare on the back of my neck.

***

Christy

I loved my job when I could place people in temp positions, and hated it when I couldn't. But that failure no longer devastated me. The feeling that I was personally responsible for all the evils in the world had long since gone and my counselor dismissed me from therapy at the end of January. I knew he was right and I've been healed.

I had a family again with Helen and Gina. And there was Kyle.

Our relationship was intensifying and that made me uncomfortable, but as my therapist and I agreed, this kind of discomfort had nothing to do with my emotional breakdown. It was just a normal reaction to the pressures of romance.

The phone rang and I answered it. "Hunt's Temp Agency. We hunt the jobs for you." It was Kyle. I never gave him my cell phone number; and I hoped he didn't know I had one. Gina thought that was weird when I told her not to mention it. But she agreed to keep my secret. I didn't know how to explain to her that I needed my privacy, especially since I told her and Helen to call me anytime.

"Hey Beautiful."

I couldn't help but smile. He always made me feel special.

"Hey back."

"You want to have lunch?"

I looked at the clock. "Okay, why not? Where?"

We met at the buffet where I took Gina the first day we met. That seemed like years ago even though it was less than six months. She and Helen and I were so close that I couldn't imagine life without them.

"This time, I'm going to remember to pay them for Gina's extra food."

"By the way, she called and agreed to teach the children's Sunday School class."

I was glad. Gina was a natural with children. Back when I taught Sunday School it was okay but I was more interested in the lessons than the children. Gina obviously delighted in kids.

Kyle reached across the table and took my hand. He put it up to his lips and kissed my fingers. I laughed and pulled away from him. "What was that all about?"

He looked at me with eyes that made me melt inside. "You are so beautiful. I want to put my arms around you and kiss you but decided that wouldn't be appropriate here and now."

"Right you are." I looked around to see who was at the surrounding tables.

"So, what do you want to do Saturday night?"

What was wrong with me? His assumption that we had a date irritated me. But I refused to let the irritation show.

I smiled at him. "What do you have in mind?"

"What I'd like is to watch a movie at your place while snuggling on the couch." He wiggled his eyebrows at me.

I kept the disgust from showing on my face. That eyebrow gesture was gross and implied stuff I was not ready to think about. Yes, when he kissed me I wanted him to keep on and there were times I wanted more. But over lunch?

I smiled and scooted my chair back. "I'm going to pay for that lunch of Gina's."

His eyebrows went up again but this time in surprise. "Now?"

"While I think of it."

I breathed deeply while I walked to the cashier's station. *Just be calm, Christy. You don't have to do anything you don't want to do.*

Trying to pay for an extra lunch five months ago proved to be an impossibility. The cashier called the manager and when I explained about the chicken breasts, he laughed. "Don't worry about it, lady. Happens all the time."

When I returned to the table, Kyle asked quietly, "Take care of it?"

"They wouldn't let me pay, but yes, it's taken care of. Now I won't feel guilty."

He wiped his mouth with the corner of a napkin. "Christy, I'm sorry I upset you. I shouldn't have suggested snuggling. It's like when I asked if I could kiss you. I'm just stupid. Those things should happen naturally, not be planned."

The repentance in his voice and eyes touched my heart. This time I reached out and touched his hand. "It's okay, Kyle. I don't know what's wrong with me. I..." *Okay, Lord, here goes.* "I think it's because I believe it's dangerous. We're Christians, you're a pastor and we don't need to be acting like teenagers. Don't get me wrong, I love it when you kiss me. You know that. But..."

He nodded. "You're right. It is dangerous and I should be kicked for putting both of us in a position to be tempted." He tilted his head and by sheer will power made me look him directly in the eyes. "I hope that will change soon. I want us to be in a position where to want each other is not temptation."

I looked down at my plate and pulled my hand back. "I don't know what I want."

He reached across the table and lifted my chin with his finger. "I know what I want and I'm going to work very hard to make you want it too."

I smiled but there was a heaviness in my stomach that had nothing to do with food.

Chapter Fourteen

2008

Gina

After work I walked toward Beckley Street and hoped Mam would be free, and not drinking. I pulled the cigarettes out of my pocket and then put them back. The last cigarette I'd smoked was while I was on the phone with Kyle Martin that morning. I wasn't going to say I'd quit, but I was going to cooperate with God if He wanted to give me the temperance to not smoke. Pastor Kyle taught on Temperance last week. He said some translations call it self control but it's not. If it was *self-control*, it wouldn't be a fruit of the Spirit. It's Spirit control, he said, and our job is to relax and let Him do His job of controlling.

When I started climbing the steps, I could hear yelling coming from my mother's apartment. I ran the rest of the way and pounded on the door.

"Mam? Are you okay?" The yelling stopped. But I kept on pounding the door. "Mam? Let me in." There was silence. Then I heard locks begin to click. Soon the door opened and my mother stood there - with blood smeared on her face.

I pushed past her. "Where is he?" Then I saw the open window. When I looked out, a man was climbing off the last rung of the fire escape and onto the street. I yelled as loud as I could. "And don't come back. You hear me? Don't you dare come back here. Ever! In Jesus name!" *Whoa! Where did that come from?* Obviously from listening to Kyle Martin teach about the Christian's authority in Christ.

Mam was sitting on the couch sobbing. "Mam? What was that all about?" I sat down and pulled her close. "Mam. I'm so sorry he hurt you." I pushed away and looked closer. "It's just a cut on the lip. I don't think we need to go to the hospital." I pulled my mother back again and held her tightly.

I thought Mam was sobbing harder but realized she had started laughing. "What's funny?"

Mam grabbed a tissue and wiped her eyes. "You. Yelling Jesus at that guy." She laughed out loud. "I'll bet that was a first. Not many people who go to hookers get Jesus sicked on 'em."

I realized my own hands were shaking but I was able to give a short nervous laugh. "Well, he deserved it."

She relaxed against my shoulder and the protectiveness that started growing in me last December filled my whole chest cavity. "Mam, we got to get you out of here."

"There's nowhere for me to go."

I drew a deep breath and thought of The Doll House. My chest tightened with protest at the thought that came to my mind. But I wouldn't be alive if Mam hadn't fought for me.

"You can move in with me. Forget the men. What do they do except keep this roof over your head and food on the table. I've got a roof and food." I swallowed the lump in my throat at the thought of giving up my bedroom. "It's just got one bedroom but you can have it and I'll sleep in the recliner."

My mother's eyes widened. "But..." She stopped and stared at me.

"But nothing. You had to do this, or thought you did, to take care of us. But that's over. I've got a job and am making pretty good now that I've been there four months. And we could probably find you a job and one day you can get your own place again. But for right now, Mam, let's just do it."

"You mean it, Baby?"

I swallowed again. "Yes, I mean it." The determination in my voice was as much to convince myself as Mam. "Will you?"

My mother laughed. "Yeah, I guess I will." Then she got a frightened look. "But, what about cigarettes and..."

"Gin?"

Mam nodded slowly.

"Okay, here's the deal. I'll buy your cigarettes. I've quit and so I won't notice the extra expense." *Okay Lord, I said it – I've quit. Now it's up to you.* "But you'll have to give up the gin. We can't afford it."

Mam looked down at the floor for almost a minute. "Okay, deal. I've thought about going to AA anyway."

I was shocked. "You have?"

"Yeah. A street preacher who comes down at the corner sometimes told me I ought to try it."

"Then it's settled?"

Mam burst into tears and her arms went around me. She cried and cried until I could feel that my own shirt was wet. All I knew to do was pat her shoulder.

Finally the storm of tears subsided and Mam blew her nose. She stood up and looked around. "Gina, what will we do with my furniture?"

Uh oh. I hadn't thought about that. "Well, hmm. Let me call my friend, Christy. Maybe she'll have an idea."

"I don't want to be a bother to your friend."

"Mom, she would want me to call her. She's a real Christian."

"So are you, Baby."

I looked at her and saw more tears in her eyes. "Thank you, Mam. That's what I want more than anything."

I went down the stairs and outside to make the call. I wasn't sure if there was better reception out there but it was an excuse to talk out of Mam's hearing.

"Oh, Christy, what have I done?" I told her about the man and the offer.

"You couldn't do any differently, Gina. And we'll get through this somehow."

When we'd finished talking, I stuck the phone in my pocket

and went back upstairs. "Okay, let's get busy. We've got to decide what you want to take and what we need to store. Christy says she knows a place where we can store it free."

Mam's eyes were slightly glazed. Probably in a state of shock. She'd lived in this apartment ever since I could remember. "Mam, do you have a lease?"

She shook her head. "No, just pay every week. Gina, this feels scary."

"I know. It feels scary to me too. But it's not as scary as thinking about you getting beat up. Or worse. I'm so glad I came by."

"Me too." Mam started crying again.

"You go in your room and see what you want to take to my place. I'll look through the kitchen."

I wished I could just throw everything out but Mam would need it when she got her own place.

***

Christy

Once again Kyle Martin and I drove to Beckley Street. This time to move Hazel Howard's furniture. It was a harder job than when we moved Gina's. There were a lot more things but the worst part was the stairs. And then there were the steps to the basement at my house. I was pretty bummed when I smelled the couch and some of the other stuff. They reeked of stale cigarette smoke, years of it. But I'd given my word, so into my basement it went.

Gina's bed from when she was a kid went to The Doll House and was put up in the living room. They also kept a few boxes of personal items, kitchen utensils, and Hazel's clothes.

Hazel was a shock. I never met a prostitute before, well not that I knew about. She had sandy hair and hazel eyes and looked a lot more normal than Gina. Well, more normal than Gina did right now. I was the only one who knew that would change soon.

Shortly after Christmas Gina confided in me that her hair was not straight and black, but dyed and straightened. She said it was really curly and auburn, just like Kyle's. I couldn't believe it at first but found out soon that it was true. We came up with a game plan and she switched from a permanent hair color to one that washed away with every shampoo. The color was almost grown out now and we giggled like school girls anticipating the night we walked into church with her new look, which was actually her old look, the real Gina. I wondered what Kyle would think.

I was grateful for Kyle; he treated Gina like a little sister and I knew part of it was because I considered her a sister. Helen and I still walked at the track every day and I admitted to myself I'd resent it if Gina joined us there, but most of the time I was happy to share Helen with her. I wondered how Hazel moving into The Doll House would affect us all.

As we were stacking the last of the things into my basement, I mentioned to Hazel that I'd been to Beckley Street once with Kyle to see a street preacher, Jim Sutton.

Her face lit up. "He's the one who led me to the Lord."

I turned at the clatter behind me. Gina had dropped a box of pans.

"Shut up!" She was staring at her mother. "You're a Christian?"

Hazel nodded. "Well, I want to be. I asked God to give me a new life."

"When?" Gina was clearly shocked.

"Right around Thanksgiving. But I'm afraid it didn't take because I kept on ...you know, just kept on with life the way it was."

"But, Mam, I could tell a difference the first time I came back. Something had changed."

Hazel shrugged. "I didn't feel any different. Or act any different."

"But look at you now. Look at us now, Mam. Life is going to be all different. God is working." When Hazel turned back to set one box on top of the other, Gina rolled her eyes toward heaven and mouthed the words, "No wonder."

I guessed she was talking about her confusion after she offered to share her home with Hazel. And saying that God led her to make the offer.

Lord, you really are an awesome God.

***

Gina

Mrs. Martin was waiting in the lobby that Sunday night when we walked in. She smiled at us all and then looked behind us.

"Christy, where's Gina?"

At that I laughed out loud. "It's me, Mrs. Martin."

The lady's mouth dropped open. "Gina? I can't believe it. What have you done to yourself?"

Christy laughed. "She's gone natural. We've been planning this for months."

"But just this morning, she had black straight hair."

We explained about the dye and straightening and Mrs. Martin laughed with us. "I'm going to have to desert my post and go to see Kyle's reaction." Then she turned to Mam. "And you must be Gina's mother?"

"Yes, Ma'am. Hazel Howard."

"We're glad to have you, Hazel."

She followed us into the conference room and waved to catch Kyle's attention. He made his way toward us.

Without a smile to give away the joke, Christy said, "Kyle, I want you to meet my friend." She pointed at me.

I held out my hand and Kyle took it. But when he looked at me, he did a double take. "Wha...Gina? Is that you?"

Before long, several regulars of the congregation were gathered around making over the new me.

But I spotted one person pouting and glaring through narrowed eyes.

"Shelby? It's me, Gina." I broke through the crowd and went toward the child.

Shelby shook her head violently. "No, you not Gina."

166

I knelt down in front of the girl. "Yes, I am. And look, now I have hair like Shelby's. I think you have the prettiest hair in the world so I wanted mine to be just like yours."

Shelby seemed to think it over and then nodded. "Okay, Gina. Shebby loves you."

I picked her up and buried my nose in the soft auburn curls. "And Gina loves Shebby too."

Pastor Kyle walked up to us. "Shelby, starting next week, Miss Gina is going to be your teacher."

The little girl beamed and hugged me more tightly.

During the service, I watched my mother out of the corner of my eye and was glad to see her captivated with the message. *Thank you, Jesus.*

It had only been two days since we moved Mam into The Doll House and I had to admit there were times when I mourned my lost privacy, but the joy on my mother's face when she saw the little house and the furnishings made up for my own personal grief.

This night the invitation was for people who wanted to be set free from addictions. I started to go up and ask prayer for smoking. *No, Lord. I believe you've already set me free. It's been three days. Thank you.*

Mam stepped across in front of me and went up toward the front. I couldn't hear what was said between them, but after he prayed, Mam's face looked as joyful as an angel.

***

Helen

I lay down the diary and stared into Sander's eyes.

It was the only picture I owned of him.

"I'm going to England in two weeks," I said aloud. "I used to dream about going there with you. Away from everything and everybody we knew."

In my daydreams and fantasies over the years, I'd imagined us in various settings free to laugh and talk and hold hands. But never any more than that. I couldn't even imagine us kissing. I tried many times to picture us getting married but it just wouldn't work. I figured that was God's way of answering Sanders' prayer to keep our love pure. He wouldn't let me pollute it even with daydreams.

I sighed. I wished God would take the love away. Or did I? I'd loved Sanders for so many years that it seemed like I wouldn't be myself without the love for him. *Forty years. That's a long time.*

The phone rang and I put the picture back in the drawer. It was Christy.

"Happy Saint Patrick's Day." The cheerful voice drew me back to a present that was good, even without Sanders.

I laughed. "Happy Saint Patrick's Day back. What's going on?"

"Helen, I've told a lie."

"Oh?" That wasn't like Christy.

"I told Kyle that you invited Gina and Hazel and me to your house for Easter." She paused a minute. "He wanted me to go to church with him and his mother Sunday morning and out to dinner afterwards."

"And you don't want to? Or do you feel obligated to spend the holiday with us?"

Christy sighed. "Honestly, I'd rather spend it with you."

"Then you didn't lie. You just anticipated the truth. Will you and Gina and Hazel come to my house for Easter dinner?"

Christy laughed. "Oh, Helen, I love you! You're the best. And yes, I would love to come and I'm sure that Gina and Hazel would love to come too. I'll ask them and get back with you."

"How does Hazel like her job?"

"She loves it. She's like a new person. Well, I guess she is a new person. She and Gina seem to be forgiven and washed clean from the past a lot better than I have." She quickly went on to explain. "I don't mean God gave more to them. I mean they receive better than I do."

"And me." I thought of my musings before the phone rang.

"Okay, that's settled. Thank you. Now, what do you want me to bring Sunday?"

"Most people bake ham for Easter dinner. I wonder why? I've never thought about that before." I wracked my brain but couldn't remember ever hearing the Easter ham tradition discussed.

"Maybe because pork was forbidden in the Old Testament, people celebrate the New Testament with ham?"

I laughed. "Maybe. But I am not a big ham fan, forbidden or not. What about you?"

"Not really. My Daddy had high cholesterol and we never had pork at home." Christy chuckled. "Mom said he used to sneak and eat bacon and eggs when he got away from her. But they never mentioned ham."

"Well, then, what would you like?"

"Why don't I ask Gina what they want?"

"Great idea. Let me know."

It was just a few minutes before Christy called back. "I've created a monster. They want Kentucky Fried Chicken."

I laughed again. "Okay, sounds good to me. Tell you what, we'll cook the vegetables and dessert ourselves but pick up the chicken."

"Sounds like a plan. So what do you want me to bring?"

"What about that oriental salad you made that time we ate at your house. That was great."

"Nappa Salad. Okay. What else?"

"Green beans?"

"I'm buying the chicken too. So that will be my part. Chicken, green beans, and the salad. You can do dessert and whatever else you think we need."

"What time will you all be here?"

"What time do you want us?"

"I'll get home from church around twelve thirty. What about one?"

"Perfect. See you then. Well, I'll see you tomorrow at the track."

When I hung up the phone, I stood still for a minute smiling. Things really were better now about Sanders. There was a resolution of sorts that had not been possible earlier. Well, maybe not resolution but resignation.

***

Gina

We had a great time on Easter. I was surprised at the way Mam talked with Helen about the upcoming trip to England. She didn't act as though a trip to the United Kingdom was a big deal. Mam was surprising me in a lot of ways these days. The spunk that caused a seventeen year old to keep her baby was back again and something else was there too. A refinement that I suspected was due to family background. One day I was determined to find out the details of Mam's past.

That night we talked Helen into going to Living Word church with us. It occurred to me that Helen was probably somewhere around the age of Mam's mother, my own grandmother. But she and Mam sure seemed to get along well.

On the way to the convention center Mam and Christy both warned Helen that the service would be very different from what she was used to. Mam? How did she know? I was realizing that I didn't know much about my mother at all.

Mrs. Martin greeted us enthusiastically and acted especially glad to meet Helen. "Christy's told us so much about you. You are truly a Godsend to her."

"As she is to me." Helen put her hand on Christy's shoulder.

We walked back to the conference room and Christy led us to four seats on the back row. Since I knew now that Christy preferred sitting closer to the front, I figured she always sat in the back with new guests to make them more comfortable.

I loved the praise music and joined in enthusiastically, and noticed Mam did too. Christy was always a little more subdued than the others and I figured it was because she went to a regular church. The sermon that night was different from Pastor Kyle's usual messages. He talked about covenants and I learned a lot but it didn't hit me as personally as usual.

"In conclusion, I want to warn you that the invitation tonight will be different. I'm not issuing an invitation to everybody present."

I thought that was weird but could tell that it definitely got everyone's attention.

"This is an invitation to a covenant. But it's the covenant of marriage. And I'm inviting just one person to join me in it." With that Pastor Kyle handed the microphone to one of the praise team and left the platform. He walked down the aisle and I saw his mother's face when he passed her and she turned to follow his progress. She looked horrified.

***

Christy

I couldn't believe my ears or my eyes. Kyle Martin was marching down the space between the folding chairs that served as an aisle in that church that didn't look like a church. And coming toward me.

No, Lord. Please, let this be a nightmare so I can wake up.

But Kyle kept coming until he reached the end of the row where we were sitting. Gina and Hazel moved their chairs back and Kyle knelt down in front of me.

"Christy, will you do me the honor of becoming my wife?" He grinned up at me and winked.

Tears were prickling my eyes and wanting to spring forth. I wanted to spring backwards and run away as fast as I could. I could feel the eyes of the entire congregation on me. Why weren't the singers doing their job? The silence was smothering.

Kyle smiled at me expectantly but I just stared at him. The silence continued. I could see his smile begin to waver. I had to do something.

I leaned over to whisper in his ear. "Kyle, I can't, not now. I'll...I'll tell you as soon as I get back from England. I promise."

When I sat back in my chair, I saw that his smile had faded. But he quickly replaced it with another as he stood up. He took my hand and pulled me up front with him. When we passed Mrs. Martin, our eyes met and I could see pity for me there.

Kyle led me onto the platform and took his mike back from the musician. "I think most of you know Christy Simpson. She is leaving for a trip to England in less than two weeks and when she returns we will have an announcement to make." Then he leaned down and kissed me on the cheek. I smiled at him. And hoped that the desire to slap him was not written all over my face.

It must not have been, because the congregation clapped and cheered. Except for Mrs. Martin. And Gina and Hazel. And Helen. They were all standing with their heads down when I looked out over the crowd.

When I pulled in the driveway after taking Gina and Hazel home, Kyle's car was already there. Once again he apologized to me, as we sat side by side on the couch in my living room.

"I asked Mom for a way to propose that would be irresistible and she gave me an idea but…"

"And what was her idea?"

"She said I should hold up a sign when we met you at the airport on your return from England. You know like people do when they're waiting for somebody they don't know? That I should have a sign asking if you'd marry me. She said I shouldn't say anything before the trip."

I waited for him to explain why he didn't take his mother's advice.

"But I was afraid you'd get over there and meet somebody else or something. I wanted you to be committed before you left."

I sighed. "Kyle, your mother was right. I wanted this trip to be just fun, not to have to make any life decisions while I'm there."

He repeated, "I'm sorry."

"And I was so embarrassed. If that was your idea of irresistible, you know nothing about women. That was the closest I've ever come to telling a friend I never want to see them again."

"A friend? Is that all I am to you, Christy?"

"I don't know, Kyle." And I didn't. I used to love the way he was so attracted to me but it increasingly made me uncomfortable. I loved to kiss him, but that increasingly made me uncomfortable too. But he still made me laugh and I enjoyed his sermons. I was very confused about my feelings toward Kyle Martin. "But I promise I'll tell you when I get back."

He nodded slowly and the sadness in his eyes made my heart hurt for him. I reached over and touched his hand. "I do care about you, Kyle. I care a lot."

"Oh, Christy." He pulled me into his arms and once again his kiss made me forget everything but the moment.

Chapter Fifteen

2008

Christy

I was in for a shock at the airport because I'd not flown since the catastrophe on 9/11/01 and didn't realize that you now had to take your shoes off and walk through security barefoot.

I hoped nobody got insulted but the words just kind of flew out of my mouth.

"You mean, walk there where everybody else walks, even people with athlete's foot and stuff?"

The security officer nodded solemnly. No humor at all, and yes he meant it.

I looked around for a reprieve - some knight in shining armor perhaps to swoop me up on his horse and carry my bare feet across the germ ridden barrier - but none was forthcoming. I rolled my eyes toward heaven and took the plunge. Inside the little walkthrough booth, a short blast of air attacked my skin. Travel had certainly changed.

When Helen joined me on the other side, we collected the luggage and headed toward our gate, me beginning to feel germs permeate my skin and crawl inward. We didn't have long to wait before the shuttle plane arrived to take us from Cincinnati to Chicago where we'd board the international flight to Heathrow. When we got to O'Hare, I was filled with excitement, remembering the departures on my earlier trips to England. And the excitement finally drove away my obsession with feet.

Finally we were aboard the jet and on our way. I couldn't sleep on the overnight flight, never could, but read while Helen dozed off and on most of the hours between midnight and six Kentucky time.

When we arrived in London it was nearly noon there and we took a taxi to South Kensington. We had rooms booked at the hotel where I stayed seven years earlier. I was starting to feel a little light headed from lack of sleep but didn't want to miss a single hour in my favorite city. It was Samuel Johnson who said, "When a man is tired of London, he is tired of life; for there is in London all that life can afford." I certainly found that to be true in 2001 and had to remind myself that I'd loved the city four years earlier also. It wasn't just David that made it exciting.

Okay, you are here to replace London memories. Stop thinking about David. The first place we headed was the Museum of London that was mentioned in a book Helen read about the city.

It was wonderful fun those weeks showing Helen the places that she'd longed to see. I loved playing tour guide as we visited the Tower and Westminster Abbey and Madame Tussaud's Wax Museum. But Helen and I also went to some places I'd never been, like John Wesley's home and church in the City Road. I got a kick out of the chair with springs that John Wesley used to bounce on for exercise the days he couldn't get out and ride his horse. Helen tried it. The whole tour group laughed at her boldness, and some others followed her example and bounced on the horse/chair.

There was also a small electricity machine in that room and I tried it because the guide said Wesley believed the little shocks were good for you. The electrical current was barely perceptible and I found it hard to believe it could cause anything beneficial, or harmful either for that matter. We met a lady from Africa who was studying nursing in England. She came on a pilgrimage to tour the house and church because it was the Methodists who provided the school and education when she was a child. One of my favorite things about traveling was to meet people and hear their stories.

We discussed going to Scotland but never made a decision. However on our fifth day in England, on our way back to the hotel from the church service in City Road, Helen decided for us.

"Christy, I want to go to Scotland. I'll probably never come back here and I'd really like to see it, especially Edinburgh. I used to have a big interest in Mary, Queen of Scots."

We kept our rooms in South Kensington for the three nights we'd be gone, and the desk clerk was very kind to help us book rooms in Edinburgh for that time. I loved the train ride north on Monday and we both especially loved talking with ordinary people who used the trains for their daily transportation.

We stayed at a quaint little bed and breakfast inn just a block from the Firth of Forth. We were tired when we got settled in so we decided to skip the city until morning. Because the reservations were made so close to arrival date we had to share a room, but there were two beds and we didn't mind for just a few days. It made me think of Gina and Hazel cooped up in The Doll House together for months now. I was beginning to realize what a private person I am. Maybe it had to do with being an only child. I wondered if Gina felt invasion of privacy the way I did.

Helen and I strolled along the shore walk to a restaurant that looked like a doll house itself from the spot where we began. The tiny garden yards of the houses there faced out on the firth and I couldn't help but envy those who lived there.

Helen breathed deeply. "This is so good. I love being here. I feel free."

I thought that was a strange statement but something in it resonated with me. Free.

"You know, I feel free too. No pressures."

"Christy, what pressures do you feel?" She stopped walking and looked out over the water. "Although I think I know the answer."

"Yeah, Kyle Martin. Helen, I hate it that he's expecting an answer when we get back. I find myself thinking stuff like – in fourteen days we have to go back and I have to give him an answer. I may change my mind but right now I don't ever want to go back."

Helen leaned over to hug me. "Tell you what. Why don't you stop thinking about that decision completely. Let's see...,maybe give yourself permission to make up your mind on the trip home?"

"That sounds wonderful. Okay. I'll do it." I held up my right hand, palm outward. "I refuse to worry about the future at all. I will live in the moment. And I will enjoy our time without letting any shadows spoil a single second."

Helen laughed and we continued our walk beside the water.

It was strange to sleep in the same room with another person. I hadn't done it since my sophomore year at college. Upperclassmen could have private rooms and my parents made sure I got one the minute it was allowed. Helen snored slightly but after a few minutes of playing my word puzzle game, I too dozed off. I woke up long enough to turn off the lamp on the bedside table.

The next morning we had breakfast in a cute little dining area with teapots all around a ledge at the top of the walls. I was disappointed that we were seated at a table for two because I was hoping to be at a larger table and meet some tourists from other places.

Helen filled me in on the history of Mary, Queen of Scots, while we walked the royal mile between Edinburgh castle and Holyrood House. Even though Helen, who was a fan of sorts, was telling the story, it seemed to me that the Scottish Queen was not very bright. She let her emotions rule her and ended up losing everything, husband, child, kingdom. But then, wasn't I a fine one to judge?

On Wednesday we took the train to Sterling and saw the castle and the William Wallace monument. It was neat to see Braveheart's sword. It was an inch taller than I am – five and a half feet long. It looked too big to pick up.

Thursday we spent more time in Edinburgh before heading

back to London. And for the rest of our time in England we took day trips out from the city – to Dover, Stratford-upon-Avon and Anne Hathaway's House, Canterbury, Warwick, Windsor, and Bath. We even took a bus tour to Stonehenge and Avebury. The days flew by.

I was so glad that we went new places. David no longer haunted England for me. I would have lots of new memories to replace the ones with him. But we didn't go to Hever Castle in Kent.

***

Gina

I got in the front seat with Kyle while Mam climbed in the back beside Mrs. Martin. I felt funny doing that but Pastor Kyle said it made sharing Sunday School lessons so much easier.

"When are you going to learn to drive, Gina?"

"You sound like Christy!" I sighed. "I guess I'm going to have to learn some time."

"I'll be glad to teach you."

"You would?"

"Sure, isn't that what big brothers are for?"

I laughed. "I guess you will be my big brother when you and Christy get married. She and I are sisters forever."

"Right. Hey, why don't you go take your test and get your permit while she's gone and surprise her when she gets home."

"That's a good idea. I've got some time I could take off work. But aren't you supposed to study first? I don't have anything to study."

"Tell you what," he said. "Why don't I go pick up a manual and find out the test times and then you could do it as soon as you're ready."

"That would be so nice, Pastor Kyle. Thank you."

"No bother. And why don't you just call me Kyle – seeing that we're going to be family and all?" He winked at me. And I laughed.

"Okay."

And he was as good as his word. Monday afternoon when I got home from work there was a Kentucky Driver's Manual on the porch beside the front door. A note inside stated that the written test was given at the courthouse every Monday and Wednesday at 8 a.m. Bummer. That meant I'd have to wait for a week.

But I began devouring the book that night and re-read it on all my breaks on Tuesday. That night I phoned Kyle Martin.

"Can you take me in the morning?"

"Take you where?"

"To take my written drivers test." What did he think? Where else would I ask him to take me on a Wednesday morning?

"Already? You've just had the book one day."

"I know but I've read it and my supervisor said I could take off tomorrow. I told her what I wanted to do."

"Gina, are you sure you're ready? A lot of people fail it the first time. I'd hate for you to waste time off work."

"I'm ready. I promise."

"I'll be there at 7:30."

"Thank you, Pastor Kyle. Bye."

When I hung the phone up, I turned to Mam who was sitting there at the kitchen table drinking a cup of coffee and smoking a cigarette. "He's coming to take me. Yay! I'll learn to drive and we'll get a car and be able to go wherever we want."

"Baby, I need to get my own place and get out of your way. I should be able to do that within a month. I'll have enough money saved."

"But Mam..." The thought of her off on her own was scary. What if she took back up with the men? But I didn't want Mam to know I didn't trust her. "It's kind of nice having you here. I feel like I'm just getting to know you."

"You are. And I guess I'm just getting to know myself too. But I don't want to be a burden on you."

I bent over and kissed her on the forehead. "You're not a burden. You are a blessing." Pastor Kyle taught about blessings last Sunday and how everyone is supposed to count them. I began the count with Mam. Christy was next and then Helen and then Pastor Kyle and Mrs. Martin. And then my job and The Doll House. So many things God had blessed me with in just seven months. And now I was going to learn to drive. Yay!

***

Kyle

Such a tiny little thing. When Gina left the room to go take her test, I smiled and put my hands together in a gesture that promised to pray. And thought that she'd need it with only one study day under her belt.

While I waited I counted the time 'til Christy would return. Two weeks from yesterday, thirteen days. Christy was going to be the perfect pastor's wife. Look what she had done with Gina Howard. And Gina's mother. Their lives were completely different because of Christy and her love. She was as effective as the street preacher. Although from what I could gather, the guy had led Hazel to accept Jesus and that prepared her for the life change that came about a few months later. But what if Christy hadn't taken Gina under her wing? Would she have insisted her mother move out? *Stop it, Martin. Pray for Gina.*

After I prayed that God would bring to Gina's mind all she needed to know to pass the test, I returned to thinking about Christy. Yes, the perfect wife. Thank God she had forgiven him for the way he proposed. When would the wedding be? I guessed most women wanted June weddings but I wished it could be sooner.

My musings stopped as Gina came back out with a broad grin on her face and waving a paper. "Passed it! Now we have to go down and get the permit."

"That's great. What was your score?"

"Perfect."

"Perfect?"

"Yeah. What'd you expect?" She did a little dance down the hall. And I laughed at her saucy smugness.

When Gina had the permit safely in hand, I asked, "You got time for a lesson? Or do you need to get back to work?"

"I got plenty of time. I took off the whole day. I figured if I didn't pass, I'd study all day so I'd pass next Monday."

"All right! Let's go." Christy was going to be very happy with me for bringing this about.

***

Gina

I was waiting for Pastor Kyle to pick me up for a driving lesson when Billy Benson walked out the door.

"Who's the guy?" His face was sullen.

"What do you mean?"

"I've seen the same guy pick you up every day for a week now. You got another old man?"

I could feel my cheeks blaze. "No! It's none of your business, but he's my pastor and he's teaching me to drive."

"Sure, he is." He leered.

I glared at him. "You just stay away from me, Billy. I used to think you were a nice guy but you're scum."

His face changed and he looked at me seriously, silent for a moment before he answered. "You're right."

"Huh?" What was he trying to pull now?

"You're right. I've acted like nothing but scum with you. And I'm sorry."

This was different. I wasn't sure how to react. Finally I nodded. "Okay, I forgive you."

"Do you think maybe we could try going out again? No pressure."

Just then Kyle pulled into the lot.

"Let me think about it, Billy. I'll let you know tomorrow." I waved goodbye as I got into the passenger seat of the blue BMW.

"Who is that?" Pastor Kyle frowned as he looked at Billy. I didn't know why; I thought Billy looked pretty good.

"A guy I went to school with. He got a football scholarship but hurt his back and couldn't play anymore so he's back from college and working here."

"Do you date him?"

"I did once but he ... well, he wanted a different kind of relationship than I did."

"You be careful."

I laughed. "I am careful. But he apologized and now he wants me to give him another chance."

Kyle's frown deepened. "I hope you're not going to go out with him again."

I looked over at him. "Well I might. I haven't decided."

"Not a good idea," Kyle said.

I sat up straighter and squared my shoulders. "I believe in giving people second chances. God does."

After a couple of seconds, Kyle laughed. "Touche!"

The lessons were going very well. I surprised myself by liking to drive and my coach seemed surprised that I was so good at it. I'd get my license soon and then the next goal would be to get a car.

When I got home that evening I realized I'd made a decision. I'd say 'yes' to Billy Benson's invitation. After all, he apologized and, face it, I'd been living with Mike. He had every reason to think I'd be easy. But now that he knew better maybe we could date like normal people.

That would be fun. I pictured Billy and me and Christy and Pastor Kyle all going out together, to a movie or something. Well, I tried to picture it. Somehow Billy didn't fit in the picture. I'd have to find out if he was a Christian. He didn't act like one so maybe God wanted me to help him know Jesus.

That night, I dreamed that Pastor Kyle was pointing his finger at me and shaking his head. "You know better," he said. And then he winked.

Billy was there as usual when I went to clock-in Friday morning. He grinned at me. "Well?"

"Okay, why not? If you promise no pressure."

He held both hands up in the air. "No pressure, I promise. After work again? Supper?"

I nodded. "I'll skip my driving lesson today."

He gave me a thumbs up.

Billy was cute when he grinned. He was a football star in high school and back then I'd have thought it was a huge big deal to have Billy Benson ask me out, even though I wouldn't have gone because of Mike. It didn't seem so big now but maybe that was because I wasn't over Mike yet.

I'd call Pastor Kyle on lunch break and also call Mam after work to let her know I wouldn't be home 'til late. Mam's new trac phone was with the same company as Christie's plan for my phone so it only cost one dollar a day no matter how many times we talked to each other.

Billy's car wasn't as nice as Pastor Kyle's and it smelled like smoke. I didn't say anything, like I didn't say anything at home to Mam, but the smell of cigarettes was starting to bother me, made my nose get all stopped up. Weird since it didn't bother me when I smoked.

"Where do you want to go?" Billy rolled down the car window and I wondered if he noticed the smoke was bothering me.

"I don't care. Wherever you want."

"How about Applebees?"

"That's fine."

"So why'd you change your hair?"

I shrugged. "I just decided to go back to being the real me. I guess I'm growing up."

I'd never been to that restaurant before, and didn't like the loud music that hit my ears as soon as we were close to the door. Since it was Happy Hour there was a crowd inside, also talking loudly.

But Billy was very polite. He pulled out the chair for me and said to order whatever I wanted. Before our waitress returned, a couple I'd seen on break at work passed by our table.

"Billy!" The guy and Billy slapped hands, "Hey, man, can we

join you?" The woman turned to smile at me.

Billy looked at me and I shrugged. Why not? The guy stopped the waitress who was leading them to a table and told her they'd be sitting here. When they were settled Billy introduced Steve Turner and Brenda Levine to me.

After we'd all ordered, the other two each having a beer before their meal, Steve started telling jokes. Off color jokes. I got more uncomfortable by the minute but Brenda shrieked with laughter. Billy chuckled quietly but I could tell he was uncomfortable, always glancing over to see my reaction.

Finally after Steve told one particularly crude joke, Billy shocked me.

"Hey, man. There are ladies here. Let's clean it up."

I sat up straighter in the chair. *Ladies. He sees me as a lady now.*

Steve looked at me as if he were looking at a new species of being never encountered before. He nodded. "Okay. Sure. Sorry

Because of all the noise around us you couldn't exactly say we ate in silence but it was true that our table contributed nothing to the noise. At all.

When the food was consumed, Steve Turner motioned to the waitress to bring his check. "We got to be jumpin' now. See you guys later."

I watched as they walked away and saw him lean down and say something to Brenda that had her double up with laughter. I guessed they were making fun of me.

Billy reached across the table and took my hand. "Sorry about that."

I smiled at him and let my hand stay in his. "Thank you. I...you made me feel special. Thank you."

The evening ended without so much as an attempt to kiss. And I felt special indeed. But there was no desire for him to kiss me and I wondered about that.

With Christy gone, Pastor Kyle picked Mam and me up for both services. True to his word, he went over the Sunday School lessons he taught during the fifteen minute drive to the convention center each Sunday morning, and on Sunday nights we discussed the children and material that I was teaching. I came to look forward to church as the highlight of the week.

And of course the driving lessons were fun too. I'd missed the one on Friday because of going out with Billy but was looking forward to Monday's lesson. It was the last one before Christy and Helen came home. Kyle and I had it all planned for Tuesday night at the airport. When they got to the car, they would get the luggage stored and then Kyle would get in the passenger's seat and I would drive them home. Christy would be so surprised and happy.

But now I turned my attention to the Lord. The song the praise team sang was one of my favorites and I let myself worship with raised hands. The realization hit me about midway through the next song as I watched Pastor Kyle lifting his arms in surrender to the Lord. I felt like someone had punched me in the stomach. My stomach didn't quite know how to react. It kept turning over and over. A sour taste came into my mouth and I was afraid I was going to throw up. I motioned to Mam that I was going to the bathroom.

When I was safely inside a stall, I latched the door and leaned back against it. And breathed deeply.

No, Lord, no. I can't be in love with Kyle Martin. Christy was frustrated with his proposal, and maybe she wasn't ready to make a marriage commitment but there was no doubt that she loved Pastor Kyle. He was crazy about her and they were obviously meant to be together. I searched my mind for pictures of Mike, and reminded myself how much I loved him. But the pictures evoked no emotions at all. I thought of Billy and how sweet he'd been on Friday, how much he wanted to make me like him. But the only face I could find in her heart had blue eyes and curly auburn hair.

Finally, I did throw up.

Chapter Sixteen

2008

Christy

"I know what let's do," Helen said. "Why don't we go to the library?" She grinned. "Busman's holiday maybe?"

"Okay. It might be interesting to find out how different they are here."

"We wouldn't have to stay long."

"Hey, I have nothing else I really want to see in London, just maybe go back to some of the old spots for a last glimpse."

We'd attended St. Martin's-in-the-Field church that morning and had the rest of that day and all of Monday to sightsee. Tuesday morning we'd need to leave for the airport fairly early in time to catch our flight. It was hard to believe that our three weeks was almost gone.

We took the tube to Euston Station and walked to the British Library but the found that the library was closed on Sundays.

"We can do it tomorrow," I said.

"What do you want to do today?"

"I don't know." Then I laughed. "This is insane. We are in the most exciting city in the world and we don't know what to do."

"I know. Let's go check out St. Martin's theatre and see what time *The Mousetrap* is showing. We should have thought of that before we even got here."

"The Mousetrap?" I was thrown back seven years without the anticipation that allowed me to steel myself.

"Oh, you don't know about The Mousetrap? It's by Agatha Christie and the longest running play in the world. It's been showing in London since the fifties."

"Okay, that sounds like fun." I refused to spoil it for Helen. Let her think it was my first time to see it too. London was known for its theatres but we'd never even mentioned taking in a play or I might have been prepared. "A play that's set a record ought to be on a tourist's list of things-to-see."

When we finally found West Street, we discovered that the theatre was also closed on Sundays.

Helen laughed and shook her head. "Who would have thought that so many things would be closed? We need to call tomorrow and see if we can get tickets. That would be a neat way to spend our last night in London. Or is there something else you'd rather do?"

"No, that sounds great. We'll do both the library and the play tomorrow. But what now?"

We just started walking and enjoying the feel of London. She told me about her lifelong love of Agatha Christie's fiction and suddenly we were in a very familiar place.

Leicester Square. *How did we end up here?* I had purposefully avoided this part of London. Since I'd never heard of it before David and I went there, it was completely linked with him in my mind. I slowed down and finally stopped.

"What's wrong?' Helen put her hand on my arm. "Are you okay?"

"I'm sorry. It's just...I wasn't expecting to be here. This is where David and I came several times." I pointed over to the patio of Bella Pasta. "That's our table."

"Come on. Let's go somewhere else."

I sighed. "No, this is stupid of me. Helen, I need to move on emotionally, not physically." I pointed to an empty bench and we sat down. As usual Leicester Square was filled with people but no one would overhear our conversation. "I know we agreed I wouldn't let Kyle's proposal ruin my trip and it hasn't. And thank God..." I reached out and squeezed her hand. "you have made this trip so much fun that I no longer think of England linked exclusively with David."

She smiled. "Good."

"I think I'm ready to make a decision about the future. I don't want to live in the past anymore. I care about Kyle and he's so dedicated to the Lord. I admire him and can't imagine anybody who'd make a better husband. And I love his mother too."

Helen looked at me piercingly. "But...?"

I was surprised. "But nothing. I think I would be stupid not to say yes."

Helen didn't answer. A little girl wandered up to us and held up a doll dressed like Sleeping Beauty from the Disney movie.

"See my princess?" She looked at me intently as if waiting for some specific reaction.

I smiled at her. "Sleeping Beauty. She's beautiful."

She squinted her eyes. "Do you know her name?"

I laughed. "Yes, it's Aurora."

The little girl took a deep breath and smiled. I must have passed the test.

Just then a woman rushed up. "Rebecca! You scared Mummy. I didn't know where you were." She hugged the girl and then turned to us. "I'm sorry if she was bothering you."

I shook my head as Helen said, "No, not at all. She's a beautiful, friendly child."

When the mother had taken her wandering daughter away, warning her of dire consequences that can come from leaving Mummy's side, I turned back to Helen.

"I think I feel like Sleeping Beauty. I had a spell cast over me for six years. And Prince Charming-Kyle.." I laughed and Helen smiled. "...woke me up a little with his kiss but I wish I were fully wide awake - and I'm not."

"Then just tell him he'll have to wait for a while. That you're not ready to make a commitment."

"But you heard him. He told everybody at church that there

would be an announcement when I got back." I thought back on that night. "And I promised him."

Helen's lips tightened. "You shouldn't be held to that promise. That was under duress if anything ever was."

I laughed. "You're right about that." But the laughter quickly left. "I just feel trapped. I don't want the consequences of either answer I can give."

Helen was quiet. That was one thing I appreciated about her. If she wasn't sure that what she had to say was wisdom, she didn't say anything. So many people talked just to fill up silence but Helen wasn't like that.

"I don't want to go back, Helen."

"Me either."

"I mean, I don't want to go back ever. I'm a terrible coward."

It was Helen's turn to laugh. "I don't think so. A coward is one who doesn't act brave when they are afraid. A courageous person acts brave despite their fear. And you will go back and you will handle everything with grace, as you always do."

I turned to look at her. "Thank you. You always make me feel so much better about myself."

April twenty eighth, the last full day of our holiday, as they say in England instead of vacation, dawned bright and sunny. Helen wanted to go to Harrods and I wanted to go to see the Peter Pan statue in Kensington Gardens so we split up and agreed to meet for lunch in Covent Garden. From there we'd go to the library, back to view the Tower of London once more from Tower Hill, and then back to the hotel to change for dinner and the theatre.

The Peter Pan statue was not exactly as I'd imagined it. Peter Pan was much younger than portrayed in the play or movie and his statue was smaller than I thought it would be. The tree trunk he stood on was taller than he was. I admitted to myself that I was disappointed and that was a first for England. What had I been expecting? A Disney version?

I found a nearby bench and sat down. It was quiet there in that part of the Garden and I enjoyed sitting there in the sunshine by myself. I meant what I said to Helen the night before; I didn't want to go back.

And I really wouldn't have to. My parents had left me very well off and I'd barely touched my inheritance. I wouldn't even have to work but I needed to. I saw a sign once that said "Born to party, forced to work" and thought at the time that it certainly didn't describe me. I could let Helen go back without me and stay here for months if I really wanted to.

Giggles drew my attention back to the Peter Pan statue. A woman stood watching a young child climb up the trunk, using the fairies and squirrels and rabbits as footholds. I could tell that she was ready to leap forward and catch him if he fell.

Lord, thank you that you are always waiting to catch me if I fall. But, Lord, I think it's time for me to grow up and not look for Never Never Land. Show me what that means, what I need to do to grow up. Please.

"Take a picture of me, Mum!" The little boy was hugging the bronze Peter Pan. His mother pulled a disposable camera out but looked nervous at having to stand far enough away to snap the picture. I stood up.

"I'd be happy to take the picture for you. So you can stand there close."

She looked relieved and smiled at me. When three shots were taken, one showing the mother standing at the base of the statue with her son above, and the others showing her son and Peter Pan, I gave the camera back and they moved on.

I'd like to have a child, Lord.

An unpleasant thought came to my mind. Had I been fooling myself about Kyle? Was my attraction for him all sexual desire and need for a normal future with a home and children? I admired him. He was a great preacher. And he was certainly attractive. But in love with him?

A sick feeling entered my stomach. No, I was not in love with him. I'd been in love and I knew what that meant. I was willing to lay down my life for David's happiness, and even for his values. But I didn't feel that way about Kyle Martin. I loved how he delighted in me but if I married him, he would be getting second best. He'd have someone who would be faithful and helpful but not someone who would delight in him.

The sick feeling passed away and peace crept over my whole body and mind. The decision was made. I didn't have to wrestle with choices. There was no choice. I couldn't marry Kyle Martin. For his sake. I breathed a sigh of relief.

But I also felt strangely like I was standing on the brink of a cliff wondering if a bridge was going to appear in front of me. From where I sat I could see the top of the Albert Memorial which represented the same thing. I didn't want to be like Queen Victoria wearing black for decades in mourning for her lost husband. Was I going to become like Helen, spending life dreaming over a doomed love? I didn't want that. But now I knew that neither did I want to go on with life by cheating some man out of finding a wife who would love him the way a wife should love her husband.

So what now, Lord?

A picture flashed into my mind of the first time I went to Kyle Martin's church and answered the call to be married to Jesus. *Thank you for reminding me, Lord.*

I looked around and saw that there was no one in sight, or in the sound of my voice, so I spoke aloud.

"Lord, I renew that vow. I want to be one with you above all things. I trust you with my future. If you want marriage and children for me, then you arrange it. But I'm not going to arrange it myself. And Lord, please prepare Kyle to hear my answer. Help him not be hurt. In Jesus name I pray. Amen."

There was something else I needed to do. "P.S. Lord. I'll do my part by refusing to daydream about David. But you'll have to take the love away and replace him with yourself in every part of my heart."

***

Kyle

I don't understand women at all. Gina was so excited about

driving lessons and especially about meeting Christy at the airport and driving her home, but Sunday night after church she cancelled both Monday's driving lesson and going with me and Mom Tuesday night. And she had no excuse, just "I can't."

And Christy. What was going to happen with us? She always responded to my kisses and I could tell she likes my company, so why was she so uncomfortable about making a commitment? A thought struck me. Could there be someone else? No. Surely I'd have gotten a hint in this past five months if there were another man in the picture.

Women! Even Mom surprised him sometimes – like with the violence of her reaction at my proposal to Christy. I thought she'd be proud of me and think how scriptural and original it was. But no...according to her, he was thoughtless and pushy.

"Son." His mother's voice broke into my thoughts as we drove toward Lexington.

"Hmm?"

"Please don't push Christy for an answer right away. Let it come from her in her time."

"Oh, okay." I tried to remember if the 'Will you marry me?' sign was upside down in the trunk so no one would see it when we packed the luggage. I'd check when we parked and make sure. That had been my mother's idea. But I guessed I blew it when I did my own proposal. I took a men's workshop once that taught, "Men think in headlines and women think in fine print." I could understand that but the interpretations of their fine print escaped me.

I pulled into short term parking and took the ticket. When the car was parked, as Mom headed toward the airport, I quickly opened the trunk. Yes! The sign was turned upside down. Nobody would ever know. I joined my mother with that burden gone, but still nervous about how Christy would greet me after an absence of three weeks. She promised to give her answer when she got back. Had she been thinking about it the whole time? I hoped so. Hoped she'd missed me as much as I missed her.

The sign showed that the flight from Cincinnati was landing. It wouldn't be long now. Mom reached over and patted me. Was my nervousness that obvious?

And there she was, coming down the elevator behind her friend. She smiled at me. Friendly but not as though she couldn't wait to fling herself into my arms. Not a good sign. Or maybe just some fine print that he couldn't read? I restrained myself from holding out my arms. I'd follow Mom's advice even farther than she gave it. I'd let Christy make the first move on everything.

***

Christy

I looked past the Martins for Gina's face but didn't see it. The plan was that she would come to the airport to greet me but...

When I reached the bottom of the escalator, I hugged Mrs. Martin first and then Kyle. *Please, God, don't let him ask my decision yet.* "Where's Gina?"

"She said she couldn't come," Kyle's words were clipped. "I don't know why."

I hoped nothing had happened to make Gina quit going to church while I was gone. "Is she still teaching Sunday School?"

"As of Sunday morning, she was." Kyle turned to smile at Helen. "Did you have a good flight?"

"Smooth as silk. But I'm glad to be on terra firma again." Helen laughed.

When our bags came around on the conveyor Kyle grabbed the biggest two and Helen and I got the smaller ones. We followed him and his mother out to the parking garage.

Mrs. Martin got in the back with Helen and I was up front with Kyle.

"Well, begin at the beginning and talk us all the way through to the end." Mrs. Martin sounded like she was truly interested and not just being polite.

"You start," I said to Helen. "I'll jump in." I wanted so much to call Gina and make sure she was okay but it would be rude when the Martins had come all this way to pick us up – and spend time with us.

Helen began by telling them about our hotel and the elegant four o'clock tea they held each day. We ordered it once and I was sure I'd undone all my exercise for the past four years. The British certainly like sweets.

"And it was wonderful being there with Christy. She was a great tour guide. Even when she wasn't familiar with the place we visited, she knew about the money and transportation and culture. It made being in a foreign country worry-free."

I jumped in. "We'd have been in bad shape if we were in a country that didn't speak English. I was never any good at foreign languages."

"Well, we were in Scotland."

I laughed and explained to the others. "Scottish brogues can be so thick that it seems sometime like a foreign language. You have to get into the rhythm of each person speaking. They all seem a little different."

Helen nodded. "But Christy was good at deciphering." She began telling them about our tours of historical sites in Scotland. Kyle was impressed that we'd seen William Wallace's sword. He was a fan of the movie "Braveheart."

My mind was not on her stories; it wavered back and forth between trying to decide how and when to tell Kyle I couldn't marry him and wondering what was wrong with Gina.

I'd turned on my cell phone as soon as the plane landed in case Kyle or Gina called to say they'd be late or something. It rang now and I looked at the id expecting to see that Gina was calling. But it was my boss. Boy she sure didn't waste any time. I frowned. I'd taken off the rest of the week so even though she knew I'd be back today, she shouldn't be calling. But I answered.

"Hey, Christie. Welcome home!"

"Thanks, Elena. What's going on?"

"I need to talk to you. Is this a good time?"

"No, I'm still in the car with the people who picked us up from the airport. We won't be home for a while."

"Call me asap?"

"Is something wrong?"

"No, I just need to talk to you."

I broke the connection. "Sorry, that was my boss. Go on, Helen, finish telling about Holyrood House."

Helen laughed. "Christy wasn't all that excited but I acted like a kid when I saw Rizzio's bloodstains. He was Mary Queen of Scot's musician and was murdered there in front of her. You know, sometimes history seems like fiction — if they are good stories. And then to see proof of things wakes you up to the pain of real people."

"That's the way I felt last time when I went to Hever Castle, but I'm interested in Anne Boleyn." I refused to dwell on the pictures in my mind of Hever; all the scenes contained David. I shook my head. I was free of all that now. I truly belonged to Jesus spirit, soul, and body. Mind and emotions.

We were on the outskirts of town when I interrupted Helen's account of Dover Castle. "Would you mind if we stopped by Gina's just for a few minutes? Once I get home, I'm not going to want to go anywhere. And I'd like to see her."

Mrs. Martin answered me. "Of course we wouldn't mind." Then she turned to Helen. "Do you want us to take you home first?"

"No, I'd like to say 'hello' too."

I pulled out the phone again and punched in Gina's number.

"Christy?" Her voice sounded fine, excited to know I was calling. Maybe my feeling that something was wrong was not accurate.

"It's me. Do you mind if I stop by for just a minute? Are you home?"

"Of course. Come on. When did you get in?"

"We're just driving into town. Helen will come with us too."

"Oh." Silence.

I couldn't say anything that would let those in the car with me know how her voice changed when she found out I wasn't alone. What on earth was wrong?

Mrs. Martin was talking. "I'm glad we're stopping. I've never seen the inside of Gina's Doll House."

"Me either," Helen said. I didn't say that since she'd donated most of the furnishings, it would be familiar to her.

As soon as we pulled up, Gina came out the front door. I leaped out of the car and ran to hug her. "Hey, I got you a present but it's all packed away. I'll give it to you later. Is it okay if we come in. Mrs. Martin and Helen both want to see your house."

"Did you warn them about the living room? About me sleeping there now?"

I hadn't but since they knew Hazel lived there too, it probably wouldn't be a surprise.

The others got out of the car, greeted Gina, and followed us in the house. She showed the two older women around and I joined them to avoid being left alone with Kyle. He sat down in the recliner and stared at the TV. When we came back in from seeing the bedroom which was now Hazel's, I saw Gina glance over at Kyle. And felt like someone punched me in the stomach. It was the kind of look I gave David years ago when he wasn't looking. Pure adoration.

He wasn't looking at her at all. I wanted to say something, to break the tension I was experiencing but I couldn't think of anything to say.

Helen came to the rescue without knowing it. "This is just beautiful, Gina. Where's your mother?"

"She's out with some friends from work. I hope..." She stopped and I knew, and guessed the others did too, that she was concerned about Hazel returning to alcohol.

I looked over at Kyle but he still stared at the TV. Surely this would be a time where a pastor should say something.

What had gone on between these two while I was away?

And why did I care? Wasn't I going to decline his proposal anyway?

I'd been going to invite Gina for dinner tomorrow night but all of a sudden I couldn't make myself do it.

Kyle helped carry my bags in the house just like he'd helped

Helen. Mrs. Martin stayed in the car so we were alone, but he never asked what my decision was about marrying him. He set the luggage in the hall right inside the door and then hesitated.

"Do you want me to put them somewhere else?"

"No, they're fine. Thank you." He wasn't looking me in the eye. "Thank you, Kyle, for coming to get us. I appreciate it a lot."

He nodded. "Hope you get settled in okay. See you later." The last statement was more a question. But I ignored that.

"Yes, see you later." I watched as he walked to the car and waved at Mrs. Martin before I closed the front door.

My stomach was churning. *What is going on?* I thought back on my prayer in Kensington Gardens. My future is in God's hand. I want only Jesus.

Then why did I feel panic?

I was almost through unpacking before I remembered that I was supposed to call Elena Hunt. The clock showed 9:45. I'd wait 'til tomorrow.

***

Gina

I stopped sobbing when I heard Mam's key in the door. I couldn't let her know what was wrong, so pretended to be asleep. But I purposefully turned my face toward the entrance so I would be able to smell gin if it came in the door.

When Mam was through the living room and into the bathroom, I breathed a sigh of relief. No gin. Heavy tobacco smell but no alcohol. *Thank you, Jesus.*

When I heard the bedroom door close, I got out of bed and went to the kitchen. Maybe some chamomile tea would help me sleep. I put a mug of water in the microwave and got out two tea bags.

"Hey, I thought you were asleep." Mam stood there in the kitchen door.

Caught! I made my voice as cheerful as possible. "You want some herb tea?"

"Okay. I was hoping you'd be up. I wanted to talk."

I put another mug in and handed my mother the first cup of tea, keeping my face turned away for as long as possible, hoping Mam wouldn't know I'd been crying. "It will need to steep for about four minutes. It's supposed to be relaxing. Help you sleep."

Mam took the cup and with her other hand turned my face toward herself. "You've been crying. What's wrong, Baby?"

The kindness and concern in her voice was too much. It broke down my resolve and tears and sobs came rushing back.

"Oh, Gina. What is it? Is there something I can do?" Mam put the hot mug down on the table and enfolded me in her arms.

After a few moments where my sobs were the only sounds in the room, I took a deep breath and moved away. "Let's sit down."

I put a teabag in my own mug and we settled at the table.

"Mam, you said you wanted to talk to me. You go first."

"Mine can wait. What on earth is going on?"

It took me a minute. "I'm afraid."

"Afraid of what?"

"Of going to hell and of losing my best friend."

Mam raised her eyebrows. "Well, I think I'd cry too."

I couldn't help but laugh. "Pretty drastic, huh?"

"Yes, but there must be a reason."

"Oh, Mam. I think I'm...no. I have..." I didn't want to say the words.

"What, Baby?"

"I've fallen in love." I looked at Mam with a plea for understanding. "With Pastor Kyle."

Mam nodded. "I'm not surprised."

"You're not?" I couldn't believe my ears. "I was."

"You've been spending every day together. He's young and good looking. You're young and good looking. You enjoy discussing the Bible. I figured you'd be attracted to each other."

"Oh no." I wanted to explain. "This is just me. He's so in love with Christy, he can hardly breathe."

"Hmph."

"It's true. And Mam, I wish I never had to be around them

together but I just can't give up church. There's Shebby." I smiled at the thought of the little girl who had so won my heart at the Christmas party. Shelby was in my Sunday School class and I couldn't desert her.

"Then just go Sunday mornings. Christy only goes on Sunday nights."

That made sense. But a pain stabbed through my heart. I'd miss the night service, the time with Christy and, face it, seeing Kyle Martin one more time each week.

The tears welled up again but at least the sobs were gone.

"Billy wants me to go out with him again and I told him I'd go again this Friday. He really is a nice boy, man. And he treats me with respect now. But I feel like...well since I realized Sunday night, I've felt like I'm being dishonest with him. He was so glad to see me Monday morning and it made me feel guilty that I didn't feel the same about him."

"Maybe you could invite him to church."

"Hey, that's a good idea. I will. But, Mam, should I tell Christy? About my feelings for Kyle?"

"No, that wouldn't be a good idea. You've got a lot of years to be friends and it could cause problems, especially after they're married."

Sometimes Mam could be very wise. I nodded. "Now what did you want to talk to me about?"

She took the last drink of tea from the mug. "I've been offered a different job. That's why I was out tonight."

"Shut up!" I didn't want to tell her I was afraid she'd gone out to party.

She nodded. "I've been offered a job in the office at Clovers. It will start out at less money than I'm making now on the floor and eventually I can work up to making more. But that's why I needed to talk to you. I'm about at the place where I can afford to move out on my own. Taking the new job would set me back. And it would be maybe six more months before I could handle it all. But I hate to keep imposing on you, Baby."

I reached for her hand. "Oh, Mam. I'm happy for you and

you're not imposing. This last few months have been the happiest time of my life." I gave a short laugh. "Well, except the past few days and that's not because of you."

"You're sure?"

"Yes. I'd still be sobbing tonight if you weren't here. Stay as long as you want. Forever if you want."

"No, that's not right. And I hate taking your pretty bedroom." She changed the subject. "Didn't Christy get back from England today?"

"Yes, and she came by – with Helen, and Mrs. Martin, and Kyle."

Mam patted my hand. "You just trust the Lord Jesus with your heart, Baby. He'll make it all come out okay."

I nodded. But my heart seemed far removed from the peace and joy that I'd known in Jesus.

Chapter Seventeen

2008

Helen

At midnight I lay in bed staring at the ceiling. Sleep wouldn't come even though I'd been up for almost 24 hours. It was a wonderful trip. I enjoyed every minute of it. But what now? The trip was what I'd clung to for the last six months. But it was over. What did the future hold? The years, how many — ten, fifteen, even twenty or twenty five — spread out before me filled with hours and days that looked dull and empty except for a few good times with Christy and Gina.

Forgive me, Lord but I'd just as soon come on to heaven.

Maybe when Christy and Kyle had children, I'd get involved in their lives, an extra grandmother.

But it wasn't the same as having my own family. My sister's children weren't the same either. They weren't interested in me at all. I'd be much more involved with Christy's. I turned on my side and adjusted the pillow. Then I remembered. Christy wasn't going to marry Kyle.

Why had I forgotten that? I sat up and turned on the bedside lamp. And picked up my Bible. *Lord, why did that completely leave my mind?*

I thought of a Bible verse and it took a few minutes to find it for the exact wording. I'd never been good at scripture addresses,

201

just remembered which side of the page they were on, and top, bottom, or middle. Ah, there it was, *The heart is deceitful above all things, and desperately wicked: who can know it?* Jeremiah 17:9

I sat very still a minute until I let myself understand what the Lord was showing me in answer to the question. "It left my mind because I didn't want to follow her example."

Christy decided to give her entire heart to Jesus and made a vow not to daydream about David at all. That decision provoked a prompting somewhere inside me to do the same, give my entire heart to Jesus and never daydream about Sanders again. But another place inside rose up and smashed that prompting in the head. It had been laying there whimpering since yesterday afternoon. Helen glanced at the clock – day before yesterday. It was now one a.m. Wednesday.

Lord, I don't know if I can do that. Just the thought of never reliving moments from the past, never thinking about him or looking at his picture, never reading the poetry, or his letter – it was too hard. I could never carry it out.

Lord, the best I can do is to confess that I have not loved you with all my heart and soul and strength and mind. And I haven't even wanted to, until now. And it's still a scary thought.

Lord, I'm sorry I've wanted to go to heaven to see Sanders more than I've wanted to see Jesus. Please forgive me and cleanse my heart of idolatry. I can't do it myself. It will take your supernatural power.

But then it came to mind what my part would be in submitting myself completely to that cleansing, purifying process. With an aching heart but a willing mind, I reached in the bedside table and picked up the book of poems. I went through them one by one reading silently, remembering how I felt when I wrote them. Then I read them aloud and tried to assess how I felt now. After they were all read twice, I tore out each page from the book and into tiny pieces. I took the pieces of paper and flushed them down the toilet.

When it was all destroyed, I sat down on the side of the

bathtub watching the remainder of the swirling water with no trace of paper left in it. I waited for the peace that should have come but was instead assaulted by another thought.

The picture and his letter. *Oh, no. I can't.* But in my mind I saw a scene of Jesus smiling. *Yes, you can. You can do all things through Me, who strengthens you.*

I retrieved the letter and picture from inside the book where I kept them. I tore the picture into pieces, feeling as though my heart was being dismantled as I did it. But just as I began to tear the letter, it was as though a hand halted my action. I thought of Abraham being stopped just before he plunged the knife into his son.

Fitting. Because the reason for not destroying the letter was not due to my own need but someone else's.

When the water was still again, I put the letter away in another book and knelt down at the bedside. I lifted my eyes and both hands, not even sure how to pray until the words from an old hymn came to mind.

"Lord, here I am. Just as I am. Nothing in my hands I bring, simply to Thy cross I cling."

And then I went back to bed. And slept.

***

Christy

"Hunt's Temp Agency, We hunt the jobs for you. May I help you?"

"Sally, it's Christy."

"Hey girl, how was your trip?"

"It was awesome. I didn't want to come back. Is Elena in? She called last night and wanted to talk to me."

"Sure, I'll put you through. Christy, when do you come back to work? Monday?

"Yes, that's the plan." But I was ready to go back now. I thought I'd want to spend lots of time alone but now...

"Christy! Glad you called." Elena's voice was cheerful and

crisp as usual.

"I'm sorry I didn't get a chance last night 'til it was too late."

"It's okay. I should have waited until today anyway. I'd like to do this in person. Would you be available for lunch?"

I hesitated. "Tell you what. If you don't mind, why don't you pick up something and come over here. I really don't want to go out today." Then I laughed. "You're not going to fire me, are you?"

"Far from it. Let's see. It's ten now. Is eleven thirty too early?"

"No. That's fine. And whatever you want to pick up for lunch is okay with me – as long as it doesn't have caffeine."

"Gotcha."

I replaced the phone in the cradle. What was wrong with me? I didn't want to wait 'til Monday to return to work - but didn't want to go out of my house for lunch?

The thought of descending again into the depression of seven years ago scared me. I refused to become reclusive. I went to the bedroom to get dressed, and the music box on my dresser caught my attention. I picked it up and opened it. The lovely strains of music floated out again. "We have the right to love again."

I have a right to love again. I have a right to a home and children. Was my decision in England all wrong? Or did God lead me to feel that way to protect me from the betrayal of Kyle and Gina?

After all I'd done for Gina, how dare she fall in love with my boyfriend! *But what about Gina? Doesn't she have the right to love again too?* I knew I was being unfair but couldn't seem to stop myself. Ungrateful thing!

And Kyle. He was just as bad. Or worse. Embarrass me by proposing in public and then barely act glad to see me after three weeks, much less eager to hear if I was going to marry him. *But didn't you ask Me to keep him from bringing it up?*

I hadn't given Kyle my answer yet. What if I said yes? It would serve him right. *But what about Me? Would it serve Me right?*

I threw the pillows, one by one, across the room as hard as I could, glad that making the bed gave me an excuse. When the sheets were all smoothed out and the bedspread on, I retrieved the pillows. But before I put them on the bed I threw them again. It felt good. Then I laughed at myself. I closed the music box, opened it again and let the tune fill the room and the words wander into my mind.

No heart should refuse love. How lucky are the ones who choose love.

What does that mean? Is my heart refusing love by turning Kyle down?

But Gina? What about her heart? I knew that she would never choose to love someone that I love. She is my friend. But she's so different. Morally. Because of her background. How did I know what she's really like when it comes to men?

And Kyle. He was probably hoping I'd turn him down. Gina's so much more exciting than me. More exotic. And she loves to teach Sunday School. She'd be a better pastor's wife that I would. But he couldn't choose who to love any more than Gina could. Any more than I could. The thought of David brought tears to my eyes.

No! I would not think about David. I could choose who to love. And I choose Jesus. Gina is my friend and no matter what she and Kyle had done, I refused to let that interfere. *But, Lord, you'll have to help me.*

Before I could change my mind, I got my cell phone and called Gina's. I was shocked when she answered. I'd been going to leave a message since she's at work on Wednesday. It turned out she was on break.

"Hey, Christy! I'm glad to hear your voice again. I missed you so much."

"Would you like to come for supper tonight – just you and me" I didn't want to invite Hazel, not tonight.

"That would be great but I thought you and Kyle would be together."

Did she know something I didn't. Like he was going to retract the proposal?

"No, no plans, except hoping you'd come over. I can pick you up from work if you want."

"I tell you what. I'll ask Billy to bring me. If he can't, I'll call."

"Billy? That scum?"

"He's not acting like scum anymore. I'll tell you about it tonight."

Well, now, that was puzzling. It sounded like she's interested in Billy and yet the look she gave Kyle was not that of a sheep looking at a shepherd.

But I was glad I got over my anger and called her.

I dusted the living room in preparation for Elena's visit. It didn't need vacuuming since no one had been here for nearly a month.

Promptly at eleven thirty, the door chime sounded.

"I got Chinese." Elena carried two huge bags and I took one from her as we walked toward the kitchen. "I knew you like it but wasn't sure which kind so I got several things. Figured you could use leftovers tonight since you're staying in today."

I'd forgotten I said I was staying in. I'd have to go out to get stuff for supper for when Gina came. Maybe I had jet lag and that was why my mind wasn't working right.

Elena got pork fried rice, sweet and sour soup, and egg rolls for herself. There were also more egg rolls, spring rolls, fried and white rice, chicken and broccoli, moo goo gai pan, stuffed mushrooms, boiled shrimp, and fried frog legs. I laughed when I surveyed my kitchen table which was completely covered with containers.

"I think I'll have enough to last 'til I come back to work next Monday."

She cocked her head and looked at me. "You may want to come back earlier."

"Okay, what's up?"

"I'm selling the business."

My hand stopped midway to my mouth with a fork full of moo goo gai pan. I almost used Gina's expression 'shut up'!

"What? Why?"

206

She grinned. "I'm getting married and moving to Boston."

I shook my head. "Where did that come from? I didn't even know you were dating."

"When I was on vacation last year, in Boston visiting with my friend, I met Hal and we've been seeing each other whenever possible since. That's where I spent Christmas. And he's flown in for several weekends. And I've been there several weekends too."

"I had no idea." My mind was whirling with thoughts. Who was buying the agency? Would I be allowed to stay on?

"The reason I wanted to talk to you was this. Are you interested in buying the business?"

I stared at her without answering. Me buy a business?

"You're so good at it. You run it perfectly. Ever since you came, and learned it, I've not had a minute's stress. You're such a good administrator." Her eyes were questioning me while she spoke.

I took a deep breath. There was enough money in the estate fund; I was sure of that. But did I want that responsibility?

"I'll have to think about it."

"Of course. And check out financing. But I'll be reasonable, I promise." She smiled engagingly. "Hal's a millionaire."

I laughed. "Go girl!" She had no idea of my own financial situation.

When we finished eating and I'd shared some about my trip, I walked her to the door.

"Elena, I feel really good about this. I'll have to pray about it and talk to my lawyer. Do you mind giving me a few days before you offer it to anyone else?"

"Not at all. It's my baby, you know. I couldn't stand to sell it to just anybody."

When she'd gone, I returned to the kitchen to put away containers of Chinese food. Her baby. *When I said I wanted children, Lord, I didn't mean businesses.*

Now the Lord chose to be silent.

***

Gina

I was a complete mixture of fear and pleasure. I loved Christy so much and wanted to see her but was terrified of betraying my own feelings for Pastor Kyle. That's why I asked Billy to take me there. I wanted Christy to know that I had my own boyfriend.

He acted thrilled. "Anytime, Babe." I'd never seen such a change in somebody. He acted like I was a princess, opened doors for me, never made a crude gesture. Maybe God was working to make them a couple.

"Billy, would you want to go to church with me and my mother this Sunday? You could pick us up." That would insure she didn't have to ride with Pastor Kyle.

He turned his head and gave me a surprised look before returning his gaze to the road. "I didn't know you went to church."

"I just started last year." I might as well come out with it. "I became a Christian. Remember, I told you my pastor was teaching me to drive."

He nodded. "I thought there was something different about you." He scratched his chin. "I'm a Christian."

"Shut up!" The expression just slipped out. I didn't mean for him to know how shocked I was.

"Yeah, I know I don't act like it."

"You didn't use to act like it but lately you do."

He looked over with a grin and a wink. "Lately I've had reason to want to be on my best behavior."

I could feel myself blushing. "So where do you go to church?"

He named a big Baptist church that was well known among high school students for it's large youth group.

"I didn't know you had a church. So I won't push you to come to mine."

"I don't mind. Church is church."

I thought back about the time I visited the youth meeting with my friend. And the church my mother told me about. All churches were definitely not alike. I laughed.

"Not necessarily. Oh! I just remembered, I teach Sunday School. You'd have to go early. And help me with little children." I grinned wickedly at him. "You up to that much good behavior?"

He laughed but kept his eyes looking straight ahead. "I think I could handle it." And a short pause, he added, "For you."

My heart turned over. This wasn't fair. I was using Billy to stay away from Kyle Martin. But I'd make sure he never knew that and be so nice to him that he'd never suspect my heart was divided.

When we pulled up outside Christy's house, I leaned over to the driver's side. "Thank you, Billy." And kissed him on the cheek, quickly before I got out of the car.

"See you tomorrow." And walked up to the house without looking back.

Christy answered the door right away and smiled when she saw me. We hugged and Christy said, "I'm so glad you came."

"Me too."

"Do you like Chinese food or shall we go out and get something?"

I stopped there in the hallway.

"Okay, here I go again. I've never eaten Chinese food."

Christy turned and looked at me. "Shut up!" We both laughed. "Tell you what, we'll heat it up later and if you don't like it we'll pick up KFC or something." She pulled out cans from the refrigerator. "All I've got are diet colas. Is that okay?"

"Sure." When we were seated at the table, Christy got up right away. "Sorry. I forgot to bring your present. Be right back."

While I waited, it was like little imps tortured my mind. *She buys you presents and you try to steal her boyfriend...soon to be husband.* That wasn't true. I would never try to steal Christy's boyfriend. And couldn't if I wanted to. Especially not Pastor Kyle. *He needs a nice wife, not street trash like you.*

Christy came back with a gift box. "I hope you like it. Maybe we'll start a tradition."

I knew what Christy meant when the opened box revealed a white castle that stood on a brass base. When I turned the castle, the strains of "Someday My Prince Will Come" from the Disney movie *Snow White.*

"How beautiful." I hugged it to her chest. "Thank you, Christy. Thank you so much. And you know, he may just have already come. I found out that Billy is a Christian."

Christy frowned. "He didn't act like one last year."

"But he is now. And he's going to go take Mam and me to church Sunday, even going to help me with Sunday School."

"Wow. That is a change."

"But that's enough about me. Tell me more about your trip. And how come you aren't with Pastor Kyle tonight? Have you told him yet when you'll marry him?"

Christy's eyes clouded over. "I'm not going to marry him."

"What?" My heart started beating wildly.

"I'm not marrying him. I can't, Gina. I've never told you about my past. And I won't go into it now. But I was in love with somebody once and I know how it feels. I don't feel that way about Kyle. It wouldn't be fair to him to marry him."

I wanted to ask what happened to the man Christy had loved but if she didn't want to go into it, I wouldn't push her. My chest was feeling more tight by the minute. If Christy didn't want Kyle, maybe...

"I haven't told him yet. How do you think he'll react?" Christy was looking at her with a very piercing gaze. As if trying to discover some information I had. All I had to give was the truth.

"He'll be devastated. I'm so sorry for him. He loves you so much, Christy. That's all he's talked about." I paused for a minute. "You might as well know. While you were gone, he's been giving me driving lessons so I was with him nearly every day. And he talked about you constantly."

"I'm sorry." Christy paused for a minute. "Oh, I'm going to tell you the truth."

I took a deep breath but it seemed like it only went half way down.

"When I got back Kyle didn't act very friendly and then when we came to your house I saw you look at him and, well, I thought you'd fallen in love with him. And I figured he wanted you too and that's why he wasn't friendly with me."

I stared at her for a few seconds and then burst into tears, put my head down on the table and sobbed. Christy quickly moved to my side and hugged me.

"Gina, I'm sorry. I shouldn't have told you what I thought. I see now, with Billy and all, that I was wrong."

I shook my head. "No, you're right." I grabbed a tissue out of my jeans. Christy sat back down without taking her eyes away from my face.

"I mean, you're right about me, not him. I didn't mean to fall in love with Kyle. It just happened. I knew it Sunday night and I'm so sorry. He was your boyfriend and I hated myself for loving him."

"But he's not my boyfriend. Not really. It's been fun to date him but I can't marry him." She smiled. "But you can."

I blew my nose. "No, he would never want me."

"Then he's crazy." Christy's voice was stern.

I laughed. But then sobered up. "But you're right about fairness. And I'm afraid I have been unfair to Billy. I asked him to come to church when I thought you loved Kyle. Now..."

Christy's eyes narrowed. "Now we've got to figure out how to catch Kyle Martin. Isn't there a fish called a martin? We've got to figure out how to land this one."

I gave a slight smile at her joke but shook my head. "No, I wouldn't want him since he's so in love with you. Maybe God will help me learn to love Billy. I thought I'd never love anybody but Mike. So I know Jesus can change things like that."

"Yes." Christy looked sad but she didn't say anything else.

For supper we used the microwave to heat up all the Chinese food, except for the egg rolls, spring rolls, and frog legs which Christy put in the oven to get them crisp again, and the shrimp which was served cold.

"Our own Chinese buffet." She waved her hand over the table.

I was surprised at how much I loved spring rolls and chicken and broccoli.

"I'm a moo goo gai pan fan myself," Christy said. "And these." She picked up another frog leg and munched on it.

I couldn't make myself try them. "What do they do with the rest of the frog?"

"I don't know, never thought about it. I guess they just throw the rest away."

"I saw a cartoon once. It showed all these frogs leaving a restaurant, on crutches and in wheel chairs. I didn't know what it meant – until now."

Christy choked. After she spit the bite into her napkin, she said, "That's awful."

"I don't think I could ever try them."

"Well, I love them but I may have to rethink it after hearing about your cartoon." Christy paused. "There's something else I want to talk to you about. I want you to pray for me."

"Sure."

"My boss is selling the agency. I have a chance to buy it. But it would mean more work. I only want to do it if it's God's will."

"Whoa. You'd own Hunt's yourself?"

Christy nodded. "And it seems like an interesting coincidence. I decide not to marry Kyle and then I'm offered this opportunity to have a real career. This could all be a part of God's plan. What do you think?"

"Gosh, I don't know about stuff like that. But I'll pray. Christy, I think you are the best Christian I know. You'll know what to do."

Christy shook her head. "I am definitely not the best Christian you know, Gina."

When Christy delivered me to The Doll House, we sat in the car and prayed together for Christy's business decision and my relationship with Billy Benson. Neither of us mentioned Kyle Martin during the prayer time.

***

Kyle

I hung up the phone and then turned to kick the kitchen

chair.

She turned me down. And didn't even have the decency to do it in person.

How was I going to face my congregation? I'd promised them an announcement.

I really never doubted, until I saw Christy coming down the escalator at the airport Tuesday night, that her answer would be yes.

Boy, was I wrong!

I picked up the phone and Mom answered on the first ring.

"Mom. Christy called me."

"And?"

"She won't marry me. She says she doesn't feel that way about me."

My mother sighed. "I was afraid of that, Son."

"Why? Is it because I messed up the proposal?"

"No. That wouldn't have stopped her if she was the right one for you."

"She is the right one." I felt stubborn. "God's just got to make her see it."

"Kyle." My mother had that warning tone of voice that I hated.

"I got to go now. See you later." I hung up, ignoring her words 'Wait, let's pray.'

I'd pray by myself. When two people prayed they were supposed to be in agreement. Mom would waver over what I intended to pray.

I kicked the kitchen chair one more time before leaving the room. When I got to the study, I fell to my knees in my favorite prayer spot in front of the window. It was too dark to see the fountain in the back yard that always reminded me of the river of living water available to God's people. But I knew it was there.

"Father, you know what's going on. You said that whatever I desire I'm to pray and believe I receive it and I'll have it. So I'm going to pray and believe I receive what I desire. You also said that a wife is a gift from you. I believe you gave Christy to me and

I am asking you to show her that she's mine. I need her. You said yourself that it's not good for man to be alone. It's not good for me. Give me my wife, Lord. I've asked and believe I receive the wife You have for me. Amen."

I remained kneeling there for a long time. And when I got to my feet, there were tears on my face. God seemed very far away.

I went into the den and turned on the television. Back to back reruns of Law and Order kept my mind occupied for two hours. But I still wasn't sleepy.

I went out the front door and locked it behind me. The street was deserted, which was not surprising since it was after midnight.

I walked a long time, thinking some thoughts, casting down others, trying to picture the day that Christy and I would be married, trying not to think about our wedding night.

Chapter Eighteen

2008

Christy

John Powell, my parents' lawyer, called me back Friday afternoon and said that he'd checked out the books Elena Hunt brought to him on Thursday and they looked good. He said the price was fair and would leave me with the majority of my inheritance still intact. He said he'd call the broker on Monday and find out the penalty for taking that much out unless I'd rather borrow the money.

"Unless the penalty is more than interest would be up 'til the time we can access it without losing money, I'd rather pay cash." Kyle Martin preached on finances earlier in the year and convinced me that it was better to remain debt free. I'd never had much to do with finances. My parents paid everything and then their lifelong friend and attorney, took care of everything after their death.

"I'll let you know. Ms. Hunt seems eager to get the transaction completed."

I laughed. "She's getting married. And thank you. I know if it was any other lawyer, it would take forever to get all this done."

"Hey, you know I'll do whatever I can to help you."

It was going to happen, I just knew it. I, Christy Simpson, was going to own my own business. I hoped Sally and Charlene would stay on. But then a thought struck me. I liked Charlene but couldn't see her as Assistant Manager. Oh, for now I'd do both jobs myself. I'd done most of it for the last year anyway. And this would keep me too busy to think about the rest of my life.

I punched in the speed dial for Gina's cell phone and left a message on her answer machine. "I'm doing it. I'm buying Hunt's. Let me know if you want to celebrate."

It was an hour later when Gina returned my call. "I just got off work. I'm with Billy. I thought I told you we have a date tonight."

"Oh." I was disappointed but I could call Helen. "Hey, have fun. Are you still going to church with him Sunday morning?"

"Yes. I'll call you that afternoon. Are you going Sunday night?"

"No. I don't think I can go back there to church."

"I'm sorry."

"It's okay."

"Congratulations on your decision. I'm impressed."

"And congratulation on yours." She'd obviously decided to continue dating Billy Benson. I wondered why, now that Kyle Martin was free.

***

Kyle

I was standing in the hallway beside the desk Mom used to greet people, when Gina walked in. She was with the man I'd seen her talking to one day outside of her work.

I cast down my instinctive reaction and called on the pastor mode to arise. With it came the smile on my face as I walked toward them.

Gina looked over at Mom and smiled. But she didn't look me in the eyes. What on earth was wrong with her? Just a week ago she was friendly and fun. What happened?

"Pastor Kyle, this is Billy Benson. We went to school together and now we work at the same place. Billy, Pastor Kyle."

I shook hands with her friend as Gina continued. "Billy's a Baptist but brought Mom and me today and he's going to help me with Sunday School."

So that was why she didn't need a ride. Mom called me that morning and said Gina had called to say she had another way to church.

"We're glad to have you with us, Bill."

"Glad to be here." He turned to Gina and touched her hair. "Anywhere our girl here goes, I'm there."

I gritted my teeth. "Well, make yourself at home." I turned to my mother. "I'll be in the office for a few minutes. You want to start without me?"

She gave me a questioning look but nodded in agreement.

When I had the office door safely closed behind me, I hit one fist into the palm of my other hand. And knelt down at the chair in front of the desk.

Lord, I'm not fit to teach or preach this morning. Just because Christy turned me down shouldn't make me want to hit somebody for touching Gina's hair. I shall not covet my brother having a girlfriend when I don't. I remembered my prayer and determination. *I don't have a girlfriend right now, Lord. But I will. A wife is a gift from the Lord and Christy will come to her senses. I believe it in my heart and say it with my mouth. Christy is my wife and I'll see that come to pass.*

I waited for peace to flood my heart, but it didn't. I got up from my knees, grabbed my Bible, opened to Psalm 51, and read aloud. "Create in me a clean heart, O God; and renew a right spirit within me. Cast me not away from thy presence; and take not thy holy spirit from me."

Still no flooding of peace.

"Restore unto me the joy of thy salvation; and uphold me with thy free spirit."

I began to feel a little less anxious. "Help me, Lord. Give your message to your people. Amen." I closed the Bible and crossed the hall to the conference room.

After the Sunday School hour, all the children joined their parents and more people came in to the room. The praise band was singing and soon all the chairs were filled. *Lord, you are blessing this ministry. Please don't let me mess it up. Give me patience.*

It was about half way through the sermon when Billy Benson put his arm around the back of Gina's chair and his hand went on her shoulder. I caught my breath. I saw that Gina's face was frozen. She looked at me with eyes that seemed to plead for me to do something. But what?

Where was I, Lord? Help.

God got me through the rest of the sermon but I was so shaken that instead of giving an invitation, I just dismissed the congregation with a prayer, and couldn't even remember the words to that.

As I was making my way to the back of the room, a little girl ran in to me.

"Sowwy." She ran on toward her goal and I saw her grab Gina's legs. "Shebby wants to go home with you, Gina." Gina reached down and picked the child up. "I wish you could go with me, Shelby. But your Mommy would miss you. I'll see you next Sunday." She kissed her and set her back down and looked around, evidently searching for the missing mother. I walked out and went back to my office.

Lust, I thought. *That's my problem. Because I can't have Christy right now, I'm thinking about other women. And of all people, Gina. Forgive me, Lord. When that guy put his arm around her I wanted to go out into the congregation and tear it off.*

Then an alien thought came to mind. What if Gina was the wife God wanted to give me. I sat down abruptly in my chair.

Ridiculous. Gina was totally inappropriate as a pastor's wife. Christy would be perfect. But then another thought came. Did it come from my own heart or from the Lord? *Are you sure?*

***

Christy

It was the end of June before the sale of the agency was completed and the business transferred to my ownership, even though Elena quit taking any part in the management after the middle of May when she moved to Boston. The name would remain Hunt's Temp Agency. I liked the play on words and decided to keep it.

Sally and Charlene both stayed on like I hoped but I wondered whether to hire a third employee. I was putting in over ten hours each week day and doing some of the paperwork at home on Saturday.

I stretched and looked at the clock. Seven p.m. on Thursday night. I picked up the phone. "Helen, it's Christy. Have you had supper?"

"Yes. Why? Haven't you?"

"No, I was going to get something on the way home and wondered if you'd want to go with me."

"I have leftovers – chicken alfredo and tossed salad. Want to come over?"

Tears prickled at my eyes. "I'd love it. Be there shortly." What was wrong with me? Helen's offer was kind but not a huge deal. I guess I needed to spend more time with her. And with Gina too. But Helen provided a parental strength and comfort that I really needed just then.

I hoped Gina didn't think I was ignoring her over the Kyle thing. I'd just been so busy. I couldn't make myself go back to that church, so our time together was not much these days. How long had it been, weeks? I locked the door and walked to my car. It was a hot July day and I'd be glad to get back in the air conditioning. Just then my cell phone rang. It was Gina.

"Are you working late again?"

"Guilty. But I'm leaving now and going to Helen's. She's feeding me leftovers."

"That was what I was going to offer. I miss you, Christy."

"I miss you too. How are you doing? How's Billy?"

She sighed. "That's one of the things I wanted to talk to you about. I tried, Christy. I really tried. But I just couldn't feel that way toward him."

"I understand. So you broke up with him?"

"Yeah. But you know, I think it was a good thing that we went out for a while. He really seems different. He says he's going back to his church. And he wasn't mad at me, just sad."

"Good." I hesitated before plunging ahead. "So how's Kyle?"

"I don't know. I see him at church but never outside. And he never talks to me anymore. I mean, he speaks but that's all. I wonder if he knows how I feel and so is afraid to be too friendly. You know, like afraid he'll encourage me or something."

"I'm sorry. Listen, if you're not dating any more how about us going out to dinner tomorrow night?"

"How about you coming over to The Doll House and letting me cook for you?"

The tears came back. "Okay. What time?"

"What time can you leave work?"

"I'll make myself leave whenever you say."

"Six?"

We agreed on supper at six at her place. When I reached Helen's she was waiting on the front porch, sitting on the swing. I wanted to run and jump in her lap, like a little girl.

It was wonderful to spend time with Helen. The alfredo was great and I felt a comfortable glow from the combination of endorphins and love.

"How are you, Christy? Emotionally, I mean."

"I think I'm okay. To tell you the truth I miss Living Word church. Mine is good but I've gotten where I love to praise and worship and Kyle is still the best preacher I've ever heard. But I don't feel like I can go back."

Helen nodded. "I understand. How's Gina? Is she still dating that boy from work?"

I'd never told Helen about Gina's love for Kyle and wasn't sure if I should. "She broke up with him."

"Did he start acting up again?"

"No, not at all." I hesitated and then told her the whole story. "She just felt like it wasn't fair to Billy to keep dating." I laughed bitterly. "I completely understand. She doesn't know how completely. You're the only person I ever told about..." I gulped. I hadn't allowed myself to think about him, much less say his name. "David." Then I changed the subject.

"I'm going to Gina's for supper tomorrow night. She wants to cook for me too." I waved at the empty plate in front of me. "I'm blessed to have such good friends."

"We're blessed to have you too, Christy. I'm glad you told me about Gina. I'll pray for her. And for Kyle Martin."

***

Gina

I insisted that Mam eat dinner with us. She agreed but said she would go to her room afterwards and watch TV so we could visit alone.

"How do you like your job, Hazel?"

Mam beamed. "I love it. I really enjoy office work. In fact they've already offered me an administrative position as soon as my six months in the office are up." She grimaced. "You have to wait that long to make a major career change. Company policy."

Christy sat up straighter in her chair. "It's none of my business but may I ask how much that pays?"

When Mam told her, Christy hesitated just for a minute. "Hazel, would you like to come and work for me? As my assistant? I'll match their salary and start you right away, whenever you can come."

Mam's mouth dropped open. "Are you serious?"

"Yes, never more. I'm working way too much and need somebody desperately. I've got good staff but nobody I trust with the administrative decisions."

"But I might not be good enough."

Christy laughed. "If Clovers has already offered you the job as soon as they can get you, you're good enough."

"Two weeks from Monday?"

Christy nodded. "Two weeks it is."

When Mam left us alone, I hugged Christy. "You are awesome. You're still changing our lives. What would have happened to us if I hadn't come to your agency?"

Christy shrugged. "God would have found a way."

"But I'm glad He found you." Then I asked the question most on my heart. "Christy, do you regret telling Kyle you wouldn't marry him?"

"No. But I regret that I don't feel comfortable going to church on Sunday nights any more. He's still the best preacher I know."

I nodded. "You still don't feel like you can come back?"

"No." Then she grinned. "When he comes to his senses and grabs you up, then I'll come back."

"I wish. But I don't think that will happen. He barely speaks to me these days."

***

Kyle

When Gina and Hazel walked in the convention center without Billy Benson, I did a double take. I wondered how they got there. Or maybe Billy let them out and was parking his car.

But when I got up to pray before the service, Billy was still nowhere to be seen. I noticed my heart rate increasing but reminded myself to be calm. The man could be on vacation. His absence didn't mean a thing.

I preached on the idolatries of the heart, using the story of the Ark of the Covenant being placed in the house of the false god, Dagon. The god's statue was found fallen and when they set it in place again, it fell and broke and they found their god on his face on the ground before the ark of the Lord, his head and hands cut off. I gave an invitation for anyone who wanted the Lord to come more fully into their heart and destroy idols.

I was surprised when the first person out of their seat was Gina. And tears were streaming down her cheeks. A phrase came to my mind from the life of a preacher centuries ago. "My heart was strangely warmed." That man had been talking about an experience with the Lord but my heart was strangely warmed by Gina's tears. I'd not been a good pastor to her. I'd been too preoccupied and then too bitter about Christy, and too afraid of my growing physical attraction to Gina to see her as a person with spiritual needs.

But now as I looked at her, all I could see was her sweetness and sincerity toward the Lord. All I could remember was her dedication to the children and her faithfulness at church. Could it be that my desire for Christy was lust instead of love? That my protectiveness and attraction to Gina was the real thing? Could snobbery and my ideas of what a wife should be like keep me from seeing clearly? *Lord?*

I went out to meet her. She looked up at me, eyes still filled with tears, and fear. I leaned down to whisper in her ear. "Is there something you want to talk about or just want me to pray?"

"Just pray," she whispered back.

But before I could open my mouth, the Lord's instruction came more powerfully than it had in months. *Ask her to forgive you.*

I gulped and then leaned down again. "First, will you forgive me for not being a very good pastor to you these past few months?" No that wasn't enough. "Ever. Please forgive me for not being a good pastor to you ever. I'm a selfish idiot."

She looked up at me with those big blue eyes so like my own and smiled, a shy, sweet little smile. Then whispered in my ear. "I don't think you're a selfish idiot. But I forgive you."

I took her hand and prayed aloud. "Lord, I thank you for Gina. Thank you for her love and devotion to You. Destroy every idol in her heart and fill her with Yourself. In Jesus name, Amen." When I looked up and saw that no one else had come forward, I didn't let go of Gina's hand. "Let's all pray. Father thank you for this night. We ask you to destroy the idols in the heart of us all, whether those idols are cultural or financial or relational. Amen."

I still didn't turn loose of the tiny hand resting in my own. It felt so good there. And so right.

***

Gina

I didn't know what to think. I went up to ask the Lord to take away the idolatry in my heart of loving Kyle Martin so much. And for the first time ever, he acted like he really cared about me. It didn't make sense.

I was pulling out my cell phone to call a taxi when Kyle caught up with Mam and me in the hallway.

"Hi, Hazel." He spoke to Mam first and then turned to me. "How'd you get here? Is Billy out of town?"

"No. We're not dating any more. We got a taxi. I'm just calling one to take us home."

"You should have called me. Remember I used to pick you up every Sunday morning?"

I could feel the heat in my cheeks. "Yes, and you taught me your Sunday School lessons on the way. I've missed that."

"And I've missed you teaching me yours on Sunday night."

His eyes were looking at me almost hungrily and I had to look away. What was going on?

"So, can I take you ladies home?"

Mam answered before I could. "Yes, sir. We'd appreciate it."

On the way home, I tried to decide whether to mention Christy or not but finally threw caution to the winds. "Mam is going to start working for Christy in two weeks. You knew she'd bought Hunt's, didn't you?"

Kyle looked at me through the rear view mirror. "No." He was obviously surprised.

"Yes. And she's been working constantly. Mam's going to be her assistant, the job she used to have for Ms. Hunt."

Kyle nodded. "Well, good for her." He glanced over at my mother. "And good for you."

As soon as we pulled up in front of The Doll House, he turned around to face me in the back seat. "How about you two going to lunch with me? Bachelors get tired of eating alone all the time."

My heart skipped a beat, or at least that's what it felt like.

Mam was the first to answer again. "I ate a big breakfast and need to take a nap. But you two go on." And Mam opened the passenger door and stepped out on the curb.

His eyes were still on me. I swallowed the lump in my throat. And nodded. I didn't trust myself to speak. Big breakfast. We both had a bowl of Raisin Bran. And Mam never took naps. Ever.

***

Christy

We were walking at the track and I was so glad to be back. From the end of April when we got back from England until a few weeks ago there was no time to meet Helen there. But I hadn't put on any weight. I'd been too busy to eat most of the time.

Today Helen was not moving as quickly as usual. I asked if she was feeling bad.

"No, but I have something I want to talk to you about."

"Sure, what?"

"Christy, I hope you won't be angry with me." Helen tugged on her ear, which surprised me. I had never seen her act nervous since I met her.

"Why would I ever be angry at you? You've been wonderful to me, always."

"But there's something I haven't told you."

I turned my head and frowned at her. "You have every right to have secrets. I won't be angry. I promise."

She took a deep breath. "Okay." Then she paused before she gave a little chuckle. "Remember, you promised."

I just waited. We walked on for a while before she continued. "It's about Sanders."

I was surprised because I thought she'd told me everything about Sanders over the past year. I didn't say anything.

"I called him Sanders, that part is true. He liked his middle name best and all his friends called him that. But it wasn't the name most people knew him by. Most people knew him as John." She looked at me as if she expected me to have some kind of reaction.

I shrugged. "And..."

"And John was how he signed in here at the track."

I could feel my mouth drop open. But no words came out. *John? Our John was her Sanders?* My knees felt weak and I quickly sat down on the bench along the wall beside us. Part of my mind thought with humor that it was a good thing no one was sitting there because I probably would have sat on them.

"Oh." *Isn't that a brilliant response!*

She sat down next to me. "I probably should have told you sooner but somehow I just couldn't. You're moving on with your life and I felt kind of like a failure, still stuck in the past. I didn't want you to judge us. About the walking, I mean. But today is the anniversary of his death and it seemed like the right time."

I finally closed my gaping mouth and found a few words. "But what? Why? I mean, you never talked to each other. Or did you talk when I wasn't around?" I felt horror pierce through me. "Did I mess up your time together?"

Helen shook her head. "Not at all. Sanders made a vow to his wife. He promised he would quit talking to me. And he honored his word. He wrote me one letter explaining to me about the promise. And he never wrote again, except once. And he never spoke to me again."

"Then how did you arrange to meet at the track every day?"

"We didn't. It was an accident." Then she smiled. "Well, I don't believe it was an accident. I think God arranged it. I didn't even know Sanders had moved here. Remember, I had moved away from him? But one day when I came to walk, there he was. He didn't say anything but the look..." She broke off talking and swallowed hard before continuing. "I knew he still loved me and he knew I still loved him."

"Oh, Helen. How awful."

"No! It was wonderful. I lived for my walk each day. Remember that I said once that I would be content to be with him, never saying anything, just being with him?"

"Yes, but..."

She interrupted me. "It was the best time of my life. I knew the rules and I didn't break them." She raised her head when she said that. "When you first started walking with us, I was irritated. I felt like you were an intruder into our private time together. But then after a few weeks..." She grinned at me. "You're going to laugh...I began pretending that you were our child."

"Just like I pretended you were my parents!"

"Yes, just like that. And Christy, Sanders did too."

"What? But how do you know ?"

"Because a few days after his funeral I received a letter and a package."

I stared at her. "He wrote you again?"

"That was the one other time. The letter had been in a safe at his attorney's office."

"Wow! How long?"

"It was dated about a year before he died. A couple of years after you began walking with us."

"And he mentioned me?"

"By name. Christy, he said. And called you 'our walking daughter'."

Tears surprised me by springing to my eyes and I reached out blindly for her hand.

She held mine tightly. "He sent some books too. Autographed to you and to me."

I just shook my head. The moment had a quality of unreality. *John Knight, feeling fatherly toward me, sending me a book. John Sanders Knight.*

"Which book?" I looked over at Helen and saw that she too had tears running down her cheeks.

"Several. *The Bride's Book, Our All in All,* and *Meet Me at the Cross*. A set of all three for each of us."

"What did the letter say? Or is that being too nosy?"

She chuckled very lowly. "No. I would have loved something too personal to show, but..." She reached in the bag she'd left there on the bench earlier, and pulled out three books, opened one of them and handed me an envelope.

I took it and opened the one sheet it contained.

"Dear Helen, You know what the last years of silent walking have meant to me. Thank you. I'm sending copies of my three favorite books. One each for you and one each for Christy, our walking daughter. If you decide to tell her about us, let her know that somehow her presence completed our communion in the spirit and provided a peace I can't explain. I pray for you both every day and will continue to do so after I'm with our Lord in person. The communion of saints is a very real truth. Know that and never doubt my love. In Him, Sanders"

I folded the letter and replaced it in the envelope. "Oh, Helen. What a wonderful thing. To be loved like that." When I handed it to her, she shook her head.

"The letter's yours." She told me about tearing up the poems. And the picture she'd cut out of the newspaper. "I'm healing. Jesus is filling up more of my heart. But was it wonderful that Sanders loved me? Oh, don't get me wrong. I love it that he loved me as much as I loved him. But love should do something, go somewhere. Oh, I know I'm not making sense." She paused and looked like she was searching her mind for the right words. "It's just that I think love should be fruitful. And our love was very unfruitful."

I thought for a few seconds. "Not really, Helen. It was the atmosphere of peace when I walked with you two that helped God heal me. And because you loved him, you understood me and helped me stop hating myself. And there are probably a lot of other good things that happened because you loved each other and made the right decision."

She hugged me and we sat there in silence.

If we had denied our heart to one another,
we would have smothered Love.
If we had given our heart to one another,
we would have contained Love.
But when we broke our heart,
Love poured out.
And the world's a different place
in ways we do not even understand.

Chapter Nineteen

2008

Christy

I didn't see Gina much these days. I had time since Hazel took over half of my work load. But Gina was busy with Kyle Martin. They'd been dating almost constantly from the time she broke up with Billy. Periodically she'd check to make sure I didn't mind.

And I truly didn't. Oh, there were times I was lonely but not for Kyle Martin. And I didn't let myself think about anybody else. I was taking an oil painting class through Community Education that I really enjoyed. The spare room was filled with easels and canvasses and paint.

And I began helping with the youth group at my church on Sunday nights. The kids were different these days, even from twelve years ago when I graduated from high school. Comparatively speaking I'd been painfully innocent. These kids were more like Gina. But I liked working with them. I realized I did better with teens than with children. Back when I taught Sunday School it was first and second graders and I always felt inadequate.

Suddenly two faces flashed across my mind. And a lump came up in my throat. They were better off that I hadn't become their stepmother. I wouldn't have known what to do with children. Then a thought hit me. That was seven years ago. The girls would be in eighth and ninth grade now. Teenagers. Candice would be thirteen and Carolyn fourteen. I wondered what had happened to them. Once, years earlier, when I drove by I saw them in the yard painting something with white paint. I couldn't tell what it was without slowing down and risking being seen.

I turned on the cd player and began singing along with Holy Are You Lord. 'Turn your eyes upon Jesus' had become my byword. And whenever I made the decision to do that, He was always there, loving me, comforting me, driving out sadness and need.

My cell phone rang and I saw it was Gina.

"You can come back to church." She giggled.

"What?"

"He proposed! Oh Christy, Kyle proposed." The joy in her voice was almost visible even through the phone.

"Gina, I'm so happy for you."

"Thank you. Thank you for my life Christy. If it hadn't been for you I don't know where I'd be. And I would never have met Kyle. Thank you. I am so happy."

"Tell him I said Congratulations."

"I will. And would you..." She hesitated. "Would you be my maid of honor?"

"Of course. I'd be honored." Then I laughed. "That must be where the term maid of honor came from. The person is honored to fill that position."

"I'm the one that's honored to have you do it."

"When's the wedding?"

"The first weekend of December. Does that seem too soon?"

It would be November in two days. "It just depends on how elaborate a wedding you want. A month's not very long."

"We don't want a big wedding. Just the congregation and family. That means you and Helen and Mam for me."

"What can I do to help?"

"Take me to Lexington Saturday to get a wedding dress."

"You got it. Hazel going too?"

"She doesn't know yet. I wanted you to be the first. And,

Christy, I'd like this trip to be just you and me. Is that okay?"

"It's perfect."

When we got off the phone, I prayed. *Thank you, Lord, for giving me sense enough not to marry Kyle Martin. You worked everything out just perfectly.*

A little voice tried to tell me that things were perfect for Gina. But not for me.

I put the cd back on and turned my eyes on Jesus.

Gina and I had a wonderful day choosing her wedding dress and my maid of honor dress. I was in a wedding once in college and the dress I had to wear was horrid – lime green, strapless, and ugly. This dress was beautiful, something I'd wear again if I ever had occasion to dress up. And it was looking as though I might. As a business owner I'd been invited to join several professional organizations. And sometimes they planned formal occasions. This dress was a silvery green with filmy sleeves and skirt, not cut too low for my taste. It reminded me of something a British Duchess would wear.

Gina's dress was breathtaking. "I don't want a modern wedding dress," she told the attendant at the Bridal shop. I want an old fashioned one." Seeing her in the beautiful lacy concoction, my eyes blurred with tears. Who would have thought fifteen months ago that the girl all dressed in black who walked in my office would have turned out to be this lovely soon-to-be preacher's wife.

I hugged her. "That's it."

The attendant nodded in agreement. "Perfect."

We went to lunch at Red Lobster at Gina's request.

"Mam's going to keep The Doll House."

"Good. I would hate to see it leave the family." I decided right then and there that I'd buy the house if the owner would sell. That way Hazel could never be kicked out. I might as well begin venturing into real estate too. "Your mother is an absolute Godsend to me."

"And you to her. Have you noticed, she's not coughing as

much?"

"Yes. When I first met her I was worried there was something badly wrong."

"Me too. But she cut way down because I was buying her cigarettes. And when she started at Clovers, she never started smoking more."

"She must just smoke on her lunch hour at work. Anyway I'm glad her lungs are better."

"I got my drivers license last month. Did I tell you?"

"No, but your mom did. I'm really proud of you."

"It was Kyle who pushed me. He talked me into it while you were in England, as a surprise to you." She told me how the plan was for her to drive us home that night but when she discovered her feelings for Kyle, she didn't come and driving was put on the back burner for months. "And Kyle's giving me a car as a wedding present."

"That's a pretty big gift. Preachers must get paid pretty well." I had no idea what pastors salaries were. I never looked at the financial statements even in my own church."

She laughed. "He says it's as much a gift to himself as to me. And he wants me to quit work."

"And do you want to?"

"Do birds fly?"

I laughed. "Then I'm glad."

"And guess what else?"

"What?" Gina was like a little child at Christmas, so excited about life that her joy spilled over on me.

"Not the next semester..." A blush spread over her face. "Kyle wants us to have a good solid honeymoon time. But the fall semester next year, he wants me to enroll in college."

"All right! I'm so glad."

"Me too. And we're excited about church too. Kyle has plans to build. Not a normal looking church. He says God doesn't want Living Word to look like a normal church. But he says we need someplace where we can meet whenever we want. And where people can come and get help, have a clothes closet and food pantry. And maybe even start a school someday. That's why he wants me to go to college. Just imagine, Christy. Me being a school teacher."

I nodded. "You'll make a wonderful one. And Living Word will be a wonderful ministry." And I mentally withdrew more of my inheritance.

The day of Gina's wedding was pretty. Even though it was winter, the sun was shining. And about an hour before the wedding soft snowflakes began falling. She looked out of my living room window. "Have you entered into the treasures of the snow?"

"What?"

Gina smiled. "Kyle taught me that verse. It's from Job. 38:22, I think. Have you entered into the treasures of the snow?"

I remembered how she loved snow. And so did Kyle. *Thank you Jesus for giving them snow for their wedding day.*

Helen and Hazel came out of the spare room, both looking gorgeous. Hazel was in a royal blue dress and Helen in a copper suit. Gina ran over to hug them both.

"It's your turn now." Helen said to her.

I got dressed first so I could be with Gina while they were dressing. "Yes, we better get on with it because the flower girl will be here in a few minutes."

We started toward the bedroom but Gina hesitated. She went over to where Hazel was standing looking out at the snow. She touched her mother on the shoulder and Hazel turned around.

"In case I don't get a chance later, I just wanted to say I love you, Mama. And I'm proud of you."

Joy flooded Hazel's face.

Gina had a blue ribboned garter that she bought at the bridal shop.

She said her bra would do for old, the dress was new, the garter took care of the blue and she borrowed pearl earrings from me. Yes, she had her other ear pierced.

Just as I was pinning the veil on the auburn curls, the door chime rang.

"Shebby's here!" Gina grinned.

Shelby bounded into the house but stopped short when she saw Gina in her wedding gown. "Gina?"

Gina laughed. "Yes, it's me."

"You're a princess."

Gina reached down and hugged the child who was looking much like a baby princess herself in pink ruffles.

"Shelby," she said. "There's a gift there for you after the wedding but I wanted to give you something special that was mine when I was a little girl. She went back in the bedroom and came out with a Raggedy Ann doll. Shelby held her arms out.

"Gina's doll."

"Now, it's Shelby's doll." Then Gina straightened up and got her coat out of the closet.

We all loaded into my new van. Gina sat in the front with me, Helen and Hazel in the second seat, and Shelby and her mother in the back. The plan was that we'd wait in the parking lot until Mrs. Martin came out and told us that Kyle was safely in the conference room. Then we'd go to his office until time for the ceremony.

Since I was committed to the youth group at my church, I never went back to Living Word and the first time I'd seen Kyle since the end of April when he took me home from the airport was the night before at the rehearsal dinner. We hugged then and it was as though there'd never been anything but friendship between us. I was relieved, since I intended to stay close to his wife for the rest of my life.

Kyle seemed anxious to introduce me to his preacher friend who was performing the wedding. He was single and I think Kyle thought we'd hit it off. The guy was very nice but I was about as attracted to him as I was to ... well, to anybody. That's something God had done very effectively for me. I no longer felt any desire for a husband.

When Mrs. Martin came to the front door and motioned to

us, we all piled out of the van and into the convention center. One year and two weeks earlier I'd walked in there for the first time to sign up to help the poor. Eight months ago I went to church there for the last time. But it still felt homey to me.

We waited in the office along with Mrs. Martin until a man from the church knocked on the door and told us both pastors were up front and it was time to begin the seating. Shelby's mother reminded her to behave and slipped into the conference room ahead of us. Mrs. Martin was escorted in first, and then Helen, and Hazel.

Then it was my turn. I looked at Gina and she smiled. "Thank you," she said.

We hugged. And I took the arm of my escort.

I looked up at the pastor and Kyle standing there. There was a time he wanted me to be joining him as his bride. But now his eyes were straining to see behind me through the open door.

When I was stationed on the left and my escort had joined Kyle on the right, the wedding march began.

First came Shelby, meticulously placing petals on one side or the other with every step. Then the music swelled. And the crowd stood up.

Unescorted by any but her unseen heavenly Father, the most beautiful bride I ever saw walked down the aisle to be given to her bridegroom.

***

The house phone rang just as I was placing the star on top of the tree. I'd been tempted to skip decorating this year but decided that, even though Gina wouldn't be coming on Christmas day, I'd invite Helen since she would be in town. And besides that, I needed to have a Christmas party for the employees and their families. It had been years since this house had been the setting for a party of any kind. Christmas was a week from today and the office party was tomorrow night. Gina and Kyle would be coming with Hazel. Charlene and Sally would bring their families too. Helen was coming as my family.

I climbed down from the stepladder, but not too quickly.

Anybody who was really important in my life knew my cell phone number and would call on that. But, if whoever it was wanted to let it ring 'til I answered, I'd talk to them.

"Hello." I hoped I didn't sound irritated, but I tend to get an impatient tone in my voice when I'm interrupted.

"Christy?" My heart leaped. There was no mistaking that voice. Even seven and a half years later. I swallowed and willed myself to answer.

"Yes."

"It's David. David Bailey." I couldn't think of anything to say. But I felt awful when he added, "We met in England." As if I could ever forget.

"Of course, David. I'm sorry. I was shocked and didn't know what to say. Of course I knew who you were."

"How are you?"

"I'm fine." I sat down on the couch because my legs were suddenly too weak to let me stand. "And you?"

"I'm fine too. Is this a bad time to call?"

"No, it's fine." *How many times are we going to use the word fine?* "I'm just decorating my Christmas tree."

"Ah. By yourself?"

"Yes." Why was he asking? Trying to find out if I'm still single? *What's going on, Lord?*

"I'll understand if you say no, but I wondered if I might come by and see you." When I didn't answer right away, he went on. "I won't stay long. I just wanted to talk to you for a few minutes."

I looked around at the chaos of boxes of ornaments and unused strings of lights. And I thought of how I looked too. Washing my hair was the next thing on the list right after trimming the tree.

But romance was out of my life anyway so what did it matter?

"Sure. You know where I live?"

He gave a short laugh. "Yes, I know where you live."

That was a strange response. "How long before you get here?"

"About ten minutes? Is that too soon."

"No. See you then."

My heart was beating fast, but my chest felt like it had shrunk and was threatening to tighten and stop the beating. I hurried to the bedroom and looked at myself in the mirror. I was okay. Not gorgeous but presentable.

Lord, why didn't you warn me? I felt a little bit betrayed. He could have let me know something was going to happen today.

I ran to the kitchen and pulled the spiced tea mix out from under the counter. I put the Christmas tea mugs out on the table and set the water on to boil. I got the shortbread down from the box on top of the refrigerator. The office party could spare a few.

The front door chime rang and I took a deep breath.

The impact of his voice over the phone was nothing compared to the shock wave that resonated through my body at the sight of him. *Lord, help me remember. Yours only.*

He stared at me as though I was the most beautiful thing in the world before he looked away. "May I come in?" I had been staring at him too.

"Of course. I'm sorry. I guess I really am in a state of shock." I took his jacket and hung it in the hall closet before leading him back to the kitchen.

"I put on water for spiced tea. It's decaffeinated. Would you like some?"

David nodded.

"I'm having a Christmas party tomorrow night for my office staff. You wouldn't know but I bought Hunt's Temp agency about six months ago."

"Yes, I knew."

I didn't look at him. Putting the mix into cups occupied my attention and I hoped he couldn't see how much my hands were shaking. He knew I'd bought the agency. And he knew where I lived.

"There's also some homemade shortbread." That was inane. The plate was clearly visible right in front of him.

"Thank you," David said.

When the tea was in the cups and the shortbread on his plate, I had no excuse not to sit down across from him.

"So. How have you been?"

"Christy. I owe you an apology."

"What for?" He had kept his word and been honorable and honest.

"I just found out about your parents."

"What?" I stared at him.

"I was unwrapping some things that were stored away for years and came across a newspaper article. I found out that your parents were killed on their way to the airport the day after I saw you last."

"You didn't know? But when you went to church..."

"I didn't. I didn't go back. I knew we couldn't see each other again or..." He paused and swallowed hard. "I couldn't see you and stay away from you. So the kids and I started going to another church."

I stared at him. "I didn't know. Except for the funeral, I never went back there either. I gave up the Sunday School class."

"Christy, I would have come to the funeral. I would have called. I would have been there for you if I had known." His eyes pleaded with me.

"Oh, David." I could feel the tears welling up in my own. "I wanted you so much. But I felt like..." I dropped my head into my hands and sobbed.

He got up from his chair and came to stand beside mine. He placed his hand on my shoulder. I wanted to tell him I understood but I couldn't stop crying. His words brought back that time when I thought he had deserted me in the worst time of my life. When I thought he too probably believed that I was morally responsible for my parent's deaths. Because I delayed my return home to stay the extra days in England with him. If I'd come home when I was first scheduled, they wouldn't have been on that road that day with the truck that ran into them.

Then he knelt down beside me and turned me around. The next thing I knew I was crying into his shoulder and he was whispering my name over and over. Finally my sobs lessened and stopped. I sat up and gave a little laugh-sob.

"Excuse me." I went to the bathroom and got a tissue and blew my nose. Then I washed my face. The picture in the mirror was certainly not a pretty one but I resisted the temptation to put on makeup. I squared my shoulders and went back to the kitchen but David wasn't there. I went into the hall and saw him in the living room looking at the ornaments waiting to be put on the tree.

As soon as he saw me, he grinned. "Want some help?"

I smiled. "Sure. But…"

"Christy, I'm divorced. I have been for nearly eight months. So it's okay to be here. If it's okay with you."

I sat down on the couch again. Same leg affliction. "Tell me."

"She left us over a year ago. Went off with some man right before Thanksgiving last year. The sad thing is the kids have never seemed to mind. They weren't surprised because she didn't love them, never had." He shook his head. "I wanted to call you then but knew it would be selfish of me. And I thought she might come back."

"But she didn't?"

He stopped staring at ornaments and sat down on the other end of the couch. "She wanted to marry the guy so she filed for divorce. I guess he must have paid for it. She never paid for anything in her life. Never worked, never had any money of her own."

"I…" I started to say I was sorry but realized it would be empty words. I wasn't sorry. She'd made him miserable. And something was starting to leap around in my chest. Hope? *But Lord, I can't. I promised to belong only to you.*

"Then when the divorce was final, last April, I really wanted to call you but got to thinking how selfish that was." He grinned sheepishly. "Tell you the truth, I did try to call the day the divorce was final. But there was no answer."

"April?" Thoughts of my own decisions last April were tumbling over in my mind like a kaleidoscope. "When last April?"

"April 28. My day of freedom."

I was stunned. It was April 28th, the day before Helen and I flew home, that I made the decision to turn down Kyle Martin's proposal.

"What's wrong? You look funny." David reached out and touched my hand. He then quickly withdrew it.

I just shook my head.

"Anyway, later I was glad you didn't answer the phone..."

"I was in England."

His eyes widened. "England?" He didn't say 'Our England?' but I caught the implication. After a few seconds pause, he continued. "I felt so guilty for leading you into an adulterous situation. Oh, I know we didn't have sex but you know what Jesus said - lusting in your heart is the same as committing adultery. I felt like I had ruined any chance of us having a healthy, holy relationship. So I decided to stay away."

"What changed your mind?"

"Your parents. When I realized that you had gone through that alone, I felt so bad that I wanted to tell you I'm sorry and that I would have been there, even if it was a sin."

I raised my eyes and we looked at each other for a long moment that made me dizzy with the intensity. The years and the heartaches and fear and guilt melted away and we sat there in silence, in peace. *Lord, you have my future in your hands.*

Then David spoke again. "I've prayed and prayed. I've asked God to forgive me for spending that time with you. And to forgive me for not regretting it." He grinned at me sheepishly. "I've asked Him to take away the feelings I have for you, to change them, to take them to Himself. I vowed never to bother you again." He shrugged. "I thought maybe you got so you hated me. But here I am."

I shook my head. "I tried to hate you. I tried not to love you. But it didn't work. And what do you think? Has he forgiven you?"

"Yes, he has. And you?"

I nodded. "Yes, I'm forgiven. So, what now? If the past is all washed away by the blood of Jesus, what now?"

The joy in his eyes was unmistakable. "I think...I think maybe He might be giving us permission to love again."

I thought so too.

Books By Amy Barkman

To Love Again

Everyday Spiritual Warfare

Which Witch?

Kentucky Adventures

You've Got to be Killing
(e-book short story)

The Patsy Patrol
(e-book short story)

A Kiss is Still a Kiss
(story in collection)

TAPESTRY COURT SERIES

Murder at Tapestry Court

Danger at Tapestry Court

ABOUT AMY BARKMAN

Amy Barkman has been writing professionally for many years but just recently got serious about book publication. She has written a newspaper humor column that ran for several years, radio programs, musical plays, short stories and poetry. In 2011 her first book, a non-fiction practical guide to victorious Christian living *Everyday Spiritual Warfare* was released by Next Step Books, and the first in the Fun To Be One Club midgrade series *Which Witch?* and *Murder at Tapestry Court* were released in 2012. *Kentucky Adventures* was released in 2014. *To Love Again* was released by Forget Me Not Romances in 2016. Amy has been a member of the American Association of Christian Counselors since 1989, pastor of Mortonsville United Methodist Church since 1998, and Co-Director with her husband, Gary, of Voice of Joy Ministries which she formed in 1979.

Visit Amy on the Web: www.voiceofjoyministries.com

Made in the USA
Columbia, SC
28 August 2017